FOREVER HOLD YOUR PEACE

With love
Caroline
x

Dedication

Thank you to my friend, Eleanor, who was the first person to read my manuscript and give me the honest feedback that I needed.

Thank you to my daughter, Anna, who helped me with the story and added the necessary drama.

A massive thank you to those of you who read Just Breathe, left me a review on Amazon or told me on social media that you enjoyed it and gave me the confidence in myself to write another book.

I hope you enjoy this one as much.

Caroline x

Other Books by Caroline Blake

Caroline Bakes Cakes for Kids

Forget me Not – a novel for young adults.

Just Breathe – a novel for adults.

Chapter One

Old Friends

June 2022 - Monday

The producer's words in Gwen's ears signalled that the end of the show was approaching. She fixed a professional smile on her face and faced the camera, like she did every morning.

"Camera two for final countdown, five, four, three, two, one."

"This is Gwen Morris for Morning News Live from the BBC. Thank you for choosing to watch us and I'll see you tomorrow, bright and early at six. Goodbye."

"That's a wrap," said Eric, the studio producer. "Good job, Gwen, darling. By the way, great interview with Sir Mark…"

Gwen snatched the ear phones from her ears before he had chance to finish his sentence and left them on the desk. Her assistant ran onto the set to pick them up and help to de-tangle all the wires from the back of her shirt, as she stood up, pushing her chair behind her.

She was sick to death of hearing his voice parroting in her ears. She didn't need to be told that she had done a great interview. Of course she had done a great job; she had been doing interviews for over ten years and everyone knew that she was one of the best in the business. She had heard enough from Eric for one day, the patronising creep. And if he called her darling one more time, she would shove the microphone so far up his arse, he'd be eating it for dinner. Charles was the only one who was permitted to call her darling.

It seemed to take forever to release her from all the wires, but at last she was free.

"Good job, Gwen!" repeated Eric, appearing on the studio floor and shouting after her as she marched towards her dressing room. "When you have a minute, I need a word about the…"

"Just give me five, Eric!" shouted Gwen over her shoulders. "Toilet break."

Gwen thankfully reached her dressing room without further interruption and closed the door behind her. It had been a crazy morning; argumentative politicians were a day-to-day occurrence, but today, because of the local election results, she had dealt with one from each of the three main parties, together with a very defensive ex-glamour model and an aggressive environmental activist and she was emotionally drained and needed to take a break before she strangled someone. Eric, the producer, was at the top of her list of possible victims. It wasn't his fault. He was harmless really, but he had the knack of grating on her very last nerve.

The break would have to be quick, just a few minutes to

herself, that's all she needed. She didn't want to be late for the team de-brief. She prided herself on being the ultimate professional and couldn't for one moment allow the production team to see that she was struggling. There was no room for any emotion or personal crisis of any kind in journalism, she knew that. She would need to sort her head out and get back out there as quickly as possible, with the biggest smile that she could manifest. A glimmer of any weakness meant that she was on the chopping board, plain and simple. She knew that she was lucky to have kept hold of this prestigious job for so long. There was a long line of young and ambitious journalists waiting to take her place, which she had no intention of giving up for a long time.

She set a reminder in the Alexa app on her phone to order some brownies and have them delivered to the team in the morning. It wouldn't do any harm to keep them sweet, including Eric, no matter now much he irritated her.

"Gwen," said a voice at the door, "I've brought you a coffee." There was a gentle knock and the door was pushed open. "I thought you might need one."

Zara, her make-up artist, hairdresser and close friend, stood in the corridor, holding out a black coffee, which she took gratefully.

"That's so kind," she said, wiping at a stray tear that was threatening to reveal how she was really feeling. It was annoying how acts of kindness brought tears more often than they brought smiles.

"Are you okay?" asked Zara.

The women had worked together and been friends for many years and Gwen knew there was no point in pretending; Zara knew when something was wrong.

"I will be," she said. "Thanks for this." She took a sip of her coffee.

Zara gave her a quick hug. "We can talk later. I'll take Eric a coffee too and get him talking, to delay him a little. Just come out when you're ready."

"Thanks. I'll be two minutes, that's all."

What the bloody hell is wrong with me, she thought, as she closed the door and checked her make-up in the mirror. I need to get a grip. Nobody can know that I've been crying.

But she knew what was wrong with her. The stomach cramps were telling her that she wasn't pregnant, again. She was another month further away from getting the baby that she prayed for every night. And she was another month closer to being forty. Her phone, still on silent, lit up and buzzed on her dressing table. It was a text message from her GP surgery.

Your cervical smear test is overdue. Please telephone the surgery and make an appointment to see a practice nurse as soon as possible.

The tears fell freely now. She didn't want to see the bloody practice nurse. At her age, she should be seeing a midwife! She wanted to lie on the bed while someone listened to the tiny beating heart inside her and told her that everything would be fine and that her baby was fit and well. She wanted to shop for maternity dresses and wear flat shoes. She wanted to decline the offer of a glass of champagne at Zara's wedding next week. She wanted to choose the orange juice instead and drink it ostentatiously, happy to explain to anyone who asked how many weeks pregnant she was, with a protective hand on her stomach. She even wanted puffy ankles and indigestion. Everything.

But you don't always get what you want.

***

Audrina looked at her watch and calculated how many hours it was until the children's bedtime. But it was only nine o'clock in the morning, she shouldn't even be thinking like that. She was a terrible mother, she knew it. Every day she tried to be better, she really wanted to be the perfect mother, happy to stay at home with her children and play with them and read to them and be amazed at the wonderful and ordinary things that they did. But every night when she went to bed, she knew that she had failed to meet her own exacting standards. She had lost her patience. She had lost her temper. Some days it felt as though she had lost her mind.

She could hear the children running around from room to room, up and down the stairs, shouting, "Goodbye bedroom, goodbye bathroom, goodbye stairs, goodbye kitchen." Today, they were all saying goodbye to their perfectly good house and moving five miles down the road into a bigger one. While they were occupied in their salutations, Audrina tried to steal another few minutes on her own in her dressing room, pretending to be busy, slowly putting on her makeup and cherishing the time to herself. The children knew the rule - if mummy's door is closed, she doesn't want to be disturbed.

Audrina's black French father and her white English mother between them had gifted her the most stunning bright green eyes, jet black hair and beautiful light brown skin. For as long as she could remember, she had always known she was beautiful; her parents had told her often and the evidence was right there for her to see every time she looked in the mirror. At least it used to be. Lately, she had discovered a few wrinkles around her eyes, which she obsessively patted every day with expensive eye cream. It was probably too late now, prevention was better than cure. She should have started with the cream years ago. More importantly, she should never have taken her beauty for granted and gone to bed with make-up on. Stupid woman! It's no wonder her work was drying up recently, she thought as she stared at herself in the mirror.

She had been spotted by a scout from Choice Modelling and Talent Agency (the most prestigious agency in the UK) when she was just sixteen years old. One Saturday afternoon, she was having lunch with her mother at a pavement cafe in Covent Garden when a man approached their table and introduced himself. He told her that she had everything that his model agency was looking for, the long flowing hair, the high cheekbones, the striking eyes, the glowing skin. He asked if she had ever thought of a career as a model. Of course she had. Her friends and all of the boys she had ever met had all told her that she could be a model. She wasn't sure, she told him. She was shy, she didn't know whether she could do it, she said. But in all honesty, she had no clue what else she wanted to do. She envied her friends who knew that they wanted to be lawyers, teachers or social workers. They could have their goal in mind when they revised for exams and chose their A'level subjects. He said he would like to find out if the camera loved her and if it did, they could take it from there. She was under no pressure.

He gave his business card to her mother, who zipped it into her purse, along with a list of maternal reservations, and asked that she call the office to arrangement an appointment for a shoot, as soon as possible. Not without a sense of unease, her mother had arranged the appointment, where they all discovered what they already knew, which was that, of course, the camera loved her. And Audrina loved the camera. Her shyness melted away and she enjoyed every minute, from the moment she entered the studio.

One month before her seventeenth birthday, she appeared on the catwalk for a small French design house at the Paris Fashion Week. After that, offers of work came in thick and fast and within eighteen months, she had appeared regularly on the covers of the best fashion magazines, including *Elle* and *Vogue* and had worked at the fashion shows in London, Milan and New York.

The following few years were a whir of photo shoots and cat walks with intermittent studying. Her mother had sagely warned her that beauty wasn't forever and urged her to go to university. Something to fall back on, her mother told her. Her Plan B. Lucky for her, she had never needed a Plan B. She scraped through her A'Levels with enough points to get her into university and when she eventually decided to drop out, she told her agency that she was willing to take on as much work as they wanted to give her. She knew that the life of a model was short and she wanted to be as busy as possible, while she could. The agency was thrilled. Even Audrina's parents had come to the conclusion that a career as a model wasn't so bad after all.

Most of the models she met told her that they loved their work, but they hated travelling so much. They hated living in hotel rooms, being away from their families for so long and they hated sleeping in strange beds night after night. But Audrina loved that aspect of the job. Throughout her life, she had travelled often between Paris and London, visiting her dad's family two or three times a year, so she was used to it. To her, travel meant independence, freedom and adventure.

At the end of an exhausting day of work, when her feet were throbbing and her legs were aching from standing for hours, she always found the energy to go for a walk around whichever city she was in before bedtime. She would put on flat shoes and enjoy a little time to herself, getting lost amongst the crowds. She walked the familiar streets of Paris quickly, more for exercise than relaxation. She loved to walk down one side of the Champs Elysees, all the way to the Arc de Triomphe, cross the road and walked back down the other side and back to her hotel. In New York, the crowds along Seventh Avenue and Forty-Second Street slowed her down, but she loved being a part of it. She slowed her pace to match that of the ambling tourists and allowed herself to become completely captivated by the city. The sirens of the passing police vehicles, the honking of the horns from the ubiquitous yellow cabs and the cacophony of voices was soothing to her soul. But her favourite city, by far, was London. Her home town. Even when it rained, which it did often, she still loved to walk. She loved the wet pavements that reflected the coloured lights from the bars and restaurants of Soho and Leicester Square, like dark skies, speckled with multi-coloured stars.

It was after the London fashion week twelve years ago that she met Devon, the new rising star of Manchester

United football team. She was almost twenty seven and he had just turned twenty three. He knew who she was; her face was becoming more and more famous, especially following the recent makeup advert she had done and she was beginning to get recognised when she went out. He had followed her on Instagram for over a year and had seen her face on billboards all over the place. But she didn't know who he was. She didn't follow football.

That night, when his team piled into the hotel cocktail bar in Mayfair the night before a match, Audrina was talking to her parents on the phone while she waited for her friend, Isla. Devon spotted her immediately and waited for her to look his way, so he could give her the killer smile that he knew usually worked like a charm. But Audrina kept her eyes firmly fixed on the window and her concentration firmly fixed on the conversation with her parents. When Isla arrived a couple of minutes later, Devon asked the barman to send over a bottle of Veuve Clicquot with his compliments. He expected an invitation to join them, but Audrina merely accepted the bottle graciously and said thank you. No invitation was forthcoming. Devon and his team mates watched open mouthed as the two beautiful women sipped the champagne between them, not once looking their way.

That night, there were dozens of other beautiful women in the hotel bar. Devon could have had his pick of any of them. He was a good looking man and he was wealthy, which seemed to be the only attributes that some women were searching for in a husband. As a footballer, he was never short of offers, but that night he turned them all down. He didn't want a one-night stand and he didn't want somebody who only wanted him for his money. He wanted Audrina. When their manager called the curfew and told the players to get an early night in readiness for tomorrow's game, Devon was gutted that he hadn't managed to get Audrina's number. She had been polite to him when he went to speak to her, but she made it clear that she wasn't interested in a relationship, or a date, or anything else. She told him she was flattered but she was busy with her work and didn't have time. All he could do was send her a message on Instagram and hope for the best.

Devon's persistence finally paid off. After dozens of messages and a huge bunch of flowers sent to her via her agent's office, Audrina agreed to go on a date. By this time, three months had passed and she was back in Paris on a photo shoot, but Devon flew to meet her and took her to dinner. They ate scallops followed by steak, accompanied by the best Chateauneuf-du-Pape that the restaurant had in their cellar. Devon was out to impress. Their first kiss was on the banks of the River Seine and as much as Audrina told herself that she was too busy for a relationship, especially a long distance one, within weeks she was in love.

Twelve years later, her life couldn't be more different. Although she still worked occasionally, it wasn't as often as she wanted. She was at home more often than she travelled and her essential beauty sleep was now interrupted by at least one of the children. Every night. Devon maintained that he was a heavy sleeper and he didn't hear the children when they woke up. Of course, his ear plugs helped.

Now, when the doorbell indicated the arrival of the removal company. Audrina braced herself for a long day.

Chapter Two

Natural Beauty

June 2022 - Monday

Gwen was pleased to see that the drizzly rain that had soaked Manchester for the last week had finally eased by the time that she left the studio, on the way for her hair appointment. It always seemed to be the way that either the rain was pouring or the wind was howling whenever she had her hair done. But today, the weather gods were smiling on her and had sent the summer sun out to chase away the rain clouds just in time. After the team de-brief, she had changed from her formal work dress into cropped jeans, a fuschia pink t-shirt and white trainers. After Zara had patched up her make-up, there was no trace of the earlier tears.

She stepped out of the BBC studio and walked to the hair dressers at the other end of Media City at Salford Quays. A little over ten minutes later, she was sitting in front of a large mirror, wrapped in a black nylon gown, while Tom, the salon owner, ran his expert fingers through her hair, frowning to himself.

"Now, I'm not saying you're not rocking the look that you already have," he said, as his assistant put down Gwen's tea and biscuits on the shelf in front of her. "But you would look *amazing* with some copper highlights. Just a few around your face, you know. It works wonders as we get older."

Gwen took a sip of tea. "I've just booked in for a trim, Tom," she said. "I hadn't planned on changing the colour. And anyway, less of the old! Just because you haven't aged a day in ten years, some of us are actually human, you know."

Tom placed a hand on each of her shoulders and smiled at her through the mirror. "Sweetheart, you are as old as the man you feel, I should know."

Gwen laughed. She could always rely on Tom to cheer her up.

"You're beautiful, you know that. A natural beauty," he said. "And you have hardly any wrinkles, but it's my job to enhance your natural beauty. I have plenty of time for a colour, what do you think?"

"Fine, I'll give it a go," said Gwen, "I'm too tired to argue and I could use some enhancements these days." She looked at herself in the mirror and tried to squash the disappointment that she felt. She could cope with the ageing process, the odd grey hair and dry skin, but she was struggling to cope with the unwelcome extra pounds. At first she told herself that it was part of the natural ageing process, but you only had to look at Helen Mirren and Joan Collins to know that it wasn't true. Recently, she had admitted to herself that her ample waistline was her own doing. She had always been curvy, but in the last month or so, her jaw line had virtually disappeared and no amount of highlights would be able to hide her double chin. Tom was right when he said that she had hardly any wrinkles, but that was down to the fact that her face was so plump, rather than good genes.

As she put her tea cup back onto the shelf, she crossed her arms, resting them on her round stomach and wished that she had refused the chocolate chip biscuit, which she couldn't help picking up and munching on. She should have asked them to take it away. She noticed that the slim lady in the chair next to her hadn't eaten hers. It was still there, untouched and completely unwanted on the tea tray. She hadn't looked at it twice. She had managed to pick up her drink as though it wasn't there. It didn't seem to be tormenting her in the way that Gwen's had tormented her, jumping up and down on the saucer and shouting *Eat me* until she had had no option but to pick it up and silence it. What she would do for that level of self control. Never mind, she thought, tomorrow will be a super healthy day. Maybe I should drink more green smoothies, spinach and kale and whatever else. Maybe then I might get pregnant. It won't do me any harm.

As Tom sprang into action, ordering colour charts to be brought over and foil squares to be cut, Gwen listened to him and nodded in agreement with all of his suggestions, mesmerized by his expertise and very slightly nervous at what she had just agreed to. But what was the worse that could happen? Her hair was a mixture of golden brown and auburn and whilst they were beautiful colours on their own, mixed together they became dull, boring and nondescript, like when you mix paints together as a child and try to invent a new colour by mixing green, orange and yellow, but it just ends up looking like brown mud. It was boring and made her look older than her years.

At university, her best friend and room mate, beautiful Audrina, had urged her to experiment with her hair colour. One night before the much anticipated fresher's party, Audrina had dragged her into town and they had spent ages in the hair section of Boots, eventually choosing a deep red hair dye. It wasn't permanent, Audrina had assured her, so she had nothing to worry about. But Gwen wasn't worried at all. In those days, she was young and self-assured and if she didn't like her new hair, she could just wear a hat until it washed out. She might even set a trend. With a carpe diem attitude, she had placed all her faith in her excited new friend, bought the hair dye, together with a cheap bottle of wine from the supermarket and they dashed back to the university campus to begin the transformation.

Two and half hours later, as a young Gwen stared at herself in their bedroom mirror, she had no intention of covering herself with a hat. The hair that she had worn short for most of her life had grown a little longer and was now brushing her shoulders and the new colour made her appear wild and exciting. Audrina had advised her to be a little bolder with her make-up too and she had carefully applied black eyeliner and a dark grey eye shadow, together with layer upon layer of mascara. She had never felt so good.

"You look amazing!" Audrina had said, as they clinked their wine glasses together.

Gwen agreed with her. She loved her red hair so much that from then on she had dyed it every month and kept the colour fresh and vibrant for the next three years. After her graduation, she had toned it down a little when she went for her first interview, and then gradually returned to the natural browny/auburn mix, which she felt was more akin to the middle-of-the-road life of a respectable journalist.

She didn't often think of Audrina these days. It was too painful to look back and stare into the past, a place where she had left her young, confident and vibrant self. The past was a place that she knew she would never be able to re-visit and she shouldn't even try. But she couldn't help wondering what Audrina would think of her today, whether she would she like her hair colour and whether she ever saw her on the television. She wished she could give her a ring, meet her for coffee and reminisce about the good times they had had at university. But she knew she couldn't. The past is a very different place and is best only visited rarely, if ever at all.

With twenty minutes to wait for the hair colour to do its magic, as she flicked through the magazines that Tom had left her, she hoped to come across a photograph of Audrina, smiling back at her from the glossy pages. But not this time. It had been a few years since she had seen her in *Elle*. It was the Christmas edition and Audrina had been advertising a deep red lipstick. It suited her perfectly. Gwen smiled when she saw the photograph, which dredged up so many memories. Audrina used to wear red lipstick all the time at university, even in lectures. It was her thing. Whenever Gwen tried it, she looked like a painted doll, completely ridiculous. But Audrina had looked elegant and classy, especially when she tied her hair back into a huge bun. She used to call it the 'no effort' look, but Gwen knew that it was a huge effort and that Audrina never spent less than half an hour on her hair and make-up.

In their first week, as they were getting ready for a morning lecture, Gwen had asked her why she was bothering with the lipstick and whether there was someone in the class that she wanted to impress. Nobody else wore lipstick during the day and if they did, it was never red. It was a soft pink or neutral beige.

"Well that's where they're going wrong," she said. "In order to be irreplaceable, one must always be different." Gwen had stared at her open mouthed and then scrabbled about in her own make-up bag for whatever lipstick she could find.

"I'm going to remember that," said Gwen.

Audrina had laughed at her and told her that she couldn't take the credit, she wasn't that inspirational and that those were the words of Coco Chanel. She said that her agent was always telling her to never aim to blend into the crowd. She was unique. Why would the designers ring the agency and ask for her if she had the same style as all the other girls? Until then, Gwen had no idea that Audrina was a model and asked her how she could possibly fit everything in. "By being different," she had said, as she left the room in a cloud of Miss Dior perfume.

After she left university and made modelling her full time career, her face seemed to be everywhere, in all the magazines and billboards and in TV adverts and once Gwen had even seen her on the side of a bus. She had been standing on the pavement on Deansgate in Manchester, outside House of Fraser, having just nipped in there for some new shoes, when the bus hurtled past with Audrina's face smiling down from the space between the windows on the bottom floor and those on the top floor. Gwen's stomach had flipped over and she wanted to turn to the woman next to her and tell her that she used to be her best friend but she hadn't seen her for a while and she missed her. But then the lights changed and everyone started to cross the road. The opportunity and Audrina had both passed.

Gwen assumed that she had probably given up modeling by now, as most models gave up by the time they were in their late thirties. She wondered what she was doing and where she lived, whether she had children and whether she was married and who her friends were. A quick Google search would tell her the answers, but Gwen resisted getting her phone out of her bag. Audrina needed to stay in the past.

On her first day at Lancaster University, when Gwen's parents had said their tearful goodbyes and finally left her alone to unpack her small suitcase, Audrina had thundered into her life. Gwen had her back to the door of their shared bedroom, neatly arranging her alarm clock and a couple of small plants on the window sill, when the door flew open and Audrina stumbled in, tripping over her suitcase, weighted down by two bulky holdalls, one on each shoulder. She flung herself onto the bed, a chaos of luggage and long arms and legs.

"Fucking hell, I'm glad that's over," she said, giving Gwen a huge grin. Gwen wasn't used to bad language. Her dad, being the old fashioned type, didn't swear in front of women and the worst thing her mum had ever said was 'bloody hell' for which she had profusely apologised at the time, blaming the profanity on the young driver who had pulled out in front of her, causing her to brake sharply.

Gwen had laughed at the time and said that it was fine, but her mum had told her that a lady should never swear, it was most undignified and she promised never to do it again. As far as Gwen could recall, she never had.

"Glad what's over?" asked Gwen.

"The long goodbye," said Audrina, rolling her eyes. "My mum's been crying in the car for over three hours, since we left London." She laughed.

"I don't think she's the only one," said Gwen, nodding her head towards the window. Audrina unravelled herself from the straps of her holdalls, leapt off the bed and went over to the window, which overlooked the car park, next to the main entrance of the university. The two girls watched side by side as dozens of parents clung tearfully to their offspring, who were all clearly desperate to escape and start their adult lives.

As Audrina watched, resting her elbows on the windowsill and her hands supporting either side of her face, Gwen stole a surreptitious glance at her. She looked much older than her nineteen years. Her light brown skin was healthy and shimmering; Gwen decided from a mixture of an expensive bronzer and natural beauty. Her long jet black eyelashes swept up and down as she blinked. Her long curly hair was tied in a loose ponytail, which hung down her back, almost to her waist. She was the most beautiful girl Gwen had ever seen.

She turned to Gwen, "I'm Audrina," she said. "Pleased to meet you." Before Gwen could object, Audrina pulled her into a hug and kissed her on both cheeks. "My dad's French," she said, by way of explanation.

"I'm Gwen," said Gwen. "I'm just boring old English,

I'm afraid."

"There's nothing boring about you, Gwendoline," said Audrina, with a mischievous smile. "You look like trouble to me."

Gwen thought the exact opposite. There was something about this girl that spelled adventure, exuberance and excitement and Gwen knew that she was in for the time of her life. She had never met anyone like her.

"Let's celebrate," said Audrina, turning to one of her holdalls and unzipping the side pocket. She pulled out a bottle of Bucks Fizz, which she expertly opened without spilling a drop. She held it up as though it were a prized trophy. "I can't bear unpacking. I thought we might need something to take the edge off the boredom."

"Wow," said Gwen, genuinely shocked that Audrina had not only thought of packing alcohol, along with her clothes, toiletries and books, but that she had the audacity to sneak it past her parents. Gwen's parents weren't in favour of alcohol at all, except for a toast at a wedding or a special birthday party. "I've only got one mug, but we can share…oh, you really are organised," she said, as Audrina pulled out two wine glasses from her bag. They were brand new and still in their box.

"A house warming gift from my dad," she explained.

"Your dad sent you with wine and glasses?"

"Of course," she said. "I told you, he's French. What my dad doesn't know about wine isn't worth knowing." She passed the box to Gwen, who opened it, pulled out the wine glasses and placed them next to each other on the bedside table, which separated the two single beds. Audrina poured the Bucks Fizz and they toasted themselves, their new friendship and finally escaping from the parents.

"We shouldn't get too pissed before the welcome meeting, but we can share this later," said Audrina, as she pulled another bottle of wine from her bag, which she put in the small fridge in the corner of the room.

"Cheers," said Gwen. "I can't wait."

Now, as Gwen looked at Tom behind her through the mirror, proudly holding up a round mirror so she could see the back of her newly coloured hair, she couldn't stop the wide smile spreading across her face. She loved it. It reminded her of her university days; the best years of her life, when she had spent virtually every day with Audrina, sharing their dreams and plans for their future. It was a shame that Audrina hadn't graduated. She had left the university in the second year and Gwen hadn't seen her since. Now that the rain had stopped, it had turned into such a beautiful day and she would love to clink a glass of Bucks Fizz with her, just like they had the first time they met. Maybe now they could sit in Audrina's garden or on Gwen's balcony, overlooking Castlefield or in one of the many cocktail bars in Manchester. But she knew that some friendships are temporary and she needed to leave the past behind.

She told Tom that he was a genius and she couldn't wait to show off her new hair. She and Charles were going to a wedding at the weekend and with her new hair, she was more determined than ever to stick to her diet. She already had the dress that she was going to wear, but a few pounds off would make it more comfortable. Starting tomorrow, she would be like the unwavering lady sitting next to her in the salon, saying no to every offered chocolate cookie. She had no choice, because Zara, the bride, had told her that one of her close friends was the official wedding photographer and she had asked her to wander about amongst the guests and 'snap' casual photographs. Zara said she hated formal photographs, where people were made to stand awkwardly in a line and smile on command. That's great, Gwen thought, except for her it meant that she had to be on guard all day and make sure her stomach was sucked in at all times. The photographer would literally be lurking around every corner and her worst nightmare would be to be snapped with a forkful of food on its way to her mouth and her stomach hanging loose.

Chapter Three

Moving House

June 2022 - Monday

Audrina hadn't wanted to move house. It was Devon who wanted a bigger house. He said he needed his own gym, even though he trained at the football club. He said they needed seven bedrooms and seven bathrooms, for when the parents came to stay. And they absolutely needed a room just for a snooker table and of course, the obligatory cinema room, complete with a popcorn machine. They didn't even like popcorn, she told him. But their friends did, he had said. It would be something to offer them when they came to visit to watch a film. As far as she knew, his friends had their own popcorn machines in their own cinema rooms, but he seemed determined to keep up with the Joneses. It seemed as though everyone in Devon's team was busy keeping up with everyone else.

She drove the twenty minutes to their new house in Alderley Edge, Cheshire with the children, leaving the removal company to get on with loading their vans, supervised by their expensive real estate agent who, for today at least, was earning his money. Devon had promised her that he would be home from training as soon as he could. Their next game was Wednesday night, in two days' time, so he had told her that the training today was only light and shouldn't last too long. She knew that she shouldn't have agreed to move house on a day when he wasn't around, but he assured her that he wouldn't be out for long, in fact he would probably be home before she had to leave and that she didn't have to do anything anyway, as the removals company did it all. That's what they paid them for. She just had to get in the car and drive from one house to the next. As he said it, she knew it wouldn't be that easy. Moving house was never easy, but three small children under six added an extra level of challenge. But she had agreed, partly because Devon always got his own way and partly because she couldn't be bothered contradicting him. If moving day was a challenge, then fine, she could cope, it would be worth it, she had thought. Their new house was truly awesome.

As she put the key into her new front door, she issued sharp admonishments to the children, "Don't run!" "Stop shouting!" "Be careful!" "Stop screaming!" And then, "Watch the paintwork!" Thankfully, the children seemed deaf to her cries and they took her angry words in their stride, as they skipped happily backwards and forwards from the car to the house, carrying their possessions. The rain was doing nothing to dampen their spirits. When the car was unpacked, Audrina bent down and pulled them into a group hug and told them how well behaved they were. No harm had been done and they all kissed her and quickly pulled away, eager to begin their exploration of the house.

As the children ran about upstairs from one bedroom to the next, Audrina wandered into the kitchen at the back of the house and began to unpack the small box of essentials, which included their kettle, a couple of large cups, a jar of coffee, the children's Disney water bottles and a bottle of orange squash. She was thankful to her mother for this little tip - as long as she had coffee, she could cope with most things. She filled the kettle with water, switched it on and began scrolling through Instagram while she waited for it to boil.

"Mummy, what are you doing?" A little voice interrupted her scrolling.

Trying to get two minutes to myself, she thought.

"Are you going to be bothering me all day?" she said with a sigh, not lifting her face from her phone.

"But mummy, I'm bored," said Harry. "Where are my toys?"

"You can't be bored already. We've literally just got here. I told you, your toys are on the removal van and your boxes will be brought in very soon. Why don't you go to window in the living room and see if you can see the van coming? They'll be here in a few minutes."

"Did you pack my dinosaurs?"

"Aha."

"And did you pack Mr Pickle?"

"Yes! Harry! I'm working, you can see that."

As soon as she said it, Audrina felt guilty. She wasn't working. Why had she said that to him? He was only three years old and she shouldn't be shouting at him. But the demands on her time were relentless and she only had a finite amount of patience. It felt as though by ten a.m., or sometimes as early as nine a.m., her patience quota for the day had run out, evaporated into the wind. Within an hour of waking, she was transformed from a kind and gentle mother, full of good intentions for an exciting day with her children to a ravaged monster, snapping and snarling at her children like a rabid dog. Every time she shouted at them, she felt guilty as soon as she looked into their beautiful faces and saw the hurt that she had caused with her sharp words. They would turn to each other for comfort and slowly leave the room, taking themselves upstairs to their bedrooms or into the garden, away from her. That's not how it should be. She knew that. She should be happy to be with her children. She had always wanted a family and now she had it. What more could she ask for than two beautiful twin girls and the cutest little boy? She was living the dream. What was wrong with her?

But nobody told her it would be so hard. She couldn't take a shower without tiny hands knocking on the door, rattling the handle and shouting for her. She couldn't leave the house without the planning of a military operation. She felt as though she had enough luggage for a weekend away, just for a trip to the shops. Her designer handbag, that used to be lightly packed with a mobile phone, her lipstick, a bank card and her keys, now held a change of clothes for three children, wet wipes, plasters, bags of sweets, toys and a plethora of crayons and pencils and bits of paper to keep them occupied at a restaurant table.

Nobody ever asked her if she was happy. They didn't have to; they presumed that she was. The content of her

Instagram feed showed her smiling every day, living her best life - on exotic holidays, her beautiful brown skin glistening under a tropical sun, her three children playing happily close by in the sand, or at home, in the kitchen, the huge garden, the master bedroom suite or walk-in wardrobe of her to-die-for dream house. She showed the world that she was a working mother who also seemed to have the perfect balance between work and play. Her Instagram account was proof of what a blessed existence she had -

 #couplegoals

#familylife

#mychildrenaremyworld

#ilovemykids.

She tried to analyse why she was always on edge, particularly these last few weeks. What more did she want? Maybe it was because she wasn't working as often as she used to. But her agent told her that jobs for forty year old models were few and far between and that she got more than most. She knew that was true. Maybe she just needed to get out of the house on her own more often. At least a couple of times a week. She made a mental note to find herself a nanny or a reliable child minder, to free up some time for herself. Now that they had moved further away from Devon's parents, she needed more help.

Devon's work schedule was certainly not conducive to family life and Audrina was alone with the children too often. Football matches on Boxing Day meant that Devon very often had to leave them after their Christmas dinner and go and stay in a hotel at the other end of the country. Football came first at the weekends and during the holidays. His short summer break was taken up with international games and some of Audrina's holidays were spent as a single parent. Her Instagram followers didn't know that. It was unlikely they would care. If they thought about it, they would probably think that Devon was taking the photographs, which explained why he was never in them. But the photos were mainly taken by waiters and friendly hotel staff who were happy to help in exchange for a few minutes chat with her cute children.

If she could just have some time to herself, she would be happy. Just a half hour every now and then. An uninterrupted bath wasn't too much to ask, was it? A few weeks ago, she had tried to explain to her closest friend, Isla, about how she felt trapped and claustrophobic by her life, but she didn't know what to say and hadn't explained it properly. The words felt wrong in her mouth. She tried to hold them back and swallow them back down. How could she explain that she wasn't happy, without sounding like a spoiled brat? She wasn't depressed, she didn't need medication, she just needed some space. She needed to get away from her kids. Just for a while. She wished that she could go back to her younger days, her university days when all she had to think about was herself, when parties, new friends, studying and modelling all took up equal space in her life. Everything was so simple then. Until the youthful naivety ended and real life smashed into her, taking her breath away.

If she could speak to Gwen, she knew that she would understand. They used to be so close. Virtually inseparable. They had spent hours and hours sitting on their single beds in their tiny bedroom in the student accommodation block, talking about their plans for their future selves. There was so much optimism. So much hope. In those days Gwen knew her better than anyone else and she had trusted her with her life. Within minutes of meeting her, she felt like she had met her soul mate. Even though people say that your soul mate is your husband, how could that be right when you spend half your time bickering with them? Gwen was like a sister to her. She missed her so much. She would do anything for one of those chats right now.

Isla had told her that she was hormonal, she was just having a bad day and that tomorrow would be better. They were in the garden of the old house, sipping cold Pinot Grigio on a warm day while the children played in the swimming pool, so who wouldn't want to spend a day like that? Isla couldn't wait to get her swimming costume on and join the children in the pool. She didn't care that her hair would get messy and would smell of chlorine, or that her mascara would run.

"Who cares?" she had said. "They won't be this small for long. In a few years' time, they won't want us to play with them in the pool. They'll be off with their friends and we won't see them all day, until they want feeding." She laughed, indicating that she loved this stage of her kids' lives but she was also eagerly awaiting the next stage. She revelled in everything they did and everything they said.

"But when do we get to have a lie in?" asked Audrina. She woke up earlier than she wanted to. Every. Single. Day. Isla laughed when she told her how she desperately needed sleep.

"You can sleep when they go to university," she had said.

"You must think that I'm so spoiled, I know I am. I have

three beautiful children, a handsome husband, more money than we need, but I feel so trapped and I don't know how to cope sometimes."

"You mean trapped by the children? Do you wish that you hadn't had them?" asked Isla, with genuine concern. She looked as though she was about to cry.

"No, no, no," said Audrina quickly. "Nothing like that, but sometimes I just want to make decisions for me, without thinking about four other people. I want to be able to say yes to an assignment without having to check the calendar and organise childcare. I want to relax when I have my hair done, instead of asking the hairdresser to hurry up because I need to get home. I want to be able to have a meal and a drink with a friend without worrying about what time I need to get home."

"So you want to be a man?"

Audrina laughed, "Oui, exactement!"

"Oh Audrina, it is the way it is because men could never cope with everything that women have to do."

"You're not wrong. If Devon had to work and look after the children as well, I don't know what state we would be in."

So Audrina had laughed along and taken a selfie, with her back to the pool, where five children and her best friend were playing with a huge inflatable ball. The hashtags #summervibes, #familygoals #bestfriendsforever showed the world how happy she was.

Isla was truly happy. She was a natural mother, born for the role. She had wide hips, a big soft chest, strong arms and enough love for a hundred children. She told Audrina to cherish every moment, time would soon fly, appreciate everything blah blah blah. Isla was already dreading living in an empty nest, whereas Audrina dreamt of hers often. Isla baked cookies and cupcakes with messy chocolate frosting, which she ate with her beloved kids at least once a week. But Isla could put on weight if she wanted to. Her body wasn't on show to thousands of people. She had given up her modelling career when her first baby had arrived, so she wasn't criticised and scrutinised every day, like Audrina was. Nobody commented if she went to the coffee shop without makeup. Nobody cared if she didn't paint her nails or wear heels. She could carry a cheap handbag, she didn't have to be 'seen' in the right restaurants and bars. Audrina envied her anonymity so much.

Audrina had once told her agent that the most comfortable jeans she had ever worn cost less than fifty pounds. They were from the supermarket, could you believe it? She had bought them on a whim and loved them. The fabric was soft and the fit was perfect.

"Darling, throw them away. Right now," Jacob had said. "And do not repeat what you just said to anyone, ever. It will damage your brand."

Audrina had laughed, but Jacob was serious. He didn't want her to be seen outside in anything other than the brands that paid her or the brands that he sanctioned.

"Darling, there are photographers everywhere and your sponsors wouldn't be happy if your perky little bottom was papped in supermarket denim. Can you imagine? If you lost your sponsorship deals, you could kiss goodbye to half term in Dubai, summer holidays on the yacht, winter holidays in the Caribbean. The whole kit and kaboodle would go."

Audrina has called him a Drama Queen and he agreed

that was a title he was proud to have. But he was serious and, as much as Audrina had loved her new jeans, she did as she was told and didn't leave the house in anything other than the clothes that her sponsors sent her. Her brand, as one of Europe's top models, had to be maintained and if this was at the cost of a cookie or two or a pair of cheap jeans, then so be it. The clothes were always a size eight and Audrina agreed with her agent that she would stay slender and "groomed" for as long as possible. In return, he worked hard to get her as many assignments as he could.

Most of the footballers' wives that she knew didn't work at all, especially after they had children. Devon's income was more than enough to fund their luxury lifestyle, but Audrina wanted her own income. The career of a footballer was short and Devon didn't have many years left before he would be considered too old. He was already worrying about whether this contract would be his last. So while she was able, Audrina kept on working.

"Harry," she called to him before he ran out of the room on his mission to watch for the removal vans. "Here, let's do a selfie."

He ran back to her and she picked him up and twirled him round. He giggled and buried his face into her neck, wrapping his legs around her tiny waist. She held him close for a moment before putting him down on the kitchen counter. She leant towards him so that their faces were side by side.

"Big smile for the camera."

She held up her phone and Harry turned his head and kissed his mother on her left cheek at the perfect time. Then Audrina put him back down onto the floor with an instruction to go and explore the living room while she posted the image on Instragram. The caption, 'Moving in day. Harry and I are loving the new kitchen. Can't wait to get baking,' was followed by:

#homesweethome

#homeiswheretheheartis

#letsgetbaking.

As Harry ran off, shouting for his sisters to join him, the removal vans arrived. Audrina spent the next few hours orchestrating the furniture and the many boxes into the right rooms. As soon as she was able, she left the house and took the children for sandwiches and ice cream. She knew that she would need to re-arrange their walk-in wardrobes at a later date, but for now, she was happy to leave the removal company to do their job.

When she got back home an hour later, Devon's car was nowhere to be seen. He had promised her that he would leave immediately after training. He only had a morning training session. Audrina sent him a message on Whatsapp.

Where the fuck are you?

Her phone rang and she answered it immediately.

"Hey baby" said Devon.

"Where the fuck are you?" She repeated, in case he hadn't just read her message.

"Baby, I'm not going to be able to make dinner tonight."

"Make dinner?" she asked, wondering whether they had dinner reservations that she had forgotten about, although she knew that was extremely unlikely. She was the one who organised everything and she hadn't booked anywhere for tonight. She was happy to get a takeaway and relax in the house.

"Josh has got this thing that I clean forgot about, so I'm gonna be late."

"You're winding me up, right?"

"Well, not that late. Before midnight, but I won't get to see the kids."

Hundreds of thoughts whizzed about inside her head.

"Baby are you there?"

"Yes, I'm here. I'm pretty speechless to be honest. You've never mentioned this thing with Josh. What even is it and why are you going without me?"

"It's a team thing, baby, just drinks and a bit of food, you know. Team bonding."

"No, I don't fucking know." She knew she wasn't being supportive, but for once, why couldn't he be here when she needed him? Why did his team come before everything? Fucking team bonding! What about family bonding? Last year, she earned more than he did, so why did their lives always have to revolve around the team? "But Josh knows that you're moving house today, doesn't he? He'll be fine with you missing it."

"Team bonding," he said slowly, as though she hadn't heard him. " You're not listening to me."

Why did he always do that? He talked to her like he was speaking to a child, which was really ironic because he hardly spoke to the children at all.

Fuck it, she thought, as she cut him off and turned off her phone. She didn't need him.

Chapter Four

Family Occasion

June 2022 - Tuesday

Gwen stretched her legs out underneath her desk and decided that it was time to go home. If she didn't leave soon, the traffic from the studio at Salford Quays into Manchester would be horrendous. If she managed to get home before four p.m. she could catch the last hour of sunshine on the balcony of her apartment, before it disappeared behind the building.

As she was putting her phone into her bag, she debated whether to ring Charles and tell him that something had come up and she would need to work late. She could tell him that she needed to check into the hotel next door to the studio, so she wouldn't disturb him by coming home after he was in bed. Relaxing on a plush king sized bed, happily catching up with Downton Abbey on Netflix sounded like a much more enjoyable evening than facing the dramas at home. Lady Mary's husband had died and she had suitors lining up to take his place and tonight Gwen would be happy to put her feet up with a plate of crackers and cheese and a glass or two of chilled Sauvignon Blanc from room service and immerse herself into Lady Mary's life and pretend that she also had her pick of wealthy eligible bachelors. Or maybe she could be Lady Sybil, the naughty one who ran off with the chauffeur. Either of them seemed to have had an easier life than hers right now.

Last night, Gwen had been excited for Charles to arrive home from work so that she could show him her new hair colour. She thought that he would like it, as he would remember when she had red hair at university, although it wasn't quite as red now. He used to love it, back in those days, when they had just met and they were in love and only had eyes for each other. He told her that nobody else had hair the same colour. It made her feel special and different, which was what Audrina was always telling her to be. So she had been anticipating him getting home from work, eagerly awaiting the compliments. That's the problem with being an optimist, she told herself when he threw himself down on the sofa, picked up the remote control and immediately immersed himself in the US Open Golf Championship. Optimists are constantly disappointed. She had gone into the kitchen and started making dinner.

She picked up her phone to him, but she checked herself and put it back into her bag. She was meant to be making an effort and if he ever found out that she had stayed away, rather than going home, for no reason whatsoever other than the fact that he didn't notice her new hair colour, it would not go down well. It wasn't as though she lived a million miles from the studio. And what could she tell him would be the thing that came up? He would know that there wasn't a major news story. She knew that she wouldn't be able to justify an overnight hotel stay. What an idiot. It was a terrible idea. It would just cause another argument.

For the past six months, their marriage had been somewhat rocky, to say the least. They were both walking on egg shells around each other, both of them on their best behaviour, or at least trying to be, most of the time. It was exhausting and Gwen wasn't sure how much longer she could keep it up. Having been through couples' counselling, she knew that communication was the key to a successful relationship, but on this occasion, you didn't need to be an expert to know that telling your husband that you would rather book into a hotel and watch television than go home to see him was not the right thing to do.

The past couple of weeks had been particularly trying. Their relationship seemed to be held together by a fine thread. Gwen's guilty conscience and Charles's wounded heart were slowly but surely pulling them apart, but Gwen's desperation for a baby made her cling on. She only had a few more fertile years left and she couldn't possibly meet someone new, start a relationship and then have a baby in that time. It wasn't a case of better the devil you know; she really did love him, but maybe she loved the idea of being a mother even more. No, that's wrong. She had loved Charles for years and would continue to love him years into the future. They had just encountered a small bump in the road, that's all. They would get over it.

Two weeks ago, they had stayed overnight at her parents' house in Leeds. It was her dad's sixty-fifth birthday and they had planned a family barbeque on the Saturday afternoon. Charles had kissed her tenderly when she came out of the bedroom and told her that she looked beautiful, the journey over there had been pleasant, not too much traffic, the conversation between them both had flowed easily, they sang along to the radio and if she had felt any portent of a calamitous weekend, she had ignored it.

They were both looking forward to the special family occasion.

They had arrived an hour or so before the rest of her dad's guests and as Gwen watched her dad giving Charles the obligatory tour of the garden, can of beer in each of their hands, she relaxed and looked forward to the weekend. As lunch time approached and her dad fired up the barbeque, the sun was hot but there was just enough cloud in the sky for it not to be too unbearable. Her dad's two brothers and their wives and their various offspring all arrived in good spirits, with armfuls of gifts and bottles of wine and beer. By the time the first round of burgers were being handed out, her parents' best friends, Steven and Fiona, were making everyone laugh with tales from their recent nightmare holiday in Majorca, when they had booked a hotel without reading the terrible Tripadvisor reviews. Fiona claimed that she now needed another holiday to get over the trauma and had booked a five star hotel in the Domincan Republic for next month.

Her younger sister, Julia, newly single, was drowning her sorrows by drinking Prosecco as though it were lemonade and by mid-afternoon, she was more than a little tipsy and was leading the dancing on the lawn. Dancing Queen was blurting out of her dad's old stereo which was plugged in near the kitchen door, but Abba's singing was drowned out by Julia, who was doing a great impersonation of an audition for Mamma Mia. She swirled around in a blaze of colour and perfume, splashing onlookers with Prosecco from her glass if they refused to join her on the 'dance floor'.

Gwen and Charles were sitting on the edge of the decking, in the shade, under the apple tree. She said, "Look at her, she's going to be ill tomorrow," at the same time as he said, "Look at her, she's great, isn't she?"

They both said "jinx" and clinked their glasses together, laughing. It wasn't until later that Gwen realised what Charles had said. It wasn't as though she hadn't heard him. Of course, she had heard the words coming out of his mouth, but the implication of them took a while to reach her consciousness. Yes, Julia was great. Of course, she was great. She was young, beautiful, sexy and vivacious, her golden hair shone and her tanned skin glistened under the sunlight where she had smoothed it with body cream - that expensive scented kind with the glittery bits. But she hadn't worn it to attract anyone's attention, certainly not her brother-in-law's and he shouldn't be commenting. She was single but she wasn't available to him. She was dancing to have fun, not so he could watch her. How dare he look at her in that way. Her sister, for God's sake! But Gwen swallowed her rising anger back down with a large gulp of wine and told herself that he didn't mean anything by it. This was Charles. She was just being silly. He loved Julia like she were his little sister.

Afterwards, when the harsh sun had set, to be replaced by a warm, gentle orange haze and when the music had momentarily calmed down and slowed to a selection of seventies and eighties ballads, the dancing stopped and the guests mingled about the kitchen, cups of coffee in hand. While Gwen's dad loaded the dishwasher, her mum produced a homemade pavlova from the fridge, overflowing with thick double cream and mountains of strawberries and raspberries, sprinkled with shavings of dark chocolate. Her dad's favourite dessert, which her mum had made for him every birthday as long as Gwen could remember. As she placed it on the breakfast bar and lit a single candle in the middle, everyone started singing "Happy Birthday." Her dad stood with his arm around her mum's shoulder and waited patiently for the singing to stop, before he blew out the candle and everyone cheered.

Gwen looked around for Charles. At first she thought he must have disappeared to the bathroom, but then she realised that she hadn't seen him for about half an hour. When her dad had been handing out the coffee, she had been talking to her Auntie Denise and it hadn't occurred to her that Charles wasn't in the crowded kitchen. Maybe that was where she had gone wrong. They should have spent more time together. Maybe she should have been aware of where he was; she should have taken greater care of him. After all, that's what the counsellor had said, wasn't it, take care of each other? She should have wanted to be with him or near him, in the way that her mum and dad wanted to be together, bound by that invisible bond of marriage and love.

Then she saw him. He was at the far end of the garden, on the old wooden swinging seat with Julia, his arm draped around her shoulders. Both of their heads were resting back against the cushion. Then Julia leant forwards as though she was going to be sick, which wasn't surprising given the amount of alcohol she had consumed throughout the day. It was nice that Charles was with her, Gwen thought. Someone older and more responsible to look after her. And after all, nobody likes to feel sick on their own. When Julia leant back again, she seemed fine. She was laughing and Charles was laughing. Then Gwen noticed his arm. He didn't move it when Julia sat back, he kept it there, not resting on the back of the cushion where it should have, but resting on her bare shoulder. One of the tiny shoe-string straps on her dress had slipped down and he gently lifted it with one finger and placed it back on her other shoulder. Such an intimate gesture. A gesture that should be reserved for husbands and wives. Just for her. He whispered something in her ear and she laughed again. What did he just say to her? Did he just stroke her arm? What the fuck! In her parents' garden, in full view of everyone. What was he doing?

"Do you want some pavlova darling?" asked her mum. She waved a small plate in front of her with one hand, the other hand still holding a cake slice covered in meringue and cream.

"No thanks," she said. "Charles! Julia! Do you want some coffee? Pavlova? Or is there something else you want?" Julia looked at her through a drunken stupor but Gwen's loaded words weren't lost on Charles. He knew exactly what she meant and what she had just seen. He dropped his hand as though Julia's skin had burnt him, got up from the swing and walked across the lawn and into the kitchen, straight past Gwen, as though he hadn't seen her.

"Did I hear you say pavlova?" he said to her mum. "It's my absolute favourite and this looks delicious." He took the plate that was moments ago offered to his wife. If she

40

wasn't forced to be on her best behaviour, she would have taken the plate from him and wiped the pavlova all over his guilty face. The way he raised his eyebrows at her meant that he knew exactly what he was doing. He knew that he had been caught, but he wasn't bothered. The bastard, was he goading her? Gwen couldn't believe that he would. Her Charles wouldn't be that cruel. But it definitely seemed like he was.

"Are you having a nice time, love?" Gwen's mum asked him. She had always loved him and treated him like a son. She'd be devastated if she knew how their marriage had been toiling.

"I'm having the best time," he said. "I'm really enjoying myself." He looked out of the window, across the garden to where Julia was still swinging on the seat, her slim legs pushing her backwards and forwards.

I bet you are, thought Gwen, struggling to keep her mouth shut.

Her dad, always aware of his daughters' emotional and physical needs, poured a strong black coffee into a large cup, stirred in a spoonful of sugar and carried it outside to Julia. She looked like she was about to curl up and go to sleep at any moment.

"The coffee'll bring her round," he said, by way of an explanation to his guests, as though she was suffering from jetlag or a particularly trying week at the office, rather than a broken heart, which she was trying to cure with too much alcohol.

While her mum was occupied serving the rest of the pavlova, Gwen dragged Charles into the living room and closed the door behind them. She had to address what she had just seen, before she exploded. Communication is key after all.

"What the fuck are you doing? I saw you stroking her arm and whispering sweet nothings into her ear, so don't even think about denying it."

"I wasn't going to," he said. He filled his mouth with more pavlova, while Gwen struggled to keep her anger under control. She refused to cry. Not today. She refused to allow him to make her upset and to ruin her dad's special day.

"What's going on? What did you say to her?"

"Nothing really," said Charles with an insolent shrug. "I told her she looked really pretty, if you must know. She needs her confidence boosting."

"And you're the knight in shining armour that's going to do that for her, are you?"

He didn't answer. He walked towards the window and looked out onto the front garden, his back to her.

"She's my sister. Would you honestly go there? In front of me?"

"It wasn't in front of you. We were on our own in the garden. It's not my fault you were watching." He scraped the fork around the plate, setting her nerves on edge, like when fingernails run down a blackboard, catching the last bits of fruit and cream that really weren't worth chasing.

"What are you doing? Are you deliberately trying to provoke me? Do you want an argument? Is that what you want? Answer me!"

"I'm not the one who slept with someone else."

There it was. The hurt, anger and humiliation that Charles had been carrying around all these months wrapped up in those few words and thrown in her face. He spat the words out, turning to her and leaning so close to her face that it was as though they were about to kiss. But the tenderness that was usually in his eyes had been replaced a cold steely glare which left Gwen feeling bereft and alone. He sat down beside her on the sofa for a moment, neither of them speaking, until he got up and walked away, leaving his empty plate on the coffee table, but taking Gwen's wine glass with him. At least he could pretend to anyone watching that he was going back to the kitchen for a refill, thought Gwen, anxious to maintain the facade to her parents. If they knew what she had done, they would be on Team Charles, that she was sure of. She couldn't bear their disappointment.

So for the rest of the evening, she kept a firm smile on her face while she worked the room. Nobody would have known the pain that both of them were feeling. Each one's caused by the other.

She had slept with someone, yes. But it wasn't as though it had meant anything. It hadn't been an affair. It was a stupid lapse of judgement at her team's Christmas party. She had been working hard all day, had barely eaten and had had too much wine. By the time the meal was delivered to her table, roast turkey and all the trimmings, she was already too drunk to eat it. So when James topped up her wine glass, leaning too close and touching her knee under the table, she didn't object. She welcomed the attention and giggled and played with her hair. It was ridiculous and embarrassing. A massive mistake. If it hadn't been for the huge argument that she and Charles had had that morning, over something and nothing, she couldn't even remember now, she wouldn't have given James the time of day. But he looked amazing in his dinner jacket and bow tie, with his shirt pulled tight across his hard chest and his deep brown eyes, which he clearly struggled to pull away from her cleavage. Why did she find him such an incredible turn-on, when he wasn't her type, he was way too young for her and they were both married, for God's sake? Why had she been so stupid?

As they stumbled their way through the hotel lobby to the lift, they attracted the attention of a low-life photographer, who managed to capture the moment that James pushed her against the wall and kissed her neck, while she clung to his young strong arms. Of course, they didn't notice him through their alcoholic haze, as he continued to snap the kissing couple as they made their way into the lift and pressed the button to take them up to the fifteenth floor, where James had booked a room.

Neither Gwen nor James had any intention of carrying on their liaison and they both agreed that what happens at the Christmas party, stays at the Christmas party. As soon as their brief encounter was over and they sat up in bed, drinking glasses of water in an attempt to sober themselves up, they agreed that they would never talk about this again and nobody would ever find out.

But, as they discovered the following day, they had no choice in the matter. Gwen Morris was a household name and the Average Joe took great pleasure in reading about the downfalls of the high and mighty. The low-life photographer probably sold the images for enough money to give him a Christmas like never before. The photographs hit the online newspapers before Gwen had time to check out of the hotel and offer her apology to her cuckolded husband.

To say that Christmas at Gwen's was fraught last year, is a huge understatement. But, as soon as the New Year brought in new intentions and fresh starts, she and Charles began couples' counselling. They decided that they loved each other too much to let their marriage go. They had something special, which was worth fighting for. She thought he had forgiven her. Since their counselling had come to an end, it wasn't something that they ever discussed. She didn't think they needed to. But clearly, they had a way to go.

On the journey home from her parents' house the day after the barbeque, Charles was apologetic but something about the way he said sorry didn't ring true. It wasn't sincere. He was beginning to build a wall around himself and Gwen didn't know how to get through it. After an hour of driving, with only the odd word said, she pulled into the motorway services, saying that she needed a coffee. Charles stayed in the car. As she walked through the services to the coffee shop, passing loving couples holding hands and families with children, the realisation that she had hurt him and was about to lose her beloved husband hit her hard. She breathed deeply and slowly, trying to dissipate the pain that was gathering in her chest. By the time she returned to the car and handed Charles his coffee, he could see from her red swollen eyes that she had been crying.

Then the sincere apology arrived. He jumped out of the car and, taking both of the coffee cups from her and placing them on the roof of the car, he hugged her tightly, whispering, "My love, I'm so sorry, I'm so sorry," into her ear. She told him she was sorry too and they sealed their apologies with a long and desperate kiss, right there in the car park, neither of them giving any thought to any passers-by.

"You know I would never have done anything with Julia," he said, when they got back in the car, each sipping their coffee.

"I know," said Gwen.

"She looked hot though. If I had to give her marks out of ten, I'd give her one!"

His cheeky wink told her that he was kidding. They both laughed and temporarily their relationship was back on track. Their marriage crisis had been averted. Although the track had been rocky and bumpy ever since.

Chapter Five

Best Life

June 2022 - Tuesday

As Audrina buttered the warm toast, cut it into soldiers and divided it between Mary, Martha and Harry, who were waiting for it patiently, eager to start dipping into their boiled eggs, she smiled to herself as she remembered how often she and Gwen used to eat boiled eggs and toast at university. It was Gwen's favourite breakfast, until Audrina showed her how to poach an egg in swirling water. Then poached eggs became her favourite.

One Saturday morning, they had just finished their breakfast and were both sat cross legged on Gwen's single bed, painting their nails dark blue.

"That was amazing, as always," said Gwen. "At least you know you can be a famous chef if you don't make it as a famous model."

"Unless there's a demand for a restaurant that sells only eggs, I don't see that as an option," laughed Audrina.

"It doesn't matter. You know you're going to be a

famous model, anyway."

"I don't think so," she had said. "There's a lot of competition you know. There are thousands of models in London and only hundreds of jobs. Maybe just dozens of jobs. That's why my mum told me to have a Plan B."

"You know fine well you don't need your Plan B, that's why you never do your assignments on time," laughed Gwen.

Audrina had tried to be humble but inside, she knew that Gwen was right. She knew that she was special. She had to turn work down every week and her agent was constantly asking her to leave university. He assured her that there was more than enough work for her, so when the time came for her to eventually leave, she knew that she would have nothing to worry about. In the meantime, she had promised her parents that she would work hard and would finish her degree.

She poured Devon's coffee for him as soon as she heard him coming down the stairs. She could tell that he was in a great mood by his awful singing as he got dressed. He had a precious day off today and he promised Audrina that he would spend every minute with her and the children. Last night, he was home just after midnight, bringing with him apologies and assurances that he understood how she was feeling and he would no longer assume that she was available twenty-four-seven to look after the children on her own, while he arranged his own social diary. Last night he had been selfish, he admitted. He said that he didn't want to be the only one who hadn't gone to Josh's house. He knew that 'team bonding' was important, but without her, he was nothing.

So she kissed him and forgave him.

This morning, as they lay in each other's arms in their giant bed with the children watching cartoons on their sixty-five inch TV, he again promised to take her into consideration more often. Audrina took his words with a pinch of salt. His contrition seemed to be real but she had heard it all before. Whilst he wasn't the worst husband on the planet, there was plenty of room for improvement, but she was getting tired of being his mentor and his teacher. She wanted a ready made husband, not one that she had to nurture and mould into the one that she wanted. But she loved him, so she had snuggled into his arms and counted her blessings.

Last night after his phone call, she had resigned herself to another evening alone and set out to make the best of it. She poured herself a glass of her favourite gin, with slimline tonic and a slice of lime, while she prepared the bath for the children. She had filled the huge tub with warm water and tonnes of bubbles and got in with Harry, playing with boats and dinosaurs for over half an hour. They had both loved it. Then she wrapped herself in her towelling dressing gown and Harry in a large towel and read him a story on the bed while Mary and Martha shared a bath. Audrina listened to the splashes and laughter of her daughters while she cuddled her son and wondered whether her life would be better with or without Devon. Would she miss him that much if he didn't come home? Did she really need a husband? He would need to see the children whenever he could between football matches, but they weren't used to him being around that much either.

As Harry was closing his eyes, her phone rang

interrupting her thoughts. It was Jacob, her agent. She tip-toed out of his bedroom onto the landing, carefully closing the door behind her.

"Hi darling, have you settled in your new house?"

"Hello Jacob, yes thank you, it's beautiful. We are just about unpacked." She didn't tell him that Devon hadn't been around all day and she had managed the move herself.

"Fantastic, well you're going to have to pack another bag, I've might have got you a job," he said.

"Amazing, where is it?"

"Paris. In two weeks. You need to leave on the Sunday night, for an early start Monday morning. I hope your passport is up to date."

"Of course, always ready and waiting."

"Great, I'll organise your flights. Call into the office on Friday morning, around nine. I need you to meet the designer and then we can go through all the details."

As she handed Devon his coffee, she told him about her assignment in Paris and he couldn't have been more supportive. Even though she had to stay overnight and wouldn't be back until late the next day, he assured her that everything would be fine and that he would cope. He said he would arrange for his parents to have the children. They would love that. He said that they might even have them all weekend, so he could go with her to Paris, as there were no games that weekend. Audrina tried not to get riled and told herself that he thought he was doing the right thing, trying to arrange time for them as a couple without the children. Plenty of couples did that and he was doing what he thought she wanted. But why couldn't he get it right? She would be working. She wasn't visiting Paris for a holiday and she wanted to go on her own. She told him that she didn't want the children to go to his mother's, she wanted Devon to look after his own children. Surprisingly, he admitted that he wasn't thinking, but yes, Audrina was right and the children should stay with him. He told her that he would plan something special for them, maybe take them to the zoo or the cinema or something while she was away.

As he pulled her into his arms and kissed the top of her head, he told her that he would miss her but if she wanted to stay an extra night, to catch up with family in Paris while she was there, then she could. Maybe he really was making an effort, she thought. She kissed him and rested her head on his chest while he stroked her hair.

***

Later that afternoon, as she knelt on the warm soil and began snipping at the dead roses and picking off some dried leaves here and there, Audrina could hear the children's voices causing a commotion inside the house. Suddenly the door to the playroom crashed open and all three children tumbled outside. The door slammed shut behind them. Audrina's few minutes of peace was over already. It was probably too much to ask them to stay inside and be quiet on such a sunny day, but Devon was meant to be supervising, just for an hour. That was all she wanted. Just one hour of peace. He promised that he would 'take his turn' to look after the children today. As though he was doing her a favour by being a father. She hadn't argued with him, there was no point. She had just told him that she would appreciate a little time to herself, while she pottered around the garden.

She could hear the children's whispered voices as they did their best not to disturb her, although their efforts were short lived and their voices were soon raised back to their normal volumes.

"Where's your daddy?" she asked them as they ran over to her, waving bits of paper splodged with paint, which they proudly held up for her to admire.

"He's making coffee," said Mary. "He said it's a surprise but, sorry, I've told you by accident. I didn't mean to."

"It's okay sweetie." Audrina scooped her up and swung her round, as she squealed in her ear. Sometimes, she could actually feel the love for them, like a physical weight in her heart. It made her heart swell, whilst simultaneously weighing it down.

"Daddy, I told mummy about the secret coffee!" shouted Mary, when Audrina put her back down. She took her accidentally spilled confession and ran back inside the house with it.

Martha picked up a football and Harry chased her down the lawn. Audrina couldn't help smiling to herself. They were so cute, but so incredibly annoying. She wondered how many mothers up and down the country were at the end of their tethers right now, and how much worse it would be by the end of the summer. The summer term hadn't even ended yet, but she imagined that most parents would be praying for September to come quickly and for Autumn to arrive and gather the children up into her waiting arms and whisk them back to school. As parents across the land exhaled a collective sigh of relief, giving thanks for the new term, teachers would be bracing themselves for what was to come. Audrina was counting the days until September when Mary and Martha started school and she could hand them over at nine o'clock.

"Hello, is anyone home?" Isla and her two sons let themselves in the garden, through the side gate. "How did your move go? You must be settled in if you have time for gardening."

Audrina wasn't sure whether she was ecstatic or aggravated to see her friend. Of course she loved Isla and was always pleased to see her, but these days they didn't seem to make the time to see each other without the children. Now, she had two more under fives to add to the noise level. Her head felt like it was about to explode. But she gave Isla a wide smile and held out her arms for the boys to run into. Kissing them both on their heads, she told them to go into the kitchen and see if Devon could get them a drink.

"Hi, yes, good thank you," she said to Isla, between air kisses. "We're all settled in now." Of course, Devon had settled in within minutes of coming home. His suits and jeans were already hanging in his wardrobe, his t-shirts were neatly folded in the drawers and his shoes were in pairs on shelves. His toothbrush was waiting for him in the en-suite. The only job he had to do was plug in his Playstation in the games room. But Audrina didn't mention any of this. She didn't need to tell Isla that she was the one who had organised and orchestrated the move, while her husband went round to his team mate's house to watch sport and drink beer instead of coming home to her and his children, because Isla's husband was part of the team too. She would have known that Devon hadn't been at home.

She didn't tell her that they had had a huge argument when he came home just before midnight and she had told him that he was the most useless husband in the world and that she would be better off without him and that all last night, he had been in the dog house. Because today was a new day.

Devon, a clutch of children around his ankles, came out of the house carrying her coffee, which he handed to her with a kiss to her cheek, perpetuating the image of a happily married couple. He gave Isla a hug and told her he would be back in a few minutes with a coffee for her too. He also promised to make the children some lunch and said that it was no problem making some extra sandwiches for Isla's boys. What the fuck, thought Audrina. He has literally never made lunch for the kids in his life and yet, here he is, enrolling himself for the Dad of the Year award. Bringing her a coffee was nice, and he was certainly on his best behaviour, but he would need to do this kind of thing more often if he wanted to keep her happy and boost her mood. This morning, when she had looked in the mirror at stupid o'clock, after Harry had woken her up, she noticed how blood shot her eyes were. She was definitely not getting enough sleep. The dark shadows under her eyes confirmed that she wasn't. If only she could figure out why she felt as though she had the weight of the world on her shoulders. If she knew why her burden was so heavy, she could cope with it.

"We live there now," said Harry, running up from the bottom of the garden and pointing towards the house.

"Yes, I know," said Isla. "I hope you have all settled in okay. Do you like your new house and your new bedroom?"

Harry nodded enthusiastically.

"Mary has the same bedroom as me," said Martha. "We share one. Mummy, why have you got big gloves on?"

"These are gardening gloves," explained Audrina. "They keep your hands clean. Okay, that's enough, aller jouer! Go and play!" Martha wandered away without arguing, seemingly unperturbed by her mother's remonstrations.

"She wasn't bothering me," said Isla, "I like to chat to the kids." She smiled at Audrina, who had taken a packet of cigarettes out of her pocket and was trying to light one, although her efforts were thwarted by the constant wind which blew out the tiny flame from her lighter.

"Fucking thing," she mumbled to herself. "I'll be right back."

She opened the kitchen door and sheltered herself from the wind on the threshold.

"I apologise," said Audrina, returning a minute later, her cigarette now lit, dangling between the first two fingers of her right hand, which she rested on the arm of the chair. "I like to chat to them too, but she never stops, that one. From morning until night, never stopping." She closed her eyes as she took a drag of her cigarette, as the smoke floated around her eyes. She blew the smoke out slowly, peering at Isla through the haze. Isla tried not to cough as it drifted across the table and into her lungs.

"I hope you don't mind me asking, but are you okay? Don't they say that moving house is one of the most stressful things ever, next to divorce and bereavement?"

"Do they? Yes, well it has been a stressful few days," said Audrina.

"It'll be fine," said Isla. "You just need a week or so to

settle in properly and get used to the place. Are you sure you're alright though? It's just that I haven't seen you smoke for ages, not around the kids anyway. I know you only tend to smoke when you're stressed."

Audrina puffed quickly on her cigarette until there was none of it left. Then she threw it down onto the floor, stamped on it and blew the acrid air out of her lungs slowly.

"I shouldn't do it, I know. Sorry. I know I need to get things into perspective. Nobody's died and I'm not getting divorced. Not yet anyway. But he is sailing close to the wind, I don't mind telling you." As soon as the words were out, Audrina wanted to grab them back. What on earth was she doing, telling Isla such personal information about her marriage when Devon could so easily overhear her? Maybe it was because she was being so kind and caring, it made her want to open up. And she did ask, after all.

The smell of recently cut grass wafted around them, a smell which should invoke joy and happiness, the contented feelings of summer. But Audrina's energy was not joyful at all. She wished that the conversation could take a lighter turn, but how could it now? It had become serious too suddenly. She wished that they could just chat about the weather and whether this was a good summer for roses. That's what she wanted to chat with her friend about, while they enjoyed the warm summer weather.

They both looked over at the children, who were all lying on their stomachs in the grass watching ants marching across the patio stones.

"They're so beautiful, aren't they?" said Isla. "Such a blessing."

"Yes, they are," said Audrina. "I know how lucky we are,

even though I haven't had a moment's peace in five years." They both laughed as an argument suddenly erupted between the two girls, confirming that peace could only be maintained for a matter of minutes at a time. "Kids, keep the noise down please."

Martha shouted that Mary had snatched a piece of Lego from her and Mary insisted that it was her Lego and Martha hadn't asked her if she could borrow it.

"Shut up!" she cried suddenly. "Just shut the fuck up!"

Silence fell. But only momentarily. Harry burst into tears, followed by Martha. Mary held tightly to Harry's hand and tugged him back to the house. Martha followed them and they closed the playroom door behind them. Isla's boys ran to her and she pulled them close to her chest, protecting them from further harsh words that may happen to float their way.

"Audrina, what on earth's the matter?" said Isla.

"Nothing, sorry. I just, I don't know, I haven't been myself for a few weeks."

"What's going on?" said Devon, as he opened the kitchen door.

"Nothing, nothing," said Isla. "Everything's fine."

"Well it's clearly not fine because I've got a house full of crying kids here."

"Look, all mothers lose their temper every now," said Isla. "Everything's fine."

Devon frowned at Audrina and waited for her to explain. She stared defiantly at him.

"It isn't Audrina's fault." Isla stepped in before an argument erupted. "They must have been pushing her buttons, driving her to extremes all morning. You know what kids can be like. They could test the patience of Mother Theresa." Even so, she was uncomfortable about what she had just witnessed.

"Fancy a glass of wine?" asked Audrina. "I think I need one."

Isla agreed and told her that it would be lovely, although she only wanted a small one, because she was driving. She wasn't used to drinking during the day, especially when she was looking after the boys, but she could see that Audrina was going through a stressful time, she told herself, even though she had had two removal vans and an army of men unpacking her furniture for her, so she wasn't sure what she was so stressed about.

But anyway, there's nothing wrong with a small glass of wine on a beautiful summer's day, is there?

She wasn't judging.

Not really.

Audrina led her into the kitchen, where she poured two large glasses of wine. She held one up to the light streaming in from the open door and took a photograph. Within minutes, it was uploaded onto her Instagram story with the hashtags

#celebratinglife
#livingmybestlife
#bestfriends.

Chapter Six

Fresher's Week

September 2003

The rain had curtailed Gwen's plans on her first weekend at university. It was still September, but it felt more like November. A cold wind from the north brought rain clouds that covered Lancashire for most of the day, confirming that summer was well and truly over. Sitting on her single bed with a mug of hot chocolate in her hands, watching the rain pounding against the window and bouncing off the window sill, she decided that a bike ride would probably not be the wisest way to spend the morning. She was excited to go for a ride on her brand new bike, which had been a gift to her from her parents, as a cheap and easy way for her to get into Lancaster town centre from the university campus. It was a beautiful azure blue with a light brown, faux-wicker basket hanging from the shiny silver handlebar and a specially designed seat, padded for extra comfort, so there was no excuse for not going on bike rides. But it could wait for another day. Wind and rain were no friends of a fair weather cyclist. She looked up to the sky, hoping to see a glimmer of blue between the dark grey clouds, but there was none. Disappointed, because she really needed to burn the calories from the chocolate eclair that she had just demolished after her breakfast, she decided that a reading day lying on her bed sounded like a reasonable alternative. There was a pilates class in the student hall in the evening and she could go to that instead of going on a bike ride. She didn't know much about pilates, but she had heard that it was just lying down on a mat and sucking in your tummy to tighten the muscles. That didn't sound too arduous.

Audrina had taken the early train to Manchester for a photo shoot and wouldn't be back until after dinner, so she had the whole day to herself.

In the corner of their small bedroom, a tall bookcase was groaning under the weight of new books. In preparation for her new life at university, in addition to the essential text books, she had treated herself to dozens of novels with money that she had saved from her summer job in the supermarket and displayed them all on a brand new bookcase, which her dad had put together, with much huffing and puffing and an over use of expletives. She had never been much of a reader, but she thought that she should be. Students should be well versed and well read, she had told herself.

She wasn't at Oxford or Cambridge and she wasn't starring in an episode of Brideshead Revisited, but there was no harm in dreaming. She liked the idea of pretending she was in an exclusive library in a top class university or even a grand stately home, where she was the only member and where she could choose a book depending on her mood.

Today, she chose *Rebecca* by Daphne Du Maurier, a special hardback eightieth anniversary edition which she had picked up from a charity shop for two pounds. She settled back onto the bed and prepared to be transported to the glamorous world of Monte Carlo.

Being a slow and discursive reader, before she had read to the end of the first page, her concentration began to wane. After a few minutes, she put her book down and ambled back over to the bookshelf and lifted the lid of her biscuit tin, which she kept on the top shelf. A mixed pile of digestives, shortbread and custard creams were squashed into the large tin. Her diet should really start today, but she had already had toast and an eclair for breakfast, so what the hell, she might as well have a couple of biscuits with her hot chocolate. She couldn't let them go to waste. Her mum had sent her with enough biscuits to feed the whole of her accommodation block. They'll help you to make friends, she had said. You can offer them round while you introduce yourself. She hadn't done that, of course. What was her mum thinking? She was more than happy to share them with friends, but she couldn't go round the corridors with her biscuit tin, offering them out. That was just weird. And seeing as how Audrina wasn't much of a biscuit eater, they would be left in there for weeks if she didn't eat them up.

Anyway, didn't they say that you shouldn't really put yourself on a diet? They make you fat, apparently. You should just follow a healthy eating regime, which is exactly what she planned to do. Nothing was off-limits and no food was on the banned list. Just eat whatever you wanted, in moderation, obviously. Shoving a custard cream into her mouth while she decided which of the other biscuits she wanted, she eventually chose one of each and put them onto a small plate. Mindful eating. That's what it's all about.

This term, she was going to transform herself. She had it all planned out. By the time she saw her parents again at Christmas, she would be a much better version of herself and would be the woman who she had always wanted to be. The diet, or rather the healthy eating regime, would be in full flow. She would be the type of person who chose to have a salad off the menu and said no to desserts. If she liked the pilates class, she would make it a regular thing. If someone asked her what gym she was a member of, she would tell them that she didn't have a gym membership, but she had a very active life. She would exercise for the fun of it, not because she thought it was a chore, something to be endured. It would be a lifestyle choice and she would have a plethora of leggings and tops to choose from. She would need plenty, as some would always be in the wash. She would make it a habit to cycle into town for the shopping, rather than having it delivered.

When she wasn't studying, she would read or do cross word puzzles. Not the easy ones from those paperback books in WHSmith. She would do the Times crossword. She would sit elegantly at the table in the students' cafe and stare wistfully into the communal garden, wearing an elegant cotton dress, a size fourteen, or even a twelve, with an expensive pen tapping on her lipsticked mouth, waiting for inspiration while she pondered the clues. The television would be used for documentaries, cerebral entertainment about nature, science or historical events or the occasional film. It would no longer be used as background noise while she worked. If she needed background noise, it would be radio four. She would be a new and sophisticated Gwen.

Of course, they could still play music while they were getting ready to go out. After all, she was a young student, not a trainee nun.

As she demolished the last of the biscuits and brushed the crumbs from her chest onto the carpet, she worked out how many pounds she could lose by the time of the Christmas party. If she tried really hard, she could lose ten, she knew it, she had done it before with a juice cleanse. But the juices were disgusting and her sister had told her never to do that diet again, because she had been "a right miserable cow and as grumpy as hell." Maybe she would give up gluten instead. Her stomach would thank her for that and there were loads of gluten free options these days.

Pleased with herself for settling on a plan, she had just settled back down with *Rebecca* when there was a knock on the door. She jumped up and quickly checked her reflection in the small mirror on the wardrobe door, making sure that there was no evidence of biscuits around her mouth, before she opened the door.

"Hi, it's Gwen isn't it?"

"Hi, yes," she said, "Audrina isn't in, I'm afraid. I'm not sure what time she'll be back, but I think it'll be late tonight. She's on a shoot in Manchester."

The handsome young man standing in front of her, nonchalantly leaning against the door frame, smiled at her. She wondered whether he made a habit of leaning against door frames while he waited for doors to be opened, so as to look cool. Had he practised the look just for Audrina, so that he didn't appear too keen when she opened the door? Whichever it was, Gwen felt for him. He had made all that effort for nothing. The performance endeared him to her.

"Well, thanks for that information," he said. "I'm sure Audrina is having a great time, whatever she's doing in Manchester, but that isn't why I'm here."

"Oh," said Gwen, "Sorry, I just assumed…"

Not unreasonably, she had assumed that he had wanted to see Audrina. Why wouldn't he? She could have her pick of any of the boys at university and some of them had asked her out already, even though they had only been there a week. So far, she had turned them all down, claiming that she was busy with her modelling. She wasn't conceited about her beauty, in fact she was quite humble. It seemed to Gwen that eyes followed her around all the time and being pursued by boys seemed to be a daily hazard for her. She claimed not to notice the ones who stared at her, or maybe she had simply learned to ignore them. But Gwen certainly had noticed the way that everyone looked at her when she walked down the corridor or entered a room, or just sat minding her own business eating her lunch or reading on the grass at the front of the university steps.

It wasn't just the boys either. Gwen had noticed that virtually all the girls stared at her, some for longer than was polite. Only yesterday morning, she had noticed one of the girls staring at her for a particularly long time in one of their lectures and then last night when they went down to the student bar, Gwen saw that the girl was wearing the same deep red lipstick that Audrina always wore. The poor girl, she must have gone into Lancaster especially to buy it, but she couldn't carry it off in the same way at all. Audrina said that she had put on too much eye make-up, that was the issue. The trick was to choose eyes or lips, not both. Gwen asked her whether she was bothered that the girl had clearly copied her lipstick. Audrina had shrugged and said that she didn't have the monopoly on red lipstick, unfortunately, but imitation was the sincerest form of flattery, so she would take it as a compliment.

"That guy over there hasn't taken his eyes off you," Gwen told her only this morning as they were having their breakfast in the cafeteria. Audrina smiled at him and he blushed furiously. Gwen giggled as the captivated boy poured sugar all over the table, completely missing his cup of coffee. He looked away quickly, embarrassed, and scooped the sugar into his hand and onto the floor.

"Boys are so easily distracted by females," Audrina said, shaking her head. "They really should concentrate their efforts on other things. They might achieve a great deal more than they do."

Gwen thought that they did concentrate on other things. All the boys she knew seemed to concentrate on football, drinking and even their studies much more than they concentrated on her.

"I'm Charles," said the boy standing on her doorstep. "I was in the market research lecture yesterday afternoon." He held out his hand and Gwen shook it, slightly taken aback by the formality of someone so young. She hadn't known his name but she had spotted him in the lecture, sitting one row behind her to the right. She had noticed his bright blue eyes and dark hair. When he looked over towards where she and Audrina were sitting and smiled, she had smiled back out of politeness, but had assumed that he was yet another of the boys who was enrolling himself into the Audrina Fan Club.

"Are you busy?" he said.

"What, right now? No, not really," she said, stepping to the side to block his view of her messy bed and the empty plate. "Just reading."

"Anything interesting?"

"Just Rebecca," she replied nonchalantly, as though reading classic literature was one of her regular activities.

"Oh, that's a great book. Where abouts are you up to?"

"Page three actually." She wished that she had started reading it earlier, so she could keep this handsome boy talking for longer. They could discuss the characters and have an in-depth conversation about the plot. But she hadn't. So she couldn't. She could feel herself blushing.

"I wondered if you wanted to come and get some lunch with me?" he said. "Unless you want to get back to your book?"

"Em, no. I mean yes, I'll come for lunch. Is the campus cafe open today? I thought it closed at the weekend?" She wished that hadn't eaten so many biscuits, as she wasn't hungry at all, but she didn't want to say no.

"I didn't mean there. I've been told that there's a really nice Greek cafe in the town centre that does the best lamb gyros around. Do you like Greek food?"

"Yes, I love it," she said. "That'll be good. I'll get my coat, just give me a second." She wasn't sure whether to invite him in, so she didn't and he didn't ask. He waited patiently for her in the corridor and a few minutes later, flashed her an amazing smile that made her stomach flip when she told him that she was ready, having quickly grabbed her coat, purse and umbrella.

"Do you know where the bus stop is?" she asked, as they

made their way down the stairs. "I haven't been into Lancaster yet. I was going to go today, but the weather put me off, to be honest." She was waffling. She needed to calm her nerves down.

"We don't need the bus. I've got a car," he said. "I'll drive. I didn't think you'd want to wait for a bus in this weather. And that umbrella definitely isn't big enough for the both of us, unless we get a lot closer."

Was he flirting with her? The way he smiled at her seemed to suggest that he was, but she wasn't sure.

As they ran across the car park and he opened the front passenger door of a brand new Range Rover for her, Gwen wondered whether this was a date. He hadn't said that it was, but then again he hadn't said that it wasn't. Whatever it was, she was happy to enjoy his company and she couldn't wait to tell Audrina that she had had lunch with a handsome boy when she got back home. Of course, she would play it cool and assume that it wasn't a date. After all, she could have a male friend, couldn't she? Just because she had never had a male friend before, didn't mean that she couldn't have one now. That's what university was all about, broadening one's horizons.

As they drove the few miles into the town centre, they chatted about where their parents lived and which schools they had been to. She told him that her parents lived in Leeds. He was from Cheltenham. She told him that she had a younger sister. He also had a sister, who was three years older. His father was the head teacher at the grammar school and his mum was a doctor. She spotted his Ralf Lauren Polo t-shirt, his well cut jeans and expensive shoes. She didn't need to ask whether his parents were wealthy, they obviously were. Not many students had their own car and those who did, didn't have one as posh as this.

She knew that her mum would be excited that she had met 'someone nice'. That seemed to be her mother's sole raison d'etre, to get her 'settled down'. But they were just having lunch, that's all. There was no need to make a big announcement to the parents yet. She was simply making new friends. It was weekend, it was raining, there wasn't anything much else to do and she was getting to know people. That's it. It wasn't a date. She would mentally friend-zone him before he friend-zoned her.

But later that night, by the time Audrina returned home, tired from her hectic day shooting and ready to jump straight into bed, there was no question about it, Gwen had been on a date. Friends don't kiss the way that Charles had kissed her.

She sat on the edge of her bed while Audrina removed her make-up, cleaned her teeth and changed into her pyjamas. Even as Audrina crawled into bed, telling her how tired she was, covering herself with her duvet and closing her eyes, Gwen carried on talking, telling her all the details of her day; about how romantic it was that Charles opened the car door for her, paid for the meal, held the umbrella over her head as they walked back to the car and then kissed her at the door of her room, as he pushed her against the wall. Audrina, without opening her eyes, told her that it sounded divine and he seemed like a really nice boy.

"He told me all about his family and his school and his hobbies and everything."

"That's nice," said Audrina.

"He asked about me, too. Don't get me wrong, it wasn't

all about him."

"That's good."

"But he hasn't asked me for a second date. Is that normal? Is he just playing it cool, do you think? Or am I meant to ask him?"

"Yes, whatever you like," said Audrina, sleepily.

"What do you mean? Should I play it cool or wait for him to contact me?"

She had never been on a date before. The only other boy she had kissed was a couple of years ago at her friend's eighteenth birthday party. Everybody had been drunk and the following morning, she couldn't even remember who it was she had kissed. She only had a vague memory of someone bumping into her as she re-filled her wine glass in the kitchen. She said sorry, even though it wasn't her fault and as she turned around, she felt herself being pulled towards someone and kissed. It was quite nice, from what she could remember, but when it was over, they had both walked away. He disappeared into the living room and she went out into the garden to re-join her group of friends. It appeared that it hadn't been special enough for either of them to hang around and ask the other person's name.

Audrina, on the other hand, had a wealth of experience with boys. Although, from what she knew of Audrina, Gwen didn't think that she would ever have to chase someone after a date. If the boy wasn't keen enough, there would be another one along in a minute.

Audrina didn't reply. She was fast asleep, but within minutes Gwen got her answer, as a text message arrived on her phone. Charles wanted to know whether she was free tomorrow. She wished she could ask Audrina whether she should text back straight away, or should she make him wait until the morning. Sod it, she thought. She texted him back and said that yes, she was free tomorrow and would love to see him.

Chapter Seven

Second Year

September 2004

Audrina was the first to arrive back in Lancaster for their second year at university. She had caught an early train from Euston and had arrived at Lancaster train station just before ten. After a short walk to the estate agent's, she had collected the keys to the new house, where she, Gwen and Charles would be staying for the next academic year. Gwen referred to it as the 'new house', when in reality it was the complete opposite. It was an old end terraced house, hundreds of years old, at least that's how it felt to Audrina. It was small and cold and damp and in need of some loving care and attention. But students didn't usually care for the houses that they occupied and the house had clearly been neglected for some time.

Audrina dumped her two suitcases and her rucksack on the hall floor and climbed the steep stairs to the first floor. The two large bedrooms each had a double bed, two bedside tables and a small pine wardrobe. The mattresses looked thin and uncomfortable and the one in the back bedroom, where she was going to sleep, had some very dark stains of a not too salubrious origin. Audrina perched on the end of the bed, got out her phone and searched for a new mattress on Amazon. Within a few minutes, she had ordered one to be delivered the following day. She had a very healthy bank balance at the moment, thanks to a long summer of prestigious modelling jobs, so she also ordered a clothes rail and a large chest of drawers, a dressing table, two stools and a full length mirror for the tiny spare bedroom, which she planned to turn into a dressing room. She hadn't told Gwen of her plans, which she wanted to keep as a surprise. But Gwen would love it, she knew she would. It would be her house warming gift to them both.

Now that they were no longer going to be sharing a bedroom, she would miss them getting ready together when they were going out for the evening. Spending hours in front of the mirror, styling their hair and putting make-up on was just as much a part of the night out as the actual night out itself. They used to spend ages getting ready, drinking wine and singing to tinny music playing through their phone speakers, choosing what clothes to wear, which shoes would match and talking about how they thought their night would pan out. Although how many nights out they would have together now, Audrina wasn't sure. Towards the end of last term, Gwen had declined more invitations to parties and nights out than she had accepted. She told Audrina that it was because she was studying for her end of year exams, but that wasn't the reason. Usually when Audrina returned home from a night out, more often than not, Charles was in their room, snuggled up with Gwen watching television like an old married couple. He would quickly get up and leave when Audrina arrived; he never out stayed his welcome and he never stayed overnight in their tiny room, but her time alone with Gwen had gradually diminished.

As the months went by from the time that Gwen and Charles first met and they became more serious, Audrina accepted that she could no longer have Gwen to herself and she needed to share her. She didn't mind one little bit. She loved Charles, he was such a kind and gentle soul and it was obvious to everyone who knew them that Gwen and Charles were meant for each other. She wouldn't be surprised if they arrived today announcing their engagement. When the end of their first student year had approached and it was time for them to start thinking about where they would live in their second year, it made sense for them to share a house. There was nobody else that Audrina was so close to and she couldn't wait for them to get here. Charles was picking Gwen up from her parents' house in Leeds and driving over.

Hi, where are you? X She sent a text to Gwen's phone.

About ten mins away. Get the kettle on x.

Fuck that. I've got Champagne x

Yayyyy!!! x

Audrina skipped down the stairs, picked up her rucksack and took it into the kitchen with her. She unzipped the back pocket, took out the bottle of Champagne and put it in the freezer to cool for ten minutes. There's nothing worse than warm Champagne, she thought. Just because we're students, doesn't mean that we drink second rate wine. She also unpacked her Champagne flutes. Even though the house was meant to be fully furnished, she knew that the contents of the cupboards wouldn't be that sophisticated. She was searching through the cupboards, checking for anything else that they needed, when there was a knock on the door.

"That was quick," she shouted, as she ran down the long hallway. She flung open the door and held her arms out wide, ready to hug her friends who she hadn't seen for two months.

"Now that's what I call a welcome," said the young man at the door. Without waiting for an invitation, he stepped into the hallway and into Audrina's waiting arms, wrapping his arms around her back and pulling her close.

"Get off me!" She pushed at his chest, but he held tight.

"You're the one who wanted a hug," he said, laughing into her ear.

"Not from you, you weirdo." She again pushed him and this time, he relented and let go. He was quite cute, she thought. Tall and well built, with deep brown eyes, shining with mischief and laughter. Even so, she didn't want a hug from a stranger, thank you very much. Not even a good looking one.

"Hey, copped off already, have you? I knew it wouldn't be long for you to be snapped up!"

Charles' Range Rover pulled up outside the house and he shouted over to her and the stranger, as he got out of the car. Ignoring the visitor, she ran down the path and hugged both of her friends at the same time.

"You look amazing," she said to Gwen. "You too, Charles, but Gwen, honestly, you look so good. Being in love obviously suits you."

"Oh don't, I feel like I've eaten my way through the whole summer. This one is always taking me out for food."

She patted her at flat stomach. "I feel fat."

"Stop being stupid. I thought you were over that dieting malarky. You're beautiful," said Audrina, giving her a kiss on both cheeks.

"I keep telling her that," said Charles, lifting their suitcases out of the boot of the car. "Anyway, who's your mate?"

"Oh shit, I forgot about him," said Audrina, leading Gwen and Charles back up the garden path towards the front door. "I'm sorry, I haven't asked you who you are and why you're here," she said to the stranger.

"I just came to say hi," he said. "I've got the house next door. I'm Sam." He nodded, but didn't hold out his hand, which Audrina was thankful for. She had had enough physical contact with him already.

"Pleased to meet you, Sam," said Charles. "This is Gwen, my girlfriend. I presume you've already met Audrina."

"We haven't properly been introduced, no," said Sam. "Hi."

"Hello," said Audrina.

He winked at her and looked her up and down lasciviously, so quickly that if you blinked, you would miss it. But she didn't miss it. She clocked it. The one short word and that one surreptitious glance turned her stomach. There was something about this man that she didn't like. Call it women's intuition. Whatever it was, her internal radar was blasting out warning signals, like a light house, illuminated and on guard. Audrina never ignored her intuition and she wanted to get away from him as quickly as possible. He was cute, some might say that he was good looking and he was definitely cheeky, but for some reason, she didn't like him.

She hoped that he would say hello and then return next door and leave them alone. Surely he would have unpacking to do too.

"So who are you sharing with, anyone we might know?" asked Charles.

Audrina cursed him under her breath for engaging him in conversation. Another time, another place, she thought. I want to get away and see you guys on your own.

"Faisal and Sebastian. We're all doing law, so you might not know them. What are you studying?"

"Business and finance. But I know Faisal, yes," said Charles. "Is he the one who plays in the cricket team?"

"Yes, that's him."

"Oh great, he's a really nice bloke. Single too. We'll have to get you two set up," he said, looking over at Audrina with wink.

Sam flashed him a look that said that he was single also. And that he was here first. Charles didn't seem to notice it. But Audrina did and so did Gwen. When Audrina looked over to her, she was grinning and a slight raise of her eyebrows and a tilt of her head told Audrina that she thought Sam would be a possible match for her. Was Audrina the only one who thought that he was smarmy?

"Don't you dare," she said, hitting him on the arm playfully. "I'm alright as I am, thank you."

"We'll see about that," said Charles. "Anyway, why are we congregating on the path? Let's get inside. Are you coming in, Sam? Have a drink with us?"

For fuck's sake, thought Audrina. Does nobody else have their weirdo spotting radar working today? Hers was on overtime at the moment.

"That'll be great, mate, thanks." said Sam, who evidently didn't need to be asked twice and followed them in with the over enthusiasm of a small puppy being introduced to a ball pool.

They all gathered in the kitchen, where all parties tend to start. Audrina was reluctant to pop open her Champagne and hoped that neither Gwen nor Charles would mention it. She would rescue it from the freezer as soon as Sam left the room. Luckily, Charles had brought some lager, which Sam seemed more than happy to share.

With a can of lager in their hands, the boys opened the back door to check out the garden, not for nice quiet cups of coffee in the morning sun, which Audrina was looking forward to, but for partying options. Audrina then took the opportunity to grab the Champagne from the freezer.

"Yes, this'll be a great space," she heard Sam say. "With being on the end, you're not likely to annoy any of the neighbours. It's perfect for parties."

"Follow me," she said to Gwen, grabbing her hand and leading her upstairs. "I'm not sharing this with that Philistine. I'm going to hide it up here until he's gone."

"You don't like him then?" asked Gwen.

"Are you serious? No, I don't like him. He's a massive creep."

"That's a shame," said Gwen. "I thought you two liked each other. I've seen the way he looks at you."

"Gwen!"

"I know, I know. As soon as I said it, I realised that all boys look at you like that. But he is super cute, you've got to admit."

"That's not what I meant at all. No, I don't think he's

cute. He's creeping me out. Anyway, when is he going? I hope he doesn't think that when his house mates arrive, that the party's going to continue over here. I've not even unpacked yet."

"Don't worry, I'll have a word with Charles. I'll suggest that he goes next door with him, if he wants, to meet the other lads and we can have a catch up."

"Yes! That sounds like a plan."

"I want to hear all about your work, where you've been and who you've met and most important of all, who you've been wearing."

Audrina laughed. "I'm not a celebrity on a red carpet."

"No, I know, but I can imagine you've been wearing some beautiful clothes."

"Yes, I have," said Audrina, as they settled onto the bed side by side.

She loved her modelling jobs and she had had a great summer, but she was so happy to be back at university with her best friend.

***

The following day, with all their belongings unpacked, the cupboards and the fridge filled with food, wine and beer and a huge new plant in the living room, which Gwen named Lily, as she gave it a jug of water, stroked its leaves and promised to care for it, their student house was beginning to look and feel like home. Audrina had opened all the windows and fresh September air blew through the house, taking the old damp smells of previous students outside. An expensive candle which Charles' mother had bought for him emitted notes of orange, geranium and bergamot around the living room and into the hall. She had also bought them matching hand soap and hand cream, which were side by side next to the kitchen sink.

"Don't let any of those smelly boys from next door use that," Audrina had told Charles when he unpacked the soap and told her that it was a gift from his mum. Charles had laughed and said that she didn't need to worry, boys didn't use soap that often. He was joking, of course, being one of the better groomed boys at the university. But she wasn't.

It was dry and sunny and after breakfast, Gwen suggested a picnic together in Williamson Park, which was one of their favourite places and gave an unrivalled view of the city and the surrounding countryside. Audrina told her that she wanted to wait in for her new mattress to be delivered, but she and Charles should go on their own. She said she would be fine and she would take the time to call home and speak to her mum and tell her that she had settled in. She needed to be in when her mattress was delivered but secretly, she also wanted to wait in for the delivery of the new furniture for the spare room and hoped to have all nicely arranged by the time Gwen got back. She would tell her that it was her moving in gift, so that Gwen didn't insist on paying her half of the money for it.

She had just ushered them out of the door when a text message from the delivery company told her that they would arrive within the next hour.

True to their word, a small van arrived thirty minutes later, a few minutes after Gwen and Charles had left, and Audrina asked the delivery men to take the furniture upstairs. As she was holding the door open for them, Sam appeared from round the corner, holding a shopping bag from the corner shop.

"Hi," he said, stopping at the bottom of her garden path. "Got a delivery?"

"You're observant," said Audrina. She couldn't help it. She didn't mean to be rude to him, but he grated on her nerves.

"One of my many talents," he said with a grin, appearing not to notice her discourtesy.

She smiled at him to take the sting out of her words. She decided she should try and be polite to him. After all, they were going to be neighbours for the best part of the next nine months, so they might as well get on. She needed to tolerate him, at least, as it seemed that Charles liked him.

"I've ordered a new mattress and a chest of drawers and a dressing table for the spare room," she said. "Gwen and Charles have gone out and I want it to be a surprise for Gwen when she gets back, so we can both use the room to get ready in."

As soon as she said it, she regretted being so open. It was meant to be neighbourly conversation but she had said too much. She didn't want to let him know that she was alone in the house, as he would offer to keep her company, she just knew he would.

"I'll help you put it together, if you like," he said, bang on cue.

"No, it's fine, honest. It's not flat packed, it's already made. Thanks though." She turned away to go back inside.

"No problem. See you later then." He opened his front gate.

"Yes, see you."

"Unless you want some company…"

"No, no, I'm fine."

"I'm not coming onto you, I just…"

"No, no, of course not, I didn't think that."

"I just thought, with Charles and Gwen being out, you might want some company, that's all."

"Another time, definitely. I've got a banging headache and after all the travel and stuff yesterday, I'm just really tired."

The delivery men came down the stairs and out of the front door.

"All done," one of them said. "We've put the chest of drawers against the side wall, to the left of the door, and the dressing table opposite. Do you want to check it? We can move it for you, while we're here."

"That would be great," said Audrina, "If you could just put the dressing table under the window for me."

"Yes, of course, no problem."

She followed them upstairs and watched until the furniture had been moved into the correct place. By the time they all went back down, Sam had gone. Audrina sighed in relief and closed and locked the front door. If he came back, she would ignore him and pretend that she was asleep.

Chapter Eight

Date Night

June 2022 - Tuesday

By the time Gwen arrived home, dark grey clouds had appeared from nowhere and blanketed the city, blocking the sun's rays and dragging the temperature down at least five degrees. Her plan to enjoy the afternoon sun on the balcony was ruined, it was far too cold for that now, so she flicked on the TV and settled down on the sofa to relax. She had an hour or so before she should start getting ready for dinner. She had booked a table at San Carlo, Charles' favourite Italian restaurant, for dinner.

After living on the west side of the Pennines for the past twenty years, she was just about getting used to the changeable weather and the amount of rain which, more often than not, forced them to change their social plans. Breakfasts on the balcony, lunch at a pavement cafe or afternoon walks by the Bridgewater Canal could never be guaranteed. Rain very often stopped play.

But this afternoon, she wasn't too bothered. She was

looking forward to their evening out and she had an hour to catch up on last night's crime drama before she had to get ready. This was her favourite time of the day. Work was finished, Charles wasn't yet home and she could do whatever she liked. When they had moved into the building three years ago, she had joined the luxury and very expensive gym downstairs, with the plan to go after work. She promised herself that she would go three times a week, when the fresh faced, enthusiastic assistant told her how much it was. The more you come, the cheaper it will be, she had told her. But it won't be any cheaper, will it, thought Gwen. It doesn't matter how many times I come, the price will still be extortionate. Even though she could afford it, it was expensive enough for it to make her feel guilty every time she checked the bank statement and saw the direct debit to West Manchester Leisure and calculated how many times she had been in the previous month. She really must make an effort to go more often. Last month, she only managed to go to two yoga sessions. It wasn't exactly the vigorous exercise she should be getting. She shouted over to Alexa to set a reminder for tomorrow to tell her to go to the gym at four p.m.

But she wasn't going to think about it tonight. Tonight was date night and if she was going to get herself hot and sweaty, it certainly wouldn't be on a rowing machine or a cross trainer.

As soon as the crime drama finished, she padded over to the kitchen, poured herself a glass of cold wine and took it with her into the bathroom.

An hour later, she was ready, make-up and hair done and wearing a new black dress.

She checked the time on the kitchen clock as she poured herself another glass of wine. Charles was almost half an hour late. As she waited for him, pacing around the living room in too-high heels because she didn't want to sit down and crease her linen dress, she practised being composed and nonchalant when he came through the door. He knew that she hated being late and that she would be anxious about missing their table booking at the restaurant, so she told herself that he wouldn't be late on purpose and that something must have happened to delay him at work. Or maybe it was the traffic. Manchester was gridlocked on most days and their penthouse apartment in Beetham Tower was situated on one of the busiest roads.

She had thought that it was a good idea for them to go out for dinner, but now she was beginning to regret her decision. As her anxiety rose with each minute that ticked by, the less she wanted to go out. She was trying to make an effort here, but he couldn't even get himself home on time. She should have booked herself into the hotel after all. At this precise moment, the only company she wanted was her own.

After a couple more minutes, she sent him a text.

Is everything okay? x

No reply.

I'm just worried. Don't panic if you're running late. Not a problem xx

Yet it was a fucking problem and the fact that he was ignoring her was a fucking problem too. When she had met Charles at university, she thought that he was different from all the others. He was kind and attentive and had never let her down. He was an old-fashioned gentleman. He put her first and thought about her wants and needs. At least he used to. These days, things were different. He appeared to like mind games as much as the next man. As soon as that thought entered her head, she quashed it. She had known him for most of her adult life and he had never played mind games with her before; what on earth was she thinking? He loved her. He was her husband. There was nothing wrong. They had a minor bump in the road, that's all. She was over thinking and it had to stop.

But by the time he finally arrived home, Gwen was pouring her third glass of wine and her blood was boiling, irrationally. She wanted to shout at him for ignoring her, scream at him that mobile phones were there for a purpose and he should use it, a quick text would take him half a second to send. The selfish prick. But she said none of these things. A calm and smiling Gwen greeted him with a hug and a kiss. If Charles was testing her, then she was very happy to say that she had not only crossed the first hurdle, she had literally leapt over it with metres to spare.

"Hi, are you ready?" he said. Not, oh you look nice or, is that a new dress?

Ready? I've been ready for over half an hour, she thought, while you've been playing your stupid mind games.

"Just about," she said. "I've opened a bottle of wine, would you like a glass before we go out?"

"We don't really have time," he said, "I thought you said that the table's booked for eight."

"Oh not to worry," she said. "I've no idea what time it is, do we need to leave now?" She knew damn well they needed to leave now. They needed to have left twenty minutes ago.

Charles looked confused. If he expected an angry and frantic wife, then he was going to be disappointed.

"Yes, we should go," he said.

As she closed the front door behind them and followed him to the lift, she took a deep breath and decided that she would enjoy her evening. It didn't matter that he hadn't noticed her new dress or how much effort she had made getting ready. After all, she did have a lot of clothes and she wore make-up every day for work. She couldn't expect him to hand out compliments every time he saw her.

They were alone in the lift and Gwen took the opportunity to be romantic, despite her annoyance at having been kept waiting. But she was too late.

"You look very handsome today," she said, taking his tie in her hand and pulling him towards her for a kiss, just at the same moment that the lift doors opened as they reached the ground floor. A middle aged couple stepped back to let them out. She didn't get the kiss, but it didn't matter, they had plenty of time to be romantic. She was going to make sure that they got over this bad patch, after all, she was the root cause.

Twenty minutes later, having arrived at the restaurant and given orders to the waiter for a large glass of Pinot Grigio for her and a large beer for him, Gwen reached over the table and took Charles's hand, hoping to show that she was determined to have a good night.

"So how's your day been?" she asked brightly. She didn't want to ask him why he was late home. Maybe he would tell her in his own time. She could tell that something was bothering him, but after a couple of beers and some good food, he would hopefully snap him out of it and enjoy the date.

"A bit frantic, to tell you the truth," he said. "One of the shipments didn't arrive, so I've had to completely re-plan the schedule for next week. I think the new project manager is finding the job too hard. He keeps moaning about working weekends so…."

The waiter arrived at their table with their drinks and asked if they were ready to order food. Gwen would have liked a few more minutes, but Charles said they were ready, so she didn't want to appear difficult, especially as they were late arriving. She quickly chose the mushroom risotto. Charles chose his regular lasagne and garlic bread.

"We've got a new woman at work too," she said. "One of the research team. She's married to Geoff, you know, the camera man? I think you met him once."

Charles nodded.

"She said they met at university. Not in the actual university, they were studying different things, but in an Italian restaurant in Newcastle where they both worked at the weekends. How funny is that? She said she almost felt obliged to start dating him, just to please her mum, who always wanted her to marry a handsome man with a steady job. I mean, it's not as though he's a doctor, but you're always going to need camera men, aren't you? I'm waffling, sorry. This wine has gone straight to my head." She took a sip from her glass, aware that it was the three glasses she had drank at home that had gone to her head, not this one. She had to be careful and slow down, although Charles didn't appear to notice that she was well on her way to being drunk.

Charles sipped his beer and said nothing. Tension emanated from every pore. Anyone glancing over to their table would think they had had an argument. Anger swirled around them like a smog. For once, Gwen wasn't the cause and if she kept talking, she knew that he would cheer up eventually. He was the type of person to bring his work worries home with him and it sometimes took him an hour or so to forget about them and calm down. Gwen kept her work worries firmly locked in her dressing room, where they belonged. The relationship counsellor had told them that they should accept and embrace each other's differences, as they were part of what initially brought them together. They fell in love with each other because they loved each other's personalities, as well as their looks. It had made sense to Gwen at the time and over the next few weeks, she had made an effort to give Charles some time alone when he came home from work. His own little portable man cave, an invisible space for him to chill. She would go for a bath or make a coffee and go into the bedroom and phone her mum, leaving him alone with the sports channel.

Gwen's wine glass was empty. She twirled the stem between her fingers and watched Charles as he stared into his beer, silently. What was he, fucking three? He was acting like a toddler. It was his fault that he didn't have his downtime after work. If he hadn't been late home, he could have had half an hour to himself. But look at all the other men in the restaurant, they weren't sulking and moody and you could bet your bottom dollar that they had come straight from work too. She didn't want to 'accept and embrace' this side of him. It was exhausting. He was a grown man, not a child.

The waiter brought their food. Charles managed a quick smile at him while he sprinkled his lasagne with black pepper and parmesan cheese and then walked away.

"So, Zara's wedding will be fun, won't it? She's so excited. She's finishing after the show on Thursday, so she can have a day off before the wedding. You know, get her nails done and do girly things. I don't know what exactly."

Gwen laughed.

Charles stabbed at his lasagne with his fork, allowing pockets of steam to escape.

"I'm looking forward to the wedding, thanks to you." She raised her glass to him.

"Thanks to me for what?" he said, not raising his glass.

"For booking the hotel and the taxi," she said, putting her glass back down on the table.

"Right," he said.

Previously, they had been good at silences. In fact, she had enjoyed them. Whether walking around Manchester on a warm summer's evening, stopping for a drink in a pavement bar, or sitting together on the sofa, either flicking through social media on their phones or watching television or snuggling in bed on a Sunday morning, there had never been a desperate need to fill the silence. It was already filled, with friendship and love. Companionship. There were never any gaps between them. So why did tonight feel so different? Was it because he had been late and hadn't explained why? She really needed to let that go. Don't sweat the small stuff. Wasn't that the name of a book or something? She took another drink of her wine, thinking of something else to say.

"She's called Grace," she said eventually. "The new woman. Isn't that a lovely name? I've always loved that name. I told her and she said she would take the compliment but really it was her mother's choosing, not hers." Gwen laughed and tried to read what Charles was thinking. Usually she could read him quite well, but tonight she was struggling. She went on, "I always thought that if we had a girl, we would call her Grace, it's lovely, isn't it? So... well... graceful."

Charles continued to eat without looking up. What was wrong with him? Gwen could feel her insides churning and told herself that it was only adrenalin. It was just a hormone. She should recognise it, acknowledge it, take a deep breath and then ignore it. That's what the yoga teacher at the gym said. Just breathe it out. You couldn't always stop yourself from feeling negative emotions, but you didn't have to give in to them. Just let them pass through and breathe them out. She could envision the yoga instructor, tight little body wrapped in lycra, breathing out negative thoughts. She really needed to do it. Right now. If she didn't, there was a very high likelihood that Charles would find himself wearing what was left on his plate.

Whatever had happened at work was clearly bothering him. He looked so tense; sad even. She hoped it would be a temporary mask and that he could return to full happiness soon. Hopefully in the next five to ten minutes. That would be great.

Yet he still hadn't said anything.

"Oh my God, I hope you don't think I'm going to go on about having a baby all night, just because I said that I like the name Grace. Is that what you're thinking?"

The waiter arrived at their table again and asked them if everything was alright with their food. They nodded quickly and he left.

"No, that isn't what I was thinking," said Charles.

"I mean, I do want children," said Gwen, "Obviously, you know I do, but it doesn't have to be the topic of every conversation." She laughed nervously.

Charles slammed his knife and fork down on the table and leant across the table to her.

"For goodness sake, Gwen. Does it always have to be about you?"

"What?"

He shook his head and tore at the garlic bread, which he dipped into the hot sauce seeping out of the lasagne sheets. Gwen waited for him to decide whether to eat it, before she pushed him for an explanation. She really didn't want to argue in public, it was so humiliating. Her face was so well known, she didn't want the world to know about every disagreement that she had with her husband. All couples argue, but not all couples get talked about in the press and Gwen could feel her humiliation building. He continued to stab the bread, again and again into the sauce before he shovelled the soaked garlic bread into his mouth, chewing quickly.

"I don't know why you're so cross," she said. "Okay, so you've had a shit day, but I should be the one who's cross, left ready and waiting for over half an hour, while you ignore my texts. I was actually worried about you." This was partly true; she was worried about him a little, but knowing that he had travelled less than two miles to their apartment, the chances of him being involved in a road accident were extremely slim. She was more annoyed at the fact that she had been kept waiting, pacing about the living room in uncomfortably high shoes.

"Un-fucking-believeable," said Charles, "You're making it about you again."

It's funny how one minute you're having a good time and the next minute you've plummeted into an argument, for no apparent reason, thought Gwen. Her mind was telling her to storm out, throw the napkin in his face, no better still, throw the wine into his face and leave him there to pay the bill. But this was Charles. Her handsome, wonderful Charles. The love of her life. So her heart kept her pinned to the chair, while it beat adrenalin around her blood stream and sent tears down her face.

"Charles?" She dabbed at her tears with her napkin, trying to be as discreet as possible.

"I was in the middle of telling you about my day, but you weren't listening. I don't know why you even asked, because you're clearly not interested in what I tell you."

"I was listening," she whispered, hoping that he would lower his voice to match hers, as the people at the next table were beginning to show far too much interest in their heated conversation. "You said that one of the shipments didn't arrive and that your project manager is finding the job hard. I did listen, see. But I didn't think it was a monologue. Conversations are a two way street." At this, she waved her index finger backwards and forwards between them. "I'm allowed to tell you about my day too."

Charles took a deep breath followed by a large mouthful of beer. "It's fucking hot in here. I need another beer. Where's the fucking waiter when you need one? Always at your table when you want privacy and then when you want to order something…There he is. Excuse me, can I have a pint of lager please."

Gwen didn't want to comment on the fact that he hadn't asked her if she wanted any more wine. She was a big girl, she could order her own, if she wanted one.

"Look, I'm sorry, okay? It's been a rough day, but everything will be sorted in the next couple of days, so I can relax at the weekend.. It'll be good."

"It's fine," she said, wiping away a tear with her finger and hoping that nobody had noticed it.

He reached across the table and held tightly her hand. "I seem to spend my life apologising to women these days." He showed that beautiful wide smile that had captivated her when they first met, that day nineteen years ago, when he had knocked on her door at university and asked her to lunch. His handsome face and his beautiful blue eyes shone in the candlelight.

"What do you mean, apologising to women?"

"You and Julia," he said.

"You've apologised to Julia? I didn't know that." She tried as hard as she could to stay calm.

"Really? Are you sure you didn't know? I sent her a card and some flowers after the barbeque. I thought I'd told you," he said.

No, you fucking didn't tell me. There was no need to apologise to Julia; she was too drunk to remember anything, but now he had made an issue of it and embarrassed them both. Now her parents would know what went on. What a mess.

"Flowers?" Gwen tried to stay calm but her thin lips

showed him that she was annoyed..

"Gwen, for God's sake, get over yourself. I was trying to do the right thing, yet you're looking at me like I've just killed your grandma. I was drunk and I was a bit too familiar and I apologised. End of."

"You absolute idiot! Julia wouldn't have remembered anything about it, she was too pissed. You should have apologised to me, not her."

"I did! All the way home, remember?"

"Stop shouting! If it hasn't escaped your notice, people are looking."

"I don't give a shit," he said, but in a quieter voice, proving that he wasn't completely comfortable with public confrontation.

They ate the rest of their meal in silence. Charles didn't drink any of his lager and the silence continued on their walk home. For the first time in their marriage, Gwen was pleased that they had a spare room in their apartment because she certainly didn't plan to share a bed tonight.

Chapter Nine

Morning After

June 2022 - Wednesday

Devon's buoyancy was irritating beyond belief. Audrina could hear him in the en-suite bathroom, singing to himself. She reached for her phone. Seven thirty. Her mouth felt like the bottom of a birdcage and she was in desperate need of some water and paracetamol. She knew she shouldn't have opened the second bottle of wine yesterday, or was it the third bottle? She had lost count. Isla only had one glass and Devon might have had one. Her headache was telling her that she must have had the rest. Jacob would go mad if he knew that she had more wine than water yesterday. She needed to make sure that she was properly hydrated today. She only had two days before she would be going to meet him in London at the agency and she knew she would be under close scrutiny, by him and the designer.

She reached a hand out to her bedside table with one eye open, but her water glass was empty. She flopped her head back on the pillow. She was usually quite diligent in filling it up before she went to sleep, but last night she obviously didn't. She couldn't even remember getting into bed.

"Feeling rough?" asked Devon, coming out of the bathroom with a towel wrapped around his waist.

"Why does that feel like an interrogation, rather than a check on my welfare?"

"I'm not judging," he said, bending down to kiss her cheek. "Nothing to do with me, but I did try to tell you to curb it."

"Did you? I can't remember." She sat up against the head board and watched Devon while he got dressed into his shorts and training top. "How much did I have?"

"Too much. Look, don't worry about it. I'll get you a tablet and some water."

He disappeared into the bathroom and came back with two paracetamol from the bathroom cabinet and a fresh glass of water. He put them down on the bedside table, picked up the remote control and flicked the television onto the BBC news channel.

"Can you honestly tell us, Prime Minister, that your policy has the best interests of the British public at heart? Inflation is sky rocketing and our viewers want to know what your government plans to do to help ordinary working people. What can you say to them this morning? Do you have any words of reassurance?"

Gwen's authoritative voice filled the bedroom and the Prime Minister fumbled his reply back at her, without actually answering the question.

"I need to stop you right there," said Gwen. "This is not a platform for a party political broadcast. If you would answer the question…"

"Turn it off, Dev, please," said Audrina. "It's too loud. You're going to wake the kids."

She rested her head on the headboard. She didn't want to see Gwen this morning and she didn't want to hear her voice. She felt tears pricking at the back of her eyes and closed her eyes tightly to stop them escaping. She missed her like crazy, even after all these years. It must be the remains of the alcohol making her emotional, she told herself.

"The kids have been up an hour. They're all downstairs already," said Devon.

"Really? I didn't hear them."

Devon laughed and kissed her forehead. "I know you didn't. You were snoring. I'll go and get you a coffee. Stay there."

As he opened their bedroom door, she could hear the faint sound of cartoons coming from the living room below. She felt awful that she wasn't there with the children, making them some toast and handing out cups of milk. But Devon can cope, she thought, as she tried to squash the guilt before it grew any bigger and engulfed her, like it did most days. She had been awake for less than ten minutes, surely she shouldn't be feeling guilty already?

She tiptoed into the bathroom. The harsh light above the mirror confirmed her fears. She looked terrible. She was dehydrated and hadn't had enough sleep. Of all the days! She tipped the two paracetamol tablets into her mouth and washed them down with two glasses of water. She knew that she shouldn't have agreed to see Jacob on Friday. She could have told him that she was busy. After all, they had just moved house. Whatever he had to talk to her about could be done over the phone and she could have met the designer on Zoom. But Jacob was old fashioned and he liked to have meetings in person, whenever possible. At any other time, she would have loved a trip to London. It was a chance to catch up with her mum and dad and have lunch somewhere nice. They always loved it when she went home. But she wasn't in the mood for it this week at all and if it was anyone else, she would cancel. But this was a new client and Jacob was keen to impress them, so she didn't want to be dropped from the job. She had been warned that she needed to look her best and get plenty of sleep between now and the shoot in Paris. As if that was possible with three kids in the house!

As soon as the thought flashed into her mind, Audrina knew that it wasn't the children's fault that she looked like death this morning. It was entirely self-inflicted. It's funny how her young body was so forgiving and however much alcohol or greasy food that she fed it in her twenties and early thirties, it had still looked healthy and glowing, even after an all-night party. But the body of someone approaching forty is a different kettle of fish and needs to be treated with tenderness and care.

She wondered what Gwen liked to drink these days. Did she still avoid red wine, like she used to at university, for fear of it staining her teeth? Audrina smiled to herself as she remembered Gwen drinking a glass of cheap Merlot using a straw. She had asked Charles to go to the off-licence to stock up on alcohol for the weekend and he had returned with the wrong wine. Gwen had fretted for the whole day about her teeth, until Audrina told her to stop. She told her that she was worried about her appearance way too much -

she was constantly on a diet and spent a fortune on expensive skin care. Audrina told her that she should be more like French women. They always looked chic and beautiful, but they were relaxed about it. They ate and drank whatever they liked, but just had smaller portions. Gwen had told her that she would try her best to take a leaf out of their book.

Audrina hoped that she had done. She was looking good these days. She noticed that she had had her hair coloured this week. It suited her. The radio had done a phone-in on whether women in the lime light needed to colour their hair to look young, as none of the male presenters did. Ms Indignant from Liverpool rang in to say that it was grossly unfair that men were able to grow old naturally, while the women were under pressure to look much younger than they actually were. Ms Angry from Birmingham rang in to say that she didn't like Gwen's new hair colour and it didn't suit her at all. She should stick to her more natural colour and stop pretending to be someone she wasn't. Audrina had wanted to call in and say that actually, Gwen might have coloured her hair just because she wanted to and not necessarily because she had any grey hairs or because she wanted to make some kind of statement to people she had never met. She had wondered whether Gwen was listening to the radio and if she was, whether she gave a fuck about what people thought. If she was still anything like the old Gwen, she would be hurt and upset by cruel words but she'd pretend that she wasn't bothered. Hopefully, she had still been at the studio and hadn't heard it.

She had asked Audrina once how she coped being a model, with loads of people looking at her and judging her.

"I ignore them," she had said. "It's got nothing to do with me being a model. People will judge you too. People will judge all women, not just models. What are we to do? Stay inside and hide ourselves away?"

"I suppose not," said Gwen. "When you put it like that."

"So, we might as well get on with it and dress how we like. Whatever we do, someone will have something to say about it."

"That's true," said Gwen.

"So put on your best smile and fuck them all."

They had said cheers, taken a gulp of wine and continued to put their make-up on, sitting side by side in the small dressing room. Girls Aloud was playing on the CD player, they had a great night out to look forward to at the university bar, where they were going to watch a reggae band, they had each other and Gwen and Charles were in love. Audrina couldn't remember ever being happier than she was at that time. Maybe it's because she had a rose tinted view of the world and she had her life mapped out in front of her, with plenty to look forward to. Or maybe it was because she was sharing every day with the best friend that she had ever had, before it all started to go wrong.

"Mummy, mummy, here you are!" Harry pounded into the en-suite and threw himself at her, clinging to her legs. "Lift me up, lift me up."

She lifted him onto the sink unit and kissed both of his cheeks and then his forehead.

"Morning my best boy, how are you?"

"Good."

"Have you had your breakfast?"

"Yes, but Daddy forgot the jam."

"Did you show him where it was?"

Harry nodded. She lifted him up and carried him downstairs. Devon was sitting in the corner of the sofa in the living room, watching football highlights on his phone. Mary and Martha were lying on the rug, side by side, watching Sponge Bob Square Pants on the television. She stood at the threshold for a moment, taking it it. Her beautiful family. She was so lucky to have them all.

"I've made you a coffee," said Devon, nodding towards a steaming mug that he had placed on the side coffee table. He had even used a coaster.

She put Harry down on the floor and he ran over to join his sisters on the rug.

"Can we turn this off now, you lot," said Devon, picking up the remote control and switching channels. "You know your mummy likes to watch the news."

Gwen's face appeared on the screen again and Audrina burst into tears.

"You daft sod, what's wrong with you?" said Devon. "That's the wine, it always makes you emotional."

And the fact that I haven't seen my best friend for years, she thought.

Mary ran over to her and wrapped her arms around her legs. "Mummy, why are you crying?" she asked. She had always been the more perceptive twin. The emotionally mature one. Audrina rubbed her hair and assured her that she was alright and that she had a headache, that's all. She said that all she needed was twenty minutes for the painkillers to start working and she would be fine again.

"Why don't you go and get a bath," said Devon. "We're fine down here and I don't have to leave for work for ages."

"Thank you, I think I will," she said.

She took her coffee upstairs and placed it on the sink in the bathroom. She lit one of her Jo Malone candles, the Lime, Basil and Mandarin one that Devon had bought her for her birthday, sprinkled bath salts into the tub and began running the water. The candle reminded her of the house that she shared with Gwen and Charles in their second year at university. Not that fragrance exactly, but any expensive candle brought back fond memories. Charles' mother, a lovely kind lady but a self-confessed terrible snob, according to Gwen, had told Charles that she wanted to make sure that they always had a collection of luxury candles in the house. She said that she knew what students were like, lazy, disgusting creatures who tended to ignore their washing pile until they ran out of clothes, so the candles would disguise the horrible smells. When Gwen had told her what she had said, Audrina wasn't sure whether to laugh or to be insulted. Gwen said she had laughed, she couldn't help it and Charles' mother had winked at her, so she was ninety-nine percent sure that she wasn't serious.

As Audrina settled into the warm bath water, she was thankful that, although she and Gwen were no longer in contact, at least Gwen still had Charles. It was nice that they were still together. They were often photographed together and they still looked so much in love. They held hands, just like they used to, and you could tell from the way Charles looked at Gwen that he was as besotted with her now as he always was.

Chapter Ten

Regular Visitors

October 2004

Sam, Faisal and Sebastian were becoming regular weekend visitors to Audrina's house, whether at Charles' invitation or their own, Audrina wasn't quite sure. What she was sure of was that she was getting fed up of it. The hall seemed to be constantly cluttered with piles of dirty, smelly trainers and the bin was forever over flowing with empty beer cans and pizza takeaway boxes. She seemed to spend every Sunday morning cleaning the kitchen, hoovering the living room carpet and plumping cushions back to normality. The boys had no respect for soft furnishings.

As she looked at one of her Champagne flutes on the floor, having become a casualty of a Sam's clumsiness, she had just about had enough. He had carelessly emptied a shopping bag of beer cans onto the kitchen unit, knocking over the Champagne flute, which ended up in a thousand tiny pieces.

If it were anyone else, Audrina would have played the

part of the gracious host and told them that it wasn't a problem, accidents happen and, no, she wouldn't dream of accepting a replacement from them, while ushering them out of the kitchen so that she could clean up the shards of glass from the floor and mop the spilled wine from the front of the kitchen cupboards, whilst at the same time maintaining a polite and diplomatic smile on her face to save her guest's embarrassment.

But Sam brought out the worst in her.

"Fucking hell, Sam!" she shouted at him. "Why can't you be more careful? You clumsy sod!"

"Well what was it doing there in the first place?" he said.

Was he for real? Did he think that, somehow, it was her fault, for putting her glass on the kitchen unit? What was she meant to do with it, carry it around with her the whole time, just to keep it out of his way? As though she was an inconvenience for using up some counter space in her own kitchen.

"Is that your way of saying sorry?" she said. "It was on the worktop, where else was it meant to be?"

"It was precariously close to the edge, I mean…"

"It was on the fucking worktop!" Audrina screamed at him. She struggled to keep the hysteria from her voice and the tears from her eyes, which had the effect of making her more angry. She didn't want him to see her crying. She didn't want him to know that he made her feel so irritable and annoyed, not just now because he had broken her Champagne flute, but every single day. When she saw him, her nerves grated and her senses went on high alert, pumping her body with unwanted adrenalin. She had no idea why. Gwen and Charles seemed to like him. Charles in particular treated him like one of his best friends, someone he had had a connection with for years, rather than a few weeks.

She had had enough of him. She had had enough of all of them, Daniel and Sebastian too, although those two were nice boys, to be honest, but it was too much, having all three of them over so often. The house was beginning to feel like a hostel, rather than a home these days. They weren't in student halls anymore. They were paying more rent for the privilege of not being surrounded by dozens of strangers all the time. And yet here they were.

"Alright you two, what's going on? You're making a lot of noise." Sebastian stood in the doorway, beer can in one hand and the menu for the Chinese takeaway in the other hand.

"I knocked a wine glass over and she's getting her knickers in a twist about it," said Sam.

"You sound like an old married couple, bickering in the kitchen." Sebastian laughed, which fueled Audrina's anger even more.

"It wasn't a wine glass," she said. "It was an expensive Champagne flute."

"I offered to replace it."

"No you didn't," said Audrina. "I never heard you say that."

"Well I was going to," said Sam. "I will do, if that's what you want."

"You blamed me for putting it…"

"Now, now children," said Sebastian. "I'm sure it was an accident."

Audrina fumed silently. There was no reasoning with

either of them, it seemed, and she didn't want to waste her breath any longer. Whether it was an accident or not, the broken glass needed to be cleaned up before someone stood on it. She crouched down and began picking up the largest pieces of glass and putting them carefully in the bin.

"While you're down there," said Sam, laughing crudely. He reached out his hand towards Audrina's head and pushed his crotch in her face, almost knocking her over. She slapped his legs as hard as she could and stood up quickly, stepping away from him.

"Even I know that you're on thin ice there, mate," said Sebastian, laughing as though he had just witnessed the funniest thing ever, in the way that only drunken men can. Lasciviously and raucously. "I think you need to leave it right there, before you say something to get you into more trouble."

More roaring laughter. She wanted to slap them both across their stupid ugly faces before they became hysterical, like people used to do in old black and white movies.

"I think you're right, mate. She must be on her period or something."

Sebastian waved the takeaway menu in the air. "Chinese food, anyone?"

Maybe he was trying to lighten the mood and cheer Audrina up, but more likely he was thinking of his own stomach.

"Not for me," said Audrina. "And you can clean that up," she said to Sam, pointing to the remaining bits of glass on the floor. She pushed past Sebastian, ran down the hall and up the stairs to the dressing room, where Gwen was still drying her hair.

"I can't cope with him anymore," she said, closing the door behind her. "He's just knocked my Champagne flute onto the floor. Aaarrrgghhh, I'm so sick of him."

"Oh no, and smashed it, I presume?"

"Yes! The big clumsy oaf. I hate him being in the house all the fucking time, getting in the way."

"What is it with you and him? I guess you're talking about Sam?" asked Gwen.

"Yes, Sam. I don't know. I just don't like him and I don't know why. Do you?"

"Well, I don't dislike him as much as you do. Charles thinks he's a laugh. He's okay when you get to know him."

"That's just it though. I don't want to get to know him. He gives me the creeps."

"It's probably because he fancies you and he's coming on a bit strong, that's all. Maybe he's trying to be funny and make you laugh, but it's irritating you instead. You can't blame a guy for trying."

"I don't know what it is," said Audrina. "I can't put my finger on it. Maybe we met in a previous life and hated each other, for some reason and my subconscious is picking up bad vibes."

"Oooh yes, maybe you were his wife and he was horrible to you and that's why you hate him now. You were probably the lord and lady of the manor and he had an affair with the serving wench and you became the talk of the town."

"I feel like I could have been his sister and we just bickered for the whole of our childhood. I don't think I would have been romantically involved with him, ever."

"Or maybe he was Louis the Sixteenth and you chopped

his head off on the guillotine and that's why you have this urge to kill him in this life, because you've done it before."

Both of them giggled.

"Here, have a sip of this." Gwen handed Audrina her glass of wine. "Something to calm your nerves."

"Thanks. The boys are ordering Chinese food, do you want any, or shall we eat at the campus?"

"Yes, let's do that," said Gwen. "I wouldn't mind getting there early and then we can get good seats for the band."

Five minutes later, they were ready to leave for their girls' night out at the university. Charles, Sam, Sebastian and Faisal were eating at home and then planning to go into the town centre later for drinks. Audrina thanked the Music Gods that none of them had good enough taste in music to like reggae, so they wouldn't be joining them at the university to watch the band. She was looking forward to a night with Gwen on her own. Or rather, she was looking forward to a night without Sam being around.

***

The Pendle Bar on campus was packed full to bursting. The band had been a huge success and when they walked off stage, the whole room erupted with students and visitors jumping up and down, clapping, cheering and shouting for an encore. After a further three songs, Gwen's feet couldn't hold her up for a moment longer.

"I've got to sit down," she shouted to Audrina over the noise. "My feet are killing me and I need some air. It's so hot in here."

They pushed their way to the door, into the corridor and

out through the fire exit door and into the cool autumn air. They collapsed onto the grass and Gwen immediately took her shoes off and rubbed the soles of her feet.

"I feel a bit pissed," said Gwen, leaning against Audrina's arm and resting her head on her shoulder.

"I know," said Audrina, laughing. "That's why your feet hurt. You've been stumbling about too much on ridiculous heels. You should wear flats if you're going to get drunk. It's a rookie mistake."

Audrina only wore heels occasionally, so she didn't have issues with blisters or throbbing soles, like Gwen did.

"I know, but I like ridiculous heels. They make me feel elegant. And I like being as tall as you," said Gwen, holding up her index finger and wagging it in Audrina's face, as though she were imparting words of wisdom.

"Stay here, you drunken bum, and I'll go and get our coats and ring us a taxi."

"Yep okay," said Gwen, lying back onto the grass and closing her eyes.

Audrina went back inside and headed towards the cloakroom at the other side of the corridor, where all the coats and bags were kept. She handed the cloakroom ticket to one of the volunteers and he began the search for their coats.

"Had a good night?" A voice behind her made her jump.

"Bloody hell, you frightened me then." She turned around to see Sam standing behind her, too close for comfort. She took a step back and forced herself to smile at him, trying not to show that he was making her uneasy. She still hadn't entirely forgiven him for smashing her Champagne flute and then being an arse about it. "I'm waiting for our coats."

"I thought you would be, what with you standing at the cloakroom." He grinned at her, looking down at her cleavage for a fraction too long.

She smiled again. "Yes, that was a stupid thing to say. Are the other boys with you?"

"I'm not sure where they are, to be honest."

Shit. Now she would have to wait before she could order a taxi home. The last thing she wanted to do was to share one with him. If he had become split up from the boys, it would make sense for him to share their taxi. But she knew that he would insist on sitting next to her, squashing up on the back seat and pressing his leg against hers. She would be stuck, unable to avoid him. Invading her personal space was one of his favourite activities, which he was doing right now. Well, she would just have to make sure that she got in first and put Gwen in the middle somehow.

The cloakroom attendant returned with hers and Gwen's coats.

"Thank you." She took the coats and held them close to her, a barrier between her and Sam. "Okay, well I'll see you later then." She walked off down the corridor, praying that he wouldn't suggest that they shared a taxi, and was almost at the exit when he caught her up.

"Is that it then?" he said.

"What do you mean?" she said. She stopped and turned to face him. She was inches away from the door. If she had just walked a little quicker, she would be there now, outside with Gwen and all the other people who wanted to get some air, rather than stuck at the end of the corridor with this creep.

"I came all this way to see you and you give me less than half a dozen words and a dirty look. I think I deserve more than that, don't you?"

Audrina couldn't tell if he was joking. She didn't know him well enough to read his mood yet or every nuance of his facial expressions, but he didn't seem to be joking. She was confused.

"What? You've come all this way? I don't know what you mean. Am I missing something here?"

"I've come all this way to see you," he said. "You know I don't like reggae, so I've not come for the music, have I?"

She laughed, but he wasn't smiling.

"Are you serious?" she said.

"Yes. I've left the boys to come to see you. We were meant to be going into town for a drink, don't you remember?"

Was he getting angry, or was she imagining it? She couldn't be sure but this situation didn't feel right at all.

"I'm sorry, saying it twice doesn't mean that it makes any more sense to me. I'm confused. We live next door to each other, so why have you come all this way to see me? You've been in our house all day."

The last sentence came out more like an accusation than she had meant it to.

"It's not the same though, is it? It's not in this setting." He waved his arm towards the bar. "I thought we could have a drink or something, you know, get to know each other properly."

"Get to know each other? Like one on one, you and me?" She could hear the derision in her words and hoped that he hadn't picked up on it. She didn't like him, but she didn't want to hurt his feelings.

"Yes, just the two of us."

"You mean on a date?"

"If you want to call it that."

"I'm sorry, no. I don't want to get involved with anyone at the moment." She turned and reached out to open the door, but within seconds, he was in front of her, blocking her exit.

"You're a tough cookie, aren't you? Is this part of the game you like to play?"

"There's no game, Sam," she said. "I'm not that childish. I don't want to go on a date, that's all. It's nothing personal."

He didn't move, but stared into her eyes.

"Sam, can you move out of my way, please? Gwen's waiting for me outside."

"She won't mind waiting for a bit. She's always wanted us two to get together."

"No, she hasn't."

"That's not what Charles said," said Sam.

"Well, I don't know where he's got that from, but I don't want a boyfriend right now. I've got my studies and my modelling and I'm too busy."

"I've got my modelling," he repeated in a high pitched voice, mocking her. "Stop playing hard to get. Life's too short for games."

He pinned her to the wall, pressing himself on her, an arm either side of her head.

"Sam, what are you doing?"

"I know you want me," he whispered in her ear.

"No, I don't, get off me!" she shouted, hoping that the

volunteer cloakroom attendant would hear her.

Sam appeared to be genuinely shocked that she didn't fancy him.

"What's wrong? Are you a lesbian or something?"

"Yes that's right, I must be a lesbian. Any woman who doesn't fancy you must be gay, is that it?"

She pushed at his arm, trying to move him to one side, but he didn't move. He stood firm like a mountain. She was trapped. She looked down the corridor, beginning to panic, but the corridor was empty. The cloakroom attendant was nowhere to be seen and there was nobody in the queue waiting for their coats. Without warning, he leant his head towards her and planted a wet kiss on her lips, pushing her back again towards the wall. She tried to push him away, but as much as she tried, he didn't budge.

Suddenly, the door to the bar flew open and three girls came, laughing and shrieking their way to the cloakroom. Sam stepped back for a second and Audrina took her chance and rushed out of the door and ran towards the grass where she had left Gwen.

But Gwen wasn't there.

"Hey bitch!"

She felt a tug on her hair. Sam was holding tightly to her hair with one hand and to her arm with the other.

"Just because you're a fucking model, doesn't make you all that, you know. You're just a fucking snotty bitch."

She felt a sharp pain to the back of head, causing her to stumble forwards onto her knees and onto hers and Gwen's coats. She realised that Sam had punched her. This was absolutely the last straw. Their coats were filthy and she was going to have a bruise on her knee, which wouldn't look good at the shoot next week. She would have to cover it with make-up. She grabbed her phone from her coat pocket. She needed to ring Gwen.

Where was she?

"That's enough, Sam. I know you're drunk but…"

She scrambled up onto her feet and faced him. That's what you're meant to do with bullies, isn't it?

"Shut it!"

A second pain shot through her head as his fist flew at the side of her head. She fell to the ground again, this time landing onto her back. Then Sam was on top of her, knocking her phone out of her hand. His face was so close to hers that she could smell beer, cigarettes and garlic on his breath. He didn't give her time to scream, before he held her mouth shut with his huge hand.

"Who the fucking hell do you think you are? You think you're too good for me, do you?"

Why was he asking her questions when he wasn't allowing her to speak?

"I'm going to show you."

And where was Gwen?

"You're nothing more than a common slut."

Where was her friend when she needed her?

"I know you want it, bitch."

Why was there nobody else about? Where was everyone.

"You want it like this, don't you?"

She couldn't speak. She could hardly breathe with his hand covering her mouth and nose.

Then she felt his other hand, rough and cold, on the delicate skin at the top of her legs.

"You like it rough, don't you?"

She couldn't tell him no.

"I know you want me."

She couldn't tell him that she didn't consent and she wanted him to get off her.

"You're just playing hard to get."

Even if she could tell him, she knew that he wouldn't listen.

Chapter Eleven

Accidental Damage

October 2004

Audrina walked home alone. Their house was no more than two miles from the university and ordinarily it was a nice walk along the long tree lined road from the university and onto the A6. But tonight, it seemed to take her an eternity. When she got there, the front of the house was in darkness, but as she put her key in the door, she realised that there was a light on in the kitchen. She didn't want to see anyone, especially one of the boys. She didn't know if Sam had managed to get home before her, she hadn't seen him on the way, but if he was in the kitchen, she wasn't sure she would be able to keep herself in check.

She wanted to sneak upstairs without anyone seeing her and get into the shower as quickly as possible. She needed to scrub the smell of him away. She felt dirty and she was dirty. Her clothes were covered in mud and grass stains. She would have to put them all on a hot wash, even her coat.

She didn't want to think about him and she tried not to,

but his big ugly faced flashed into her mind. He was imprinted onto her consciousness. The thought of what he had done to her made her feel sick. She had used every ounce of self control to stop herself from being sick on the way home. She had never been one of those people who vomited on the pavement on a night out, no matter how drunk she had been. So she wasn't going to start now. He wasn't going to make her into that person. She wasn't common and uncouth, like he was. She could control herself.

"There you are," said Gwen, coming out of the kitchen, holding a glass of water. "I've been home ages, I was starting to worry about you."

"I couldn't find you," said Audrina, bending down and concentrating on taking her shoes off, so that she wouldn't have to look Gwen in the face. "Where were you?"

"I needed the toilet, so I went back in and then I got talking …"

"You weren't there." Audrina interrupted.

"I know, I - aww, don't cry. It's alright." Gwen put her glass down on the bottom stair and reached out her arms to hug Audrina. "Sorry if you were worried about me, but I'm fine."

"I looked for you." Audrina sobbed. She pushed Gwen away angrily.

"I did call you but you didn't answer so I thought I'd just get a taxi and then see you at home. I'm sorry, I…"

"You could have left me a voicemail or something."

"I did," said Gwen.

"Well, I…" Audrina patted her coat pockets to search for her phone again, although she knew already that it wasn't there. "I don't know where my phone is."

"Look, we're fine and we're home safe" said Gwen. "Why don't we have a plan for next time, in case we get separated again?"

Audrina gave up the futile search for her phone and sank down to sit on the bottom stair, next to Gwen's glass of water.

"I've lost my phone," she said, tears now streaming down her face.

"It's okay, I lose mine all the time. It'll turn up. Someone will have handed it in at the bar."

"He raped me." She spat the words out suddenly.

Gwen wasn't sure that she had heard the words correctly. There was so much pain, fear, shock and repulsion tied up in those three short syllables. She wished it wasn't true, but the look on Audrina's face told her that something horrible had happened to her. It was true.

"He raped you."

It wasn't a question. It was more of a statement. She hoped that Audrina would tell her that she was being silly, she had misheard her and, of course, she hadn't been raped. She was perfectly fine. She wasn't hurt, soiled or bruised. She wasn't frightened, shocked or dazed. She wanted Audrina to lead her into the kitchen where she would make them both a cup of hot chocolate which they would take to bed. She wanted to sit with her on the bed and wait for Charles to come home, while they dissected the events of the evening. She wanted to have a normal conversation about the band and how good they were and who was there and what they had seen. Like that girl who was serving behind the bar and kept getting the drinks orders wrong because the band was too loud and she hadn't heard properly. And what about the boy who sat at the corner of the bar and kept staring at her? Did he gather up enough courage to ask her out by the end of the night, or did her incompetency at making drinks put him off? She wanted to laugh about it. But she knew that she wasn't going to.

"Oh my God? Was it Sam?" she asked.

Audrina nodded. "How did you…?"

"I saw him outside, when I was on the grass. He asked me where you were."

Audrina closed her eyes and Gwen watched a solitary tear fall down her beautiful face. Then she rested her head on her knees and wrapped her arms around her legs. Now Gwen was crying too.

"Oh my God, I told him you had gone to get the coats. It's all my fault. If it wasn't for me, he wouldn't have found you."

"No, no, no," said Audrina. "You're not doing that." There was a sudden unexpected anger in her voice.

"Not doing what?"

"I'm the one who's been attacked, but now for some reason, you think you're the victim?" She waved an angry hand in Gwen's direction to stop her coming any closer. "I can't cope with your emotions as well as my own. You can fuck off. Everybody can just fuck off. I'm going to bed." She stood up suddenly, knocking Gwen's water onto the floor and ran upstairs.

"Audrina!"

Audrina ran into the bathroom and slammed the door shut behind her. There was no lock on the door, so she sat on the floor with her back to it. Her heart was pounding so much that she felt dizzy. She desperately needed to be on her own.

"Audrina, I'm sorry, I'm so sorry," said Gwen, running up the stairs after her. She knocked gently on the bathroom door and whispered into the crack between the doorframe and the door. "Audrina, please come out. I'm sorry."

Audrina didn't answer.

"Okay then. It's okay, you don't need to talk to me. But I'll wait here for you, until you're ready, okay? I'm here for you."

Audrina could hear Gwen's gentle crying and sniffling through the door. The sound floated through the cracks and filled the bathroom, suffocating Audrina's anger and squashing it. She knew that she shouldn't have shouted at her like that. Gwen wasn't trying to be a victim, of course she wasn't. What she had said was cruel and unnecessary and she knew that Gwen would be hurting as much as she was. Gwen was the biggest empath she had ever met. She stood up slowly and pulled open the door. Her friend rushed into her arms and they held each other while they both sobbed. Eventually Audrina pulled away.

"I need a shower," she said.

"No!" said Gwen fiercely. "You can't do that, you'll wash away all the evidence. I've seen it on the telly. Having a shower is the worst thing you can do."

"I don't care about evidence, I need a shower." Audrina was suddenly tired, emotionally worn out and desperately needed to go to bed. She had no idea what time it was but tomorrow would be a new day and she could get on with the rest of her life as though this horrible thing had never happened. She wasn't ever going to think about it ever again.

"We've got to ring the police," Gwen persisted. "They'll be here within a few minutes. Then when you've given your statement, then you can have a shower." She looked into Audrina's face with such love, stroking her hair, like a mother does with a child who is having a tantrum because they can't have sweets before dinner.

Audrina shook her head. "But it won't be like that, will it? I'll have to go to the police station and get examined and everything. It'll take all night."

"Well, yes but.."

"No, I'm not doing that. I don't want to report it," she said.

She walked over to the bath, pulled the shower curtain to one side and turned on the tap. Gwen immediately pushed past her and turned it off.

"You have to report it. He needs to go to prison. He's dangerous. You said yourself that he's creepy, he could do this to someone else. You owe it to women kind."

Gwen thought that would appeal to Audrina's sense of justice and integrity, which she knew was in there somewhere. She was the ultimate feminist and surely she would want this misogynistic bastard punished.

"Gwen, I don't want to report it and I don't want to talk about it anymore, alright? Look, I know you think I'm making the wrong decision, but I've been working my socks off all summer, getting myself a portfolio together and a decent client base, I don't need this kind of publicity. My career is too important to me to let him ruin it."

Gwen wasn't sure whether this would ruin it or, after all Audrina hadn't done anything wrong, but she held her hands up in surrender. It was clear that Audrina had made her mind up and after what she had been through, it was her choice. "Fine, whatever you want to do. I understand."

"Thank you," said Audrina.

"I'm here for you," said Gwen. "Whatever you need, I'm here."

Audrina nodded. "There is something you can do for me."

"Yes, anything."

"I'm worried about my phone. It's got all my contacts on it, so I need it back. I think I know where it might be." The memory of it being slapped out of her hand flashed into her mind. "So, if you wouldn't mind coming in the taxi with me, so I can look for it? I don't want to be alone with a man…"

"Yes, yes, of course," said Gwen. "You have a quick shower and I'll ring for a taxi. I'll ask them to come in ten minutes."

"Thank you," said Audrina, closing the bathroom door behind Gwen.

Ten minutes later, when Audrina came downstairs, dressed in clean jeans and a jumper, and carrying all the clothes that she had been wearing earlier, Gwen was waiting for her in the kitchen, her mobile phone in her hand.

"There's no taxis for at least an hour," she said, waving the phone as if it was confirmation. "They're mega busy with the gig at the uni, as well as the usual Saturday night business, they said."

"It's fine, I'll look for it tomorrow," said Audrina. "There'll be nobody there on a Sunday morning, so it'll still be there. It's not like anyone's going to find it." She pushed her clothes into the washing machine, poured powder into the drawer and turned it on.

"We don't have to wait until tomorrow, if you don't want to," said Gwen. "I can borrow Charles' car. The keys are in the hall."

"Where is Charles?"

"Oh I don't know, he went out with the boys. But he won't mind if I borrow it."

"But you've had a drink, Gwen."

"We're literally going two minutes down the road and I didn't have that much." She stood up. "Come on, let's go. We'll be back before you know it."

Audrina didn't argue. She needed to get her phone back, so she ignored the little voice inside that was warning her that it wasn't a good idea to, firstly, take someone's car without asking their permission and secondly, to allow a drunk driver behind the wheel. After all, her inner voice hadn't protected her so far tonight, so she could just shut the fuck up.

"Okay then, let's go," she said, following Gwen out of the kitchen. "The sooner we go, the sooner we get back. Do you want to text Charles though and just ask him if it's okay?"

"He won't mind," said Gwen, grabbing his keys from the shelf underneath the mirror in the hall.

"But should we ask him though?"

"No," said Gwen, taking a deep breath.

"Because he might say no? Is that what you're thinking? I can tell you're not completely sure about this."

"Look, if he knew what had happened, then one hundred percent, he would say yes, so do you want to tell him?"

"No, of course I don't want to tell him," said Audrina,

panicking that Gwen wouldn't be able to keep the secret.

"Then let's go."

They closed the front door behind them and walked around the corner to where Charles had left his Range Rover in a side street, away from the main road.

"The trickiest bit will be to park it again in this tiny space," Gwen laughed. There was a slight hint of nervous hysteria in her voice and Audrina knew that it was a real problem. Both of them had passed their driving tests but neither of them had their own car and their parking experience was minimal.

"We'll manage somehow," said Audrina. "The trickiest bit is to get there and back without Charles realising that his car has gone missing and reporting it stolen." As soon as she said it, she could see the panic on Gwen's face. "But don't worry though, I know exactly where my phone will be, so we won't be long."

"Do you?"

"Well I think so, it must be on the grass somewhere close to the fire exit. Close to where you were sitting."

"Okay, fine," said Gwen decisively.

With a plan to park the car in the nearest car park to the Pendle Bar and run across the grass towards the fire exit, locate the phone and get back as quickly as possible, Gwen started the engine, manoeuvred out of the parking space and set off towards the university.

After just a couple of minutes, they turned left off the main road and drove up the long drive towards the campus.

"I don't think I've ever seen it this quiet," said Gwen.

"No, me neither," said Audrina.

"Or this dark," said Gwen. "I didn't know this lane didn't

have any street lights."

"I know. I suppose you don't take any notice when you're in the back of a taxi, do you?"

Audrina turned her head to look at Gwen and spotted Sam, coming out from behind a tree and stumbling towards the pavement, trying desperately to walk in a straight line. He was fiddling with the zip on his jeans, clearly having just used one of the trees as a urinal.

"Shit, that's Sam!" she said.

She ducked down in the seat instinctively and Gwen put her foot down and speeded past him.

"Did he see us?" asked Gwen

"I don't think so," said Audrina. "He probably went behind the tree for a wee. It looked like he was struggling to keep upright, so he's way too drunk to register the car. Don't worry about it."

But she knew that he had seen them. She saw him begin to raise his arm in a wave as the recognition of his friend's car slowly dawned on him through his drunken haze. Gwen had enough to worry about right now. If they could get the phone and get the car parked safely back its spot at home, then they would deal with the issue of Sam at a later date, if he ever said anything, that is. The likelihood was that he was too drunk and wouldn't remember in the morning. If necessary, they will have to confess to Charles that they borrowed his car, promise to buy him some beers as a thank you for the unexpected loan and all will be well.

As soon as they reached the car park and Gwen stopped the car, Audrina opened the door and ran out across the grass towards where she thought her phone might be. There was no sign of life in the bar, in the cloakroom or in the corridor. The whole building was in darkness. The light from the windows which had illuminated Sam's wrathful face as he threw her to the ground and forced himself on her had now disappeared. The band had packed away, the staff and the revellers had gone home. Peace had returned and there was no sign of the violence and hatred that had occupied the site only an hour before. Audrina looked up to the dark sky that was free of clouds and sprinkled with stars. But she knew that there would no longer be any joy in star gazing for her. Never again would she be able to look up to the night sky with joy and wonder at the beautiful universe that they were a tiny part of. Sam had ruined that for her. Every time she looked up, she would remember this night.

She tried to control her wandering mind and began hunting for her phone. It would have been virtually impossible for her to find her phone on her own in the dark, but thankfully she never left it on silent and Gwen rang it from her phone, helping her to locate it within just a few minutes.

"I've got it!" she shouted, picking it up from the grass and wiping it on her jeans. "Thank you Gwen, I don't know what I'd do without you."

Gwen burst into tears. "I'm sorry I wasn't here when you needed me. I'm a terrible friend."

Suddenly being at the scene of the crime made it all too real. She didn't want to imagine what Audrina had gone through, while she was laughing and chatting about some silly insignificance. Audrina hadn't told her exactly what Sam had done and she was glad because she didn't think she could cope with the details. What she did know was that he would have been strong and powerful and horrible and cruel. To violate her beautiful Audrina like that. The bastard.

Audrina hugged her quickly. "Come on now, we've no time for this. Be strong, stop crying and take me home."

Gwen nodded and they walked back to Charles' car hand in hand, with Audrina's phone safely tucked away in the front pocket of her jeans. Neither of them spoke as they climbed into the car and began the journey home. Gwen was busy concentrating on navigating the long, dark lane that led from the university to the main road, whilst avoiding the dozens of rabbits that had decided to play in the light of the headlights and Audrina was concentrating on looking out for Sam. If they could just get to the main road and if they saw him before he saw them, everything would be alright. They would need to turn around and think of another way home, but at least they could get home undetected.

But there he was. Still on the lane, close to where he had been ten minutes ago.

"Oh shit, it's him again," said Audrina.

Gwen followed Audrina's line of sight and saw Sam leaning against one of the trees that lined the lane. As soon as he became aware of the sound of a car, he pushed himself up and stumbled towards the road. This time, there was no doubt about whether he recognised the car or not.

"Oi, stop!" he shouted, waving his arms over his head, as though he were trying to stop a steam train that was lumbering towards him.

"He wants us to stop," said Gwen, taking her foot off the accelerator and slowing down.

"Don't!" shouted Audrina. "He probably thinks it's

Charles driving. Just ignore him."

"But he'll see us. He'll see that it's me driving," said Gwen.

As the catastrophic stars aligned, Gwen intended to stop but, in her panic, she put her foot down hard on the accelerator instead of the brake, at the same time as Sam stepped off the pavement and lunged towards the car. Both she and Audrina saw his face, white with shock, so close to the windscreen that for a moment, it appeared as though he would come right through it. Then he was gone and they both felt the bump as the left front wheel drove over him and they both heard his ear piercing scream.

Audrina watched his crumpled body fall to the ground through the mirror on the front passenger door.

"Now we're going to have to come up with a reason as to what caused the damage to the car," she said. Her mind didn't want to begin to process what damage had been caused to Sam.

Gwen screamed and brought the car to a stop.

"I've got to go and help him," she said, although she made no attempt to get out of the car. Her shaking hands clung to the steering wheel and she stared straight ahead of her, as though frightened of what she would see if she looked in the mirror. "Audrina, help me!" she said. "What shall we do?"

"Drive on!"

Chapter Twelve

No Sleep

October 2004

When Gwen thought back over those fateful few seconds, in the following days, months and years, she thought that she might have stopped the car and got out. If anyone had foretold what would happen that night, she would have expected herself to jump out of the driver's seat and run over to the unintended victim and see if he was okay. She could have administered first aid. She wasn't sure if she would be any good, but she knew the basics and surely this was one of those situations where the phrase 'a little knowledge can be a dangerous thing' doesn't apply. Any knowledge of first aid is better than nothing. She could have stopped any bleeding, ripped her shirt to make a temporary tourniquet, in the way that she had seen them do on television hospital dramas. The best case scenario would be that he would have heavy bruising around his foot, which would be sore and swollen for a while. His stomach would be bruised too, where the front bumper of the Range Rover hit him. The worst case would be that some bones were actually broken, in which case she would have no option but to take him to the hospital.

Which she would have done, gladly.

But none of that happened, because she didn't stop. Which was just as well, because there was nothing she could have done to help him, even if she had.

She had considered stopping, of course she had, and she had discussed it with Audrina as they reached the end of the lane and turned right onto the A6 towards Lancaster town centre. They had only a few minutes before they would be home, so the decision had to be made quickly. Audrina was adamant that they should go home, park the car, get into bed and forget that this horrible night had ever happened.

"Are you crazy?" Gwen had shouted at her. "We can't just forget that we have knocked somebody over. I'm going to remember this night for the rest of my life, whether I want to or not."

"It was an accident," said Audrina. "You haven't done anything wrong."

"I know it was an accident!" screamed Gwen. "But you can't say that I haven't done anything wrong. Leaving the scene of the accident is illegal and I'm pretty sure that running someone over is illegal too."

"I'm not sure about that," said Audrina, calmly. "I don't think it is." She took her phone out of the pocket of her jeans and tapped onto the screen.

"What are you doing?" asked Gwen.

"I'm googling whether it's illegal to run someone over," said Audrina. "I think it depends on your intent…"

Gwen had knocked the phone out of her hand and it had

landed in the foot well of the car.

"That's the second time someone has knocked this phone out of my hand tonight, for fuck's sake," she said bending down to pick it up.

"I'm sorry," said Gwen. "But you can't do something so stupid. You can't google things like that. If the police check our phones now, you've just given them enough evidence to put us in prison."

Audrina had laughed and told Gwen that the police in a sleepy Lancashire village such as this wouldn't be so clever. They weren't dealing with MI5. Gwen couldn't believe that Audrina had laughed. She put it down to shock, but even so, she told Audrina that it was no laughing matter. There was a man lying injured on the road and probably wouldn't be found until the morning and it was all their fault. Audrina looked at her stonily and said that there was only one victim from this evening's events and Sam would be just fine.

When they got home, they both went straight to bed and no more was said.

This morning, as Gwen lay in bed, next to a sleeping Charles, she felt as though she had been awake for hours. She wasn't sure that she had slept at all. She got out of bed quietly and tiptoed to the bathroom. Audrina was still asleep. At least, her bedroom door was closed. She wasn't convinced that Audrina would have slept much at all either. How could she? In an ideal world, they would ignore last night's events and get on with the rest of their lives as though nothing had happened, like Audrina had said. But that wasn't reality.

As she came out of the bathroom, Audrina was waiting for her on the landing. They hugged each other.

"Did you sleep alright?" Gwen whispered.

Audrina shook her head.

"I'll put the kettle on," said Gwen. "See you downstairs in a minute."

She walked downstairs, picking up Charles' car keys from the shelf in the hall as she went and took them into the kitchen. She put them down on the small kitchen table while she filled the kettle with water and switched it on. She took two cups from the cupboard and put a tea bag in hers and two teaspoons of coffee in Audrina's. If this was a normal Sunday, she would take her tea into the living, wrap herself with a blanket and watch trashy television until at least eleven o'clock, by which time everyone would be up and someone would put bacon under the grill for their brunch. Usually, it was Charles. It was one of the things that he was quite particular about. He said that neither of the girls made his bacon the way he wanted and they certainly didn't put enough sauce on the sandwich. He liked his bacon crispy but not burnt and there were precious seconds between those two stages when the bacon had to be watched with eagle eyes. Gwen didn't have the patience for such foibles and Audrina refused to cook it, on the basis that she had usually done all the tidying up from the boys' mess from the night before. So they had settled into their routine, with each member of the party accepting their vital role in the smooth running of the house.

But today, Gwen wasn't in the mood for television and she certainly couldn't face any food.

Audrina came into the kitchen and sat down at the table. Gwen had never seen her look so bad. Her eyes were red rimmed and swollen and she looked like she hadn't slept a wink. She picked up the car keys from the table and held them in her outstretched hand.

"What are you doing with these?" she said. "You need to put them back on the shelf. I think I heard Charles stirring, he'll be down soon." She waved the keys towards Gwen, urging her to take them from her.

"Oh shit," said Gwen. "I thought he was still asleep. I wanted to check the damage on the car before he comes down. I couldn't see it properly last night. I don't know how I'm going to explain …"

The ringing of the doorbell followed immediately by heavy knocking startled both of them and Audrina jumped up quickly. Gwen took the keys from her and held them behind her back, as though whoever was at the door had x-ray vision and could see all the way through the door, down the hall and into the kitchen.

Audrina hadn't ordered any shopping to be delivered and neither of them were expecting any visitors this early.

"Who's that?" she whispered to Gwen.

"It sounds urgent, whoever it is. Is it the police, do you think? They've coming to arrest us both, I just know they have."

"Gwen, get a grip," said Audrina, pushing past her.

"Okay, fine, I'll go. I can do this," said Gwen, walking to the front door. She placed the car keys back on the shelf, took a deep breath and pulled back the bolt on the door.

"Oh hello," she said, as she opened the door, her worst fear confirmed by the sight of a tall policeman on the doorstep.

"Good morning," he said. "I'm sorry to disturb you so early, but we're doing some house to house enquiries in the area, looking for witnesses to an accident that happened last night."

"What kind of accident?" said Gwen. She tried to keep her voice neutral and hoped that the policeman didn't hear the shake or see the guilty look which she was adamant was as clear as day on her face. She had never been able to hide her facial expressions. Her mum had told her that she always knew when she had done something wrong as a teenager, by the look on her face. She hoped that this policeman wasn't as perceptive as her mother.

"There was an accident at the university," said the policeman. He fiddled in his jacket pocket for a note book, as though any questions he may want to ask potential witnesses were written in there. "We've been told that this house is student accommodation and that there are three of you living here, is that right?"

"Yes, this is my address," she said. "I do live here with my boyfriend, Charles, and my friend, Audrina."

"Are they both at home? I will need to speak to all of you, if you don't mind."

"Yes, they…"

"Gwen, is everything alright?" Charles appeared at the top of the stairs, wrapping his dressing gown around his waist.

Gwen turned around to see where Audrina was, but she had disappeared back to the kitchen.

"I'm sorry to disturb you so early," repeated the policeman, "but I need to have a quick word with all the residents of the house, if that's okay? Can I come in?"

"Yes, of course," said Gwen, opening the door wider and standing to the side.

"I won't keep you long," said the policeman, wiping his feet on the door mat and filling the hall with six foot two inches of authority, despite the fact that he wasn't much older than all three of them.

"Let's go into the kitchen," said Charles, coming down the stairs and taking charge. Gwen noticed that his posh private school voice had been dialled up a notch. He held out his right hand to the policeman. "Charles Morris, pleased to meet you."

The policeman looked slightly taken aback and swapped his note book from his right hand into his left, so that he could shake the proffered hand.

"PC Dawson," he said, following Charles and Gwen into the kitchen, where Audrina was sitting at the small table, trying to appear calm and relaxed, quietly drinking her coffee.

She stood up as they all entered the kitchen. "Hi," she said, "What's going on?"

"Audrina, this is PC Dawson, he wants to ask some questions about an accident. Did I hear you say it was at the university?" said Charles.

He was still using his upper class authoritative voice, which seemed so natural that Gwen was beginning to wonder which one of his accents was real; this one or the more neutral one that she was used to hearing.

"Yes," said the policeman. "A young man was found in the road this morning and it appears that he was involved in an RTC."

"Sorry, a what?" asked Audrina, knowing full well what the letters RTC meant. She smiled at the policeman, causing him to blush slightly, as she twirled a strand of her hair and tucked it behind her ear. She caught Gwen looking at her, silently reproaching her for attempting to flirt with him. Audrina's glare and raised eyebrows told Gwen to back off. She would do what she needed to do.

"A road traffic collision," said the policeman. "One of our patrol cars found him in the early hours of this morning and we're trying to trace any possible witnesses. It looks like it may have been a hit and run."

"How awful," said Charles. "I do hope the poor chap is alright."

You're Charles Morris, not Prince Charles, thought Gwen. So stop trying to sound like him.

"Well, I can't divulge that kind of personal information at this stage, I'm afraid," said the policeman. "Not until his family have been informed."

"You have to inform his family? You mean he's dead?" Gwen blurted out the words before she could stop them. He couldn't be dead, could he? He had only fallen a few feet and she wasn't driving fast. She felt the blood beginning to rush from her head into her feet, making her feel light headed. She rushed over to the kettle, knowing that the policeman would be able to read her every guilty thought, if he could see her face.

"I'm afraid I can't divulge any information," he said again. "But the family do need to be told about his accident."

"Yes, of course. Would you like some tea?" Gwen asked, over the noise of the water rushing into the kettle, which she hoped would hide the tremor in her voice. She desperately wanted him to say yes, to give her something to do. But she also desperately wanted him to say no, so that he would be out of the house as quickly as possible.

"No, thank you," he said. "If I can start by asking your full names, please."

Gwen put the kettle down and leant against the kitchen unit, rested her hands on the door behind her back, to stop them shaking. Charles took charge again.

"As I said, my name is Charles Morris. This is Gwen Wilson, my girlfriend, and this is Audrina Petit, our close friend. We're all studying Business and Marketing at the university." He flashed the policeman a self assured smile, without a hint of deference.

"Can I ask where you were last night?" asked the policeman. "Did any of you go to the university last night? I believe there was a band on?"

"Yes, weren't they amazing?" said Audrina. "Modern reggae, but with some of the old classics from Bob Marley, Black Slate and…"

"Did you all go?" the policeman interrupted.

"Just us two," said Audrina, "Me and Gwen."

"And what time did you leave?" he asked, pen poised over his open note book.

"I'm sorry, I don't know," said Audrina. "It was when the band finished, I went to get our coats and we left, isn't that right, Gwen."

Gwen nodded and the policeman scribbled in his note book.

"And you don't know what time the band finished?"

"No, but I'm sure the university could tell you that," said Audrina, getting up from the table. "Excuse me, would you mind, I need some water." She reached behind the policeman and opened the door to the wall cupboard directly behind him, holding onto his arm while she did so, as though she needed to steady herself while she reached up to get a glass.

What the bloody hell is she doing? thought Gwen. Leave the man alone and let him get on with his job. Flirting with him isn't going to keep us out of prison. She could see that the policeman was struggling to maintain his thought process.

"Can I ask you how you got home?" asked the policeman, keeping his eyes on Audrina as she tiptoed to the sink and filled her glass with water.

Since when did she walk on her toes like that, thought Gwen. Wasn't she tall enough? She wasn't on a catwalk now. This was serious stuff. What with Charles and his impossibly posh voice and Audrina flirting, Gwen couldn't cope with much more. She was struggling to hold her emotions in check as it was.

Audrina took a sip of her water before turning round to answer the question. "We walked home," she said. "I think Gwen tried to get us a taxi, but they were all busy."

Good thinking, thought Gwen. If they tracked their phone calls, they would be able to see that she had phoned the taxi company, so there was no point in telling lies.

"Did you see the accident? Or did you hear anything? Any car speeding away, or anything like that?" asked the policeman.

"No," said Gwen, a little too emphatically. "I mean, if we did, we would have stopped and given our names or tried to help or something."

The policeman nodded and Gwen was happy that she had given him the correct answer.

"And you, Mr Morris, where did you go last night?"

"I went into Lancaster with my friends, Sam Thompson, Sebastian Browne and Faisal Patel."

"Sam Thompson?" asked the policeman, suddenly looking up from his note book.

"Yes, why?" asked Charles.

"Give me two minutes," he said, walking into the hall and talking into his radio.

"Where's he going?" asked Gwen.

"Do you think this is about Sam?" said Audrina, hoping that Charles believed their story as much as the policeman seemed to. Charles didn't say anything, but kept his eyes on the policeman who was standing close to the front door.

A few moments later, the policeman returned to the kitchen and asked them all to sit at the table, which they did dutifully. Gwen picked at some dry skin next to her thumbnail, waiting for the bad news which she knew was coming.

"I've checked with my sergeant, who tells me that the young man's family have now been informed, so I am able to divulge some more details."

Gwen wondered whether police officers were given special training on how to use specific words. They all seemed to talk in the same unnatural way. She knew what divulge meant, but she couldn't think of a single time in her life that she had ever used it. But this policeman had said it three times already.

"I'm afraid the victim of the RTC was your friend, Sam Thompson."

"Sam?" asked Audrina, with as much surprise as she could muster.

"Yes, I'm sorry, but he didn't survive his injuries and he was pronounced dead at the hospital in the early hours of this morning."

Gwen let the torrent of tears flow at last, unable to contain them for a second longer. The policeman patted her hand and said that he was sorry to be the bearer of bad news and that he didn't realise that they were friends, although he should have guessed that they would be, as they lived next door to each other. He said that his colleague had gone next door and would be imparting the bad news to Sam's house mates.

"When was the last time you saw Sam?" the policeman asked Charles.

"I don't really know," he said. "We were drinking in the Old Bull for quite a while, but it gets busy, so we moved on to the White Horse, probably some time after eleven, I would think. I think that's when I last saw him."

"So you became separated?" asked the policeman.

"Well, yes," said Charles. "I don't think I registered that he had gone for a long time. We weren't just sat together, the four of us, we were chatting to other people. Then when I decided to go home, I couldn't find either of them, so I walked back without them."

"I see," said the policeman. He stood up. "Well, I'll not take any more of your time. And again, I'm sorry about your friend."

"Thank you," said Charles, standing and shaking the policeman's hand again before leading him to the front door.

Chapter Thirteen

Church Service

October 2004

It rained on the morning of Sam's funeral. Not the light autumnal rain that's refreshing and cooling to walk in after a hot summer, but the heavy and persistent rain more akin to a cold day in the middle of January. Charles, Gwen, Sebastian and Faisal had hardly said a word throughout the hour long journey to Preston, each of them lost in their own thoughts. The boys looked as though they had a cloud of misery hanging over them. Faisal stared out of the back passenger window of Charles' car, every now and then taking a deep breath and wiping away tears. Sebastian sat in the middle of the back seat and stared through the windscreen, his back as rigid as his stiff upper lip. Audrina knew that he was upset and that he would be putting on a brave face. He had shared a room with Sam last year at the university and they were as close as she was with Gwen. As they got out of the car, she touched his hand and asked if he was okay. He told her that he was, but then pulled his hand away quickly and walked on, towards the church. Audrina wondered whether Sam had said anything to him about going to look for her at the university that night.

As she walked to the church, Sebastian and Faisal in front, followed by Gwen and Charles, with each step getting colder and wetter, she felt herself becoming more and more annoyed. Trust Sam to get under her skin and make her agitated, again. She had never been to a funeral before, so she didn't have a suitable black coat. Her winter coat was white, padded and thick, only to be worn for protection from wintery storms. Despite the rain, she decided that she would have looked stupid wearing that today and she would be far too warm in the church. In addition, she refused to allow Sam to dictate what she was wearing, even from the grave. So when she had stood in front of her open wardrobe doors this morning, she decided to choose a pale blue tea dress, which she had bought online from John Lewis, beige flat pumps from a boutique in Lancaster and a dark blue cashmere cardigan, which her mum and dad had bought her for her birthday, which she put over her shoulders. She hated black and she refused to wear it. Funeral or no funeral.

You can take your black clothes, Sam Thompson, and you can shove them where the sun doesn't shine, not that it will shine for you any longer.

She was carrying an umbrella with one hand and trying to keep her cardigan around her shoulders with the other hand, but the wind was strong and incessant and it was impossible to keep herself dry. By the time she reached the church, she was wet, dishevelled and angry and she wished that she hadn't agreed to go. She had told Gwen that morning that she didn't think it was a good idea for either of them to go, but Gwen said that was rubbish and of course they should go. She said that Charles would think it was very odd if he had to go on his own, and he wouldn't dream of missing the opportunity to pay his last respects to Sam. Audrina had mumbled under her breath that he didn't deserve any respect but Gwen had shushed her, putting a forefinger to her lips, and reminded her that Charles was downstairs and he might hear them.

Charles had taken Sam's death quite hard. Audrina hadn't realised that they had been that close, but he was genuinely upset. In a way, that was a good thing, as it had diverted the attention away from the damage to his car.

Within minutes of dropping the bombshell of Sam's untimely death on them, the young policeman had returned to the house and knocked on the door again. He had asked Charles to confirm that he was the registered owner and keeper of the black Range Rover parked around the corner. Charles told him that he was and he then asked him to explain the damage to the front nearside headlamp unit and the front bumper. Before Gwen could think of an explanation and put forward her confession, Charles told the policeman that he had parked too far forward in a multi-storey car park and that the damage was his own fault. Gwen couldn't believe what she was hearing. He said that he would have it booked into the garage for a repair early next week. He hadn't got round to it yet. It could have been Charles' confident and convincing manner, together with his I'm-far-too-posh-to-be-guilty accent that caused the policeman to accept his words and back away, or the fact that Charles was crying so much. Whatever it was, the policeman didn't ask any further questions, apologised for disturbing them again and left them to it.

"Charles," said Gwen, as soon as the front door had been closed once again, "I need to tell you something."

"It doesn't matter, Gwen," said Charles.

"But it does matter. The damage to your car, it was my fault. I borrowed…"

Audrina rushed over to them, anxious to save Gwen from herself.

"Well, it's my fault really," she said. "I asked Gwen if we could borrow your car to go and get us a bottle of wine last night. I'm so sorry, we shouldn't have done it. I'll absolutely pay for the damage."

Charles, ever the gentleman, had told them both not to worry about it. He said that he had assumed that Gwen had borrowed the car and he had made up the story about the multi-storey car park to avoid her being questioned further by the policeman. He said that he didn't want to talk about it anymore and he disappeared next door and spent the rest of the morning with Sebastian and Faisal. He hadn't even asked them how the damage to the car had occurred.

Gwen sank to the floor and cried like a baby. Audrina sat on the bottom step, in the same position that she had sat the previous night and waited for her to finish. Eventually Gwen's tears were spent and they both got up and went into the kitchen. Audrina said they should try and eat something, so she put two slices of bread into the toaster.

"I feel like this is a dream," she had said to Gwen. "It doesn't feel real."

"I know," said Gwen. "I don't know what to do. Now Charles has lied to the policeman about the damage, it will make it even worse if I tell them the truth."

"Right, let's get one thing straight," said Audrina. "He can't ever know the truth."

Gwen stared at her, trying to process how she could even begin to live with this secret.

"You won't be telling anyone the truth. Nobody needs to know."

"I don't know if I can carry this guilt around with me," said Gwen. "Forever is a long time."

"I know it is, but you're going to have to," said Audrina. "If you want to confess, go to church."

From that day two weeks ago, neither of them had spoken about it, but now as they walked into the church and sat down in one of the pews close to the back, Gwen got on her knees and began to pray. Audrina could imagine that she was confessing and she hoped that it gave her friend some solace, but she couldn't do it. She didn't feel as though she had anything to be sorry for. It wasn't their fault that Sam had walked in front of the car. It wasn't their fault that he was too drunk to steady himself and, as far as she was concerned, he got his just desserts that night. She then put her hands together in prayer and apologised to God for being so un-Christian and for not showing compassion and forgiveness towards another human being.

"I'm sorry God, please forgive me, but we can have this conversation again when you've dealt with him for five minutes. See how much patience you have with him then." She followed with the Lord's Prayer, just in case He was listening.

As she opened her eyes and looked around at the busy church, she felt a sudden weight in her heart and had to take short, shallow breaths to stop herself from sobbing, right then and there. It's just the church, she told herself, you know you always feel emotional in church. It's just the atmosphere. It's the spiritual energy of tears and laughter from hundreds of people over hundreds of years. That's all it is.

She heard the church doors open behind her as another group of people arrived. One of the women, who looked to be in her fifties, walked down to the front and said something to a woman of a similar age. They looked alike and could possibly be sisters. She wondered whether it was Sam's mother and aunt. The two women clung to each other silently, each one lost in their own thoughts for a moment. By the time they broke apart, they were both crying.

"Do you think that's Sam's mum?" she asked Gwen.

"I would imagine his parents will come in with the coffin," said Gwen, "But it looks like family members. Maybe aunties or something."

This morning, as she was getting ready, Audrina thought that she might have to force some tears so that Charles wouldn't wonder that it was odd that she wasn't upset. Gwen hadn't stopped crying all morning and it would look strange if she sat through a whole funeral service with dry eyes. But as she looked at the mourners, she surprised herself at how much she cried and that her tears were genuine. Those poor women. She wondered what Sam was thinking now, seeing her crying over him. The arrogant little shit. She hoped that he had gone to Heaven for a lesson in how to behave and that if his soul was ever sent back down to earth for a second chance, he would be a better person.

He seemed to have been a good friend, which was his only saving grace. Sebastian, Faisal and Charles were all devastated. The four of them had all been close in the short time that they had known each other. Even Gwen had genuinely liked him. On occasions, Audrina had been jealous of their friendship, which was preposterous. But when she saw them together, how they laughed and were clearly so comfortable in each other's company, she couldn't help wishing that she felt the same. She had never seen Gwen flinch when Sam had been near her. She never saw any repulsion in her eyes when she spoke to him. Audrina couldn't put her finger on why she hadn't liked him, but it seemed that the more she disliked him, the more he was drawn towards her.

Although she was crying, as the whole situation was so dreadfully sad, she wasn't sorry that he had gone. She was glad that she never had to see him ever again and, when the last of the bruises that he had caused on her arms had finally disappeared, she would never have to think of him ever again either.

Sam's parents had arranged for a buffet in one of the pubs close to the church and although Audrina had agreed to go, she knew that she wouldn't be there. She just wanted to go home and close the door on that chapter of her life and begin the healing process.

Today, she wanted to close the door on the whole world.

As she heard the sound of car tyres on gravel and the sound of the doors opening and closing, she knew that the funeral cars had arrived at the church. She took a deep breath and wiped away stray tears, telling herself that she had cried enough now, she must stop. Enough was enough.

As she heard the footsteps from outside, approaching the door of the church, her heart raced. She didn't want to turn around and see his coffin. She didn't want to imagine him inside a wooden box, lifeless and cold. She knew that it had been an accident, but if they had never met, he wouldn't be dead.

Gwen grabbed hold of her hand and squeezed it tightly. "Are you alright?" she asked.

"I'm fine, thanks."

"You look a little pale."

"I'm fine."

"Are you sure?"

"I do feel a bit sick," she admitted. "I don't want to do this."

"I know, I know," said Gwen. "It's horrible."

So why aren't we leaving? I mean it, I don't want to be here, she thought. But she didn't say that out loud, because nobody wanted to be there, did they? Funerals were horrible for everyone, not just those who had been close to the dead person, but for all of the people who had touched the dead person's life in some way. Nobody looked forward to a funeral. She was being stupid. She needed to get a grip and just sit tight and get through it. It would be over soon.

As the organ music started, her heart began to beat so fast that she felt as though she had just ran up a flight of stairs. Her thoughts raced around her head with questions that she couldn't answer.

Why am I so upset? Is this grief I'm feeling? Or is it guilt? Or fear? Probably a mixture of everything, she decided. He was a horrible and nasty bully and I hate him. So why are there so many tears? Is it just the church and the empathetic emotions making me cry? Don't they say that there are seven stages of grief and that you deal with one at a time? I wonder what stage I'm at now? It's not disbelief or denial. I do feel bloody angry though. I'm so angry with you Sam, you absolute bastard! Why did you do that to me? Just because I didn't fancy you, you felt it was your right to force yourself onto me? I don't want to feel like this. I don't want to go through any stages of grief, never mind seven stages. Whatever this is feels so heavy - I feel like I'm in two stages at once. I've got one in each hand and I can't put either of them down.

I hate you for what you did to me.

The coffin was carried by the funeral directors and followed by close family members. It looked like his mum, dad and a younger brother. They all looked pale and devastated, dressed from head to foot in black. His mother's eyes were red and blood shot, one hand tightly gripping a crumpled tissue and the other hand gripping the strap of her black handbag.

When they got to the front of the church and took their seats on the front pew, Audrina stood up suddenly, before the funeral directors had time to close the church doors and before the vicar started his speech, addressed to the dearly beloved, or whatever they said at funerals.

"I'm going," she said.

"What are you doing?" asked Gwen in a whisper. "Wait, I'm coming with you."

They walked out as quickly as they could without attracting attention, leaving Charles with Sebastian and Faisal, and Gwen made sure that the church were closed behind them. Two funeral directors were standing to one side of the path, having a sneaky cigarette and didn't give them a second look.

"I couldn't stand it for another minute," said Audrina. "I need to go home. I'm sorry Sam," she said, raising her eyes to the sky. "But you don't deserve my tears. I'm done."

Whether that was true, she wasn't sure. It might take some time to get over the trauma of everything that had happened in the last couple of weeks, but she knew that she didn't want to stay in church and pretend to mourn for him a second longer.

"I don't think I can leave Charles," said Gwen. "He's quite upset."

"Of course, of course," said Audrina. "You go back inside and I'll get the bus back home."

"What shall I tell him?" asked Gwen, already panicking that Charles wouldn't believe another lie.

"Just tell him that I found it too traumatic because it reminded me of a family funeral that I went to over the summer. I don't know, you'll think of something."

Gwen wasn't sure that she would, but Audrina had already started to walk away, her cardigan wrapped tightly around her shoulders and her head down.

***

Half an hour later, Audrina was beginning to feel a little calmer.

She had spoken to her mum, who had assured her that she had done the right thing by leaving the church. She said that the boy's poor family wouldn't have noticed one way or the other whether she was there or not, but it was important that she looked after her own mental health. Audrina told her mum that she would be fine, not to worry and although it had been an upsetting day, she didn't really know the boy that well and had only agreed to go to the funeral to support Charles, but he was fine with Gwen. She said that she felt better now that she had spoken to her and promised to ring her mum again tomorrow.

But after the phone call, she buried her head in the cushion on the sofa and sobbed and sobbed until she didn't have any tears left. She fell to her knees, hands resting on the sofa and sent her apologies to God. She told Him that she was sorry that Sam was dead and she would try her hardest to forgive him for what he had done to her. She asked God not to be too hard on him, he was young and thoughtless and he probably deserved forgiveness. She hoped that He was listening. She didn't think that she could cope with the guilt of killing him, together with the guilt of sending him to Hell too. If God didn't exist, then it didn't matter, but if He did, then she had done all she could do.

She got up and went into the kitchen to make herself a coffee. As she waited for the kettle to boil, she wondered how the funeral had gone and what the eulogy had been like. She had no regrets about missing it. It wasn't the right time for her to sit and listen to speeches about what a wonderful and kind person he had been. But now, she would never know whether the Sam who had attacked her was his true self. He had been very drunk and he could have taken drugs too, which would explain why he did such a terrible thing. But she hadn't known him well enough to know whether he had acted out of character or not. It could have been because he was a born psychopath and he had always been evil, or it could have been because he was just immature and thoughtless. And now she would never know how he would have reacted the following day. Would he have knocked on their door with a heartfelt apology, pleading for forgiveness? Or would he have continued to be horrible to her, teasing and mocking her and swearing to anyone who would listen that their sexual act was consensual? Would he have remembered at all? Or would the alcohol have erased the memory?

She was sorry that Gwen had become involved and she was sorry that they had both lied to Charles. She was sorry that Charles, Sebastian and Faisal had lost their friend and that his family had lost him. But most of all, she was sorry that she had ever come to Lancaster University. She had never wanted to be a student. She wasn't a big fan of the course, she never intended to use it and as far as she was concerned, she was wasting time and had completely wasted the last year by missing out on modelling assignments. Of course, if she hadn't come, she would never have met Gwen. But was their short friendship, wonderful and full of love and laughter as it had been, worth this secret that they now both had to keep? Because of her, Gwen had a burden to carry for the rest of her life. Would she be able to handle the weight of it, or would she confess to Charles at the first opportunity?

Chapter Fourteen

Let's Talk

June 2022 - Wednesday

The morning always arrived before Gwen was ready and today was no exception. She was in a deep sleep when her alarm clock went off at four thirty. Even the birds weren't properly awake. A few of them had begun some tentative singing, but most of them would still be in bed for another half an hour. But at least she has reached the mid-point of the week. The end of the week was in sight and she then had two days to catch up with her sleep, before Monday rolled around again. Charles had booked two nights in the beautiful Grand Hotel in Chester for the wedding and she was looking forward to spending some quality time with him. She might be able to persuade him to join her in the spa on Friday afternoon, after they had checked in, and then they could relax in their room with a bottle of wine and room service the night before the wedding. She couldn't wait.

As she turned over to cancel her alarm, she wasn't surprised to find his side of the bed empty. He wasn't a great sleeper, especially when it was hot and humid, like it had been this week and if he was finding it hard to get to sleep, he very often de-camped into the spare room so that Gwen wouldn't wake him when she got up early. Today, she knew that he wanted to make an early start, as he had a big project on at work, so after she had showered and got dressed, she made him a coffee and gently opened the door of the spare bedroom.

"Morning darling, I've made you a coffee…"

The room was empty. The bed hadn't been slept in.

Gwen stood for a moment, unable to process what she was seeing. She knew he hadn't fallen asleep on the sofa last night, he wasn't in the spare room and he wasn't in her bed, so there was only one other place he could be. But surely he wouldn't have done that? Alright, they had argued last night and she had stormed off to bed without him, but even so, they had had worst arguments in the past. What on earth was wrong with him? She could feel the anger growing inside her as she realised that, more than likely, he would have checked into one of the rooms in the Hilton Hotel below their apartment. He had done that once before, years ago when they had had a stupid argument over something and nothing. He had stormed out like an angry teenager. The day after, he had crawled back with a huge bunch of roses, her favourite truffles from Hotel Chocolat and an apology. He promised that he wouldn't do it again. She had taken the apology reluctantly but told him that it was embarrassing for her. Everyone in the hotel knew who she was and now everyone would be gossiping about the state of their marriage. He had assured her that he had been discreet. She had shouted that it wasn't discreet at all. A night alone in a hotel room plus gifts of chocolates and flowers the morning after equalled a troubled marriage.

If he had done the same thing again, she would be more than furious. He might as well telephone the tabloids and tell them all their personal business. People would already be talking about them after their heated conversation in the restaurant last night.

She dumped his coffee on the bedside table and stamped into the kitchen, where her phone was charging. She pressed his number, not caring whether he was awake or not. It went straight to voicemail. She didn't leave him a message. What on earth could she say? She didn't want to ask him to come home, she had to leave for work in a minute anyway, so it wasn't as though they had time to talk. As far as she was concerned, she didn't have anything to talk about. Their stupid argument in the restaurant was exactly that, stupid. He said he had had a bad day and that was it. It was in the past. So what on earth was he playing at?

And now she was going to be late. She had to be in the studio in less than half an hour. She grabbed her handbag and the door keys and left the apartment. Thankfully the lift down to the basement car park was empty. There was nobody else usually around at this time of the morning, so she had a little time to compose herself before she had to put her professional face on and smile into the cameras.

She arrived at the studio only two minutes later than her normal time. How she made it in that time, she would never know. Lady Luck had made sure that the roads were empty, the police had all gone in for their tea break and all the other drivers were still asleep. She didn't condone fast driving, but the adrenalin fueled anger surging through her veins made sure that her foot stayed firmly pressed onto the accelerator throughout the short journey.

Intermittently she stabbed at the screen on the dashboard to dial Charles' number, but each time it went to voicemail. On the fourth time, she left an angry voicemail asking him where the fuck he was and he eventually returned her call just as she was pulling into the studio car park.

"Hello," he said, sleepily.

Just hearing his voice irritated her beyond belief. How could he still be asleep? By staying in the hotel last night, he was making a statement to the world that their marriage was teetering on the edge of collapse and he still managed to sleep?

"So, you decided not to sleep at home last night. Is that perhaps something I should have been consulted about?"

"Hey, calm down, calm down," he said. "Are you driving?"

"Of course I'm driving. I'm just about to go into work, don't you know what time it is?" She couldn't help shouting at him. She knew deep down that she should have been calm and possibly even conciliatory and she should have asked him gently why he hadn't stayed at home and what could she do to make him feel better. But fuck the couples' counsellor. She wasn't in the mood for peace talks.

"I was just worried about you driving and using your phone..."

"Oh fuck off, Charles. You're on loud speaker. I'm not holding the fucking phone to my ear, I'm not stupid." She didn't usually swear; it wasn't her style at all and she knew that Charles didn't like it. He thought that it wasn't ladylike but right now, she couldn't help it. Sometimes, only swear words would do to express inner feelings.

"Okay, well I can tell this isn't a good time for you and, to be honest, it isn't a good time for me either. You know I've got a busy day at work, so I'll speak to you tonight. Drive carefully." He cut her off.

Aaaaarrrrggghhhh! She slammed her fist onto the steering wheel and screamed at the *Call Ended* words on the screen.

Taking a few deep breaths to calm herself, she parked the car, got out and walked towards the studio. By the time she reached the fourth floor and said good morning to her colleagues, she was in professional mode and nobody would have guessed that there was anything amiss.

***

Gwen managed to get through the day by not thinking about Charles at all. She put him to the back of her mind and every time he popped to the front, she squashed him back down by telling herself that there was nothing to worry about. They would sort it out tonight. They would talk over a bottle of wine, have make-up sex and carry on as usual in happily married contentment. At least, that's what she wanted to do.

It was late afternoon by the time his text finally arrived and she had finished work and was back at home. Her heart pounded as she read his words.

We need to talk x

She knew that 'we need to talk' was relationship speak

for 'we need to talk about us'. He clearly wasn't planning to talk about the weekend, or their next holiday or what they should have for dinner tonight. She tried not to panic. After all, she knew that they needed to talk. It wasn't normal for couples to spend nights apart, one of them in a hotel and one of them at home. So, yes, they needed to talk. But it would be fine.

I'm at home, where are you? X she replied.

On my way. I'll be there in a few minutes.

Within ten minutes, he was standing in their hallway, not smiling, not pulling her into a hug.

"I walked out without my key," he said, as she opened the door.

She looked him up and down and noted that he was wearing the same suit and the same tie as last night, but with a different shirt. He looked down at his shirt and opened his mouth to say something, but then didn't. She couldn't be bothered asking what he was going to say. Where he had bought his shirt wasn't important.

"Come in," she said.

Come in? When did they get so formal? He lived there, he didn't need an invitation to come in. She didn't think she had ever said those words to him before. When they were dating, before he had a key to her apartment, he used to knock on her door and once the door was opened, he would just walk in; he didn't need to be asked. In fact, they usually didn't speak until they had finished kissing. It was normal for him to press her against the wall, holding her tight and kissing her mouth, her neck, her ears, greeting her like a long lost and much missed lover, even if he had seen her just the previous night, before they broke apart, giggling, and said hello. Of course, it was different now that they were married. Some of the heat had died down, but it wasn't unreasonable to expect a little warmth. Right now, the air around him was cold and unpenetrable. She walked away, down the hall and into the kitchen, unwilling to break down his walls at this stage. She needed to wait and see what he had to say first.

"Do you want tea?"

She smiled at him and occupied herself with getting two cups out of the cupboard, teabags from the tin and milk from the fridge. She wanted to pretend things were normal. She didn't want to stand idle, waiting for affection that clearly wasn't coming her way. She didn't want to wait for words which she knew would hurt her. She would cling to normality for as long as possible.

"Yes please," he said, walking over to the window and peering out at the view across the city. He had his back to her and she longed to touch him, turn him around and kiss him.

She made the tea and then put the cups on the dining table, one at each side, so they could sit opposite each other and talk. The gravitas of the situation deserved the formality of the seating arrangement.

"Do you want to sit down?" she said. Another invitation that previously hadn't been necessary. She waited for him to speak.

"You know the counsellor told us that communication was key?"

She nodded.

"Well I've been thinking all night of the things I want to say, but now I don't know where to start," he said, pulling out a chair and sitting down, resting his arms on the table.

I think you probably do, she thought, preparing herself for the words that, suddenly, she knew were coming. It was obvious that he hadn't planned to make things up with her, otherwise they would be kissing by now. He hadn't brought flowers or chocolates, like last time, just his new shirt and a cloud of misery.

"I can't do this anymore," he said. As he said the words, he didn't meet her eye but concentrated hard on his tea cup, tipping the mug and swirling the hot liquid around.

Even when the expected words came, she felt completely unprepared. Her dry mouth wouldn't allow her to speak. There were no easy words to break someone's heart. She felt sorry for him, as she knew that he would have thought long and hard about what to say. She shook her head, waiting for him to continue, willing him to change his mind. He looked up at her and her heart broke when she saw his tears. She hadn't seen him cry since Sam's funeral. She pushed her chair back and ran to the other side of the table. He didn't move, so she flung her arms around him from behind and leaned into him, so that her head was resting on his back.

"We can work it out," she whispered into his ear. "We don't need to split up, we just need to talk. I love you."

"Thank you," he said, taking a deep breath, "But I'm sorry, it's over."

He was meant to say that he loved her too. Not thank you! As though she was giving him a gift, rather than her whole heart, her whole precious heart that he has just used and then returned, crumpled and damaged like some unwanted online shopping. She had heard of girls at work, before a Christmas party, they would buy a dress, wear it for one night and then return it. The difference being that they treated the dress with care and attention and return it undamaged. But now Gwen was damaged. Very damaged.

She let go immediately and ran into the hall and into the bathroom. She buried her face into the towel so that he didn't hear her crying. After a moment, she took a deep breath and went back into the living area, taking the towel with her. She knew that she would need it again. Charles was in the same position at the table. He hadn't moved at all. She had expected him to follow her, to wrap his arms around her, to comfort her and make it better. But he didn't. How could this be happening? The man who was meant to give her solace was the one causing this pain. Who would she turn to now? He was her cushion against the world. They were a team.

"Why are you still here? I thought you said it was over. You can leave now." She was suddenly angry at him for hurting her.

"Gwen, my love," he said. She loved it when he called her that. He used to whisper her name and 'my love' to her when they were having sex. Had they done that for the last time? She couldn't remember it properly. Was it last weekend? Saturday? No, it was Sunday morning. If she had known this was coming, she would have etched it onto her memory with more care, for her to look back on. Had they kissed for the last time? When was their last kiss? She had tried to kiss him last night before she went to bed, but he didn't respond. She thought that he was distracted by the Formula One Highlights, when all along, he was planning on leaving her. So she had stormed off without him. If only she had known, then maybe they could have talked.

She tried to remember their last proper kiss, but her mind was panicking and she couldn't recall. Should she kiss him now? No, he clearly didn't want her arms around him, so it was highly unlikely that he would welcome a kiss and she couldn't bear any more rejection.

This felt like a nightmare.

It was unreal.

It couldn't be happening.

And yet it was.

"I'm sorry," he said. "I've tried to get over it, but I can't. I just keep seeing you two together and it drives me crazy."

"Who? James?" she asked. She knew that's what he meant, she didn't need to ask him, but she felt she needed to be absolutely sure that they were both on the same page.

"Yes fucking James, who do you think I'm talking about?"

Now he was angry again, like that day back in December when he saw the photo of her and James kissing. It was all over social media and the gutter press pages online. It was so humiliating for him, she got that. He had stormed off, leaving her abandoned and feeling lost and stupid. How could she have been so naive as to think that someone as well known as her could get away with kissing another man in public? She should have known better; she had spent her whole career being professional and aloof, but she managed to completely make a balls-up of everything with one drunken mistake. She should have known that he wouldn't be able to get over it. If they were Mr and Mrs Nobody, then he might have done. But to have the whole country know that you have been cuckolded, it was too much.

"But we've talked about him before," she said. "Darling, you know it was a moment of madness and it meant nothing. I was drunk."

"I know, but you weren't unconscious, were you? You were still capable of giving consent."

She didn't reply.

"Yes?"

"Yes, but it was drunken consent, which is completely different," she said, desperately clutching at straws.

"No," he said, "It isn't different. We've had drunken sex plenty of times. You know what you're doing, even when you've had a drink." His tears were falling freely now.

"But I don't think about James anymore," she said. "Honestly, I don't. He's in my past and I never give him a second thought. He doesn't even work with me now."

"You don't get it, do you? It's like I said the other night, it isn't always about you. Unfortunately, I do give him a second thought. I can't get the bastard out of my head. He's there, every day." He tapped at the side of his head with an angry forefinger. "So, we need to end it. I'm sorry."

She dropped down onto her knees in front of him and buried her head in his lap. She would beg; he was worth begging for.

"Charles, please don't. Please."

She looked up at him and through her tears she could see the imperceptible shake of his head. He lifted one hand and stroked her hair.

"I've only ever loved you, you know that. There has been nobody else. This is us. We can't end it."

"We can. Whenever I touch you, I see him doing it. If I touch your hair, your face, anywhere on your body, I wonder whether he has touched the same place. I can't bear to think that he probably has. You've ruined us."

With those words, she knew that she could never get him back. It was her fault, one hundred percent, and despite the fact that he had tried to move on, he couldn't forget what she had done and he certainly couldn't forgive her. Google held the evidence. There was no point in asking for one more chance. Charles wasn't a betting man and he wasn't prepared to give her any more chances.

She got up from her knees, embarrassed that she had even thought about begging him to stay. She knew that she couldn't force him to change his mind. If he wanted to stay, they wouldn't even be having this conversation.

At this time, they would usually be eating dinner, at home or at a local restaurant. She asked him if he wanted anything. Her little ploy to keep him there a few moments longer. Neither of them had eaten since breakfast, but the knots in both of their stomachs made it impossible for them to consider any food and she found that she was relieved when he said he couldn't eat. If he couldn't eat, then it must mean that he was upset and if he was this upset, then it must mean that he could change his mind. Maybe. Maybe not today. Not right now, but at some point. He had to.

Eventually they moved from the dining table and snuggled on the sofa, his arm around her one last time. She rested her head on his chest for the last time. She knew that she could raise her head slightly and kiss his face, one last time, but she didn't. She was frightened to move unless it prompted him to leave. For hours they sat and talked, about their relationship, about the wonderful times they had had and the places they had been. They laughed and cried and hugged and kissed and when all of their emotions were spent, he left.

It was dark by that time, but she didn't ask him where he was going to stay.

She walked him to the door and politely said goodbye and told him to take care of himself. Then she had sank to the floor in the hall, her back resting against the wall and sobbed. Everything happens for a reason, she could hear her mother telling her. But what's the reason for this? What was the point in her falling in love, getting married, planning future children, just for it to be thrown back in her face years later. She couldn't see the point in it at all.

Who would give her a baby now?

Chapter Fifteen

London Trip

June 2022 - Thursday

"That's my packing done and the kids are fed and quiet," said Audrina. "They're happily playing too, which is a change. No arguments for Daddy to have to deal with."

"As soon as you walk out of that door, World War Three will erupt, you can guarantee," said Devon. He poured himself a black coffee from the cafetiere. "Have you got time for one before you go?" he asked, holding up his cafetiere towards her.

"No. The taxi will be here in a few minutes, so I'll get one at the train station," she said. "I'll just have a mouthful of yours."

"Is there anything else that you want before you go?" asked Devon, pulling her into a hug and kissing her neck.

"Absolutely not," she said, laughing and pushing him away. "You'll have to wait until tomorrow for that."

"You're cruel," he said.

A ping on the Uber app on her phone told her that the taxi

had arrived and was waiting outside the gates at the bottom of the driveway.

"It's here," she said. "Time to go." She put her phone safely away in the front pocket of her handbag and then kissed Devon. She was excited to get going. She always loved visiting London and it would be nice to see Jacob again. It felt like she hadn't seen him for ages. But even so, she would miss Devon and the kids.

Devon walked her to the front door, resting his hand on the small of her back.

"I'm going to miss you," he said, as he opened the front door for her.

"No, you're not," she said. "As soon as you get the Playstation on, you won't even remember my name."

"Possibly. What's your name again?"

She slapped him gently on the arm. "I'll be back tomorrow night and I'll call you the minute I get to the hotel." She gave him another long kiss and then shouted her goodbyes upstairs to the children, while Devon put her suitcase in the boot of the taxi.

"Mummy, mummy," shouted Harry. "Wait there." He appeared at the top of the stairs and beckoned to her to come to him.

"What, darling?"

"Bye again."

She laughed and ran up the stairs, scooping him up into her arms and kissing him until he squealed and begged to be put down. She ran into Mary's room where she and Martha were watching Frozen, sitting by side on her bed.

"Girls, give me another hug," she said, "Quickly, the taxi's waiting for me outside."

The girls scrambled off the bed and ran to her and wrapped their little arms around her neck as she squatted down in front of them. As she breathed in the wonderful smell of their hair, she knew that she was one of the luckiest people in the world. She was truly blessed to have three healthy and happy children. By the time she ran back down the stairs, kissed Devon one more time and climbed into the back seat of the taxi, she had lost count of the number of blessings she had been given. Her children, her husband, her wonderful and supportive parents, the huge house they had just bought, two new cars and the jobs that they both loved. She had been overly grumpy this week and she needed to snap out of it. She didn't want the children to be shouted at for the smallest of things. They didn't deserve that. Only this morning, she had shouted at Mary for leaving a puddle of water on the bathroom floor after she had washed her face and cleaned her teeth. As soon as she had said it, she had apologised to her and told her that she was worried that someone might slip, that's all. She said that she didn't mean to sound so cross, but she was trying to prevent an accident.

"Sorry, mummy," Mary had said, with tears in her eyes. "I didn't see it."

Of course she didn't see it. She's five years old. She shouldn't have to concern herself with domesticity. If there are some drops of water on the floor, it doesn't matter. It's not the end of the world and it is easily fixed. There are much more important things to be worried about. As Audrina took the towel from her hand and wiped the floor, she told herself that she needed to change and today was the day that she was going to do that. She knew what had been bothering her for a while, more particularly this week, and she needed to deal with it. Her children and her husband didn't need to suffer and be whipped by her tongue every time she opened her mouth.

As she settled into the back seat of the taxi, she decided to do some reflecting while she was away for this short trip to London. She would find a decent meditation app and download it and promise herself that she would do it every day. She might even book herself a personal trainer, to get the endorphins pumping. Devon always felt much better when he had been to training, whether it was because he had spent the morning with a huge bunch of his friends or whether he had endorphins from the exercise, Audrina wasn't sure. But any self improvement was worth the effort. She should seriously think about some counselling too. She had never dealt with the trauma of what Sam had done to her and then what had happened to Sam all those years ago at university and maybe now was the time. She had cut herself off from Gwen and Charles and buried her feelings, along with the truth of what had happened that night. Of course, she would never talk about Sam's accident with anyone except Gwen, not even a counsellor, but at least she could learn how to begin to accept what had happened. All these years, she had been telling herself that she hadn't done anything wrong and neither had Gwen. But deep down, she knew that wasn't true. They should have stopped after the accident and they should have tried to help Sam. If they had done, he may have survived. They were told that he apparently died suddenly from a head injury and he didn't suffer, but Audrina didn't believe that. She thought that the young policeman was telling them what they wanted to hear, so they wouldn't be upset. As far as she was concerned, she was responsible for forcing Gwen to drive away and as a consequence, she was the one who was responsible for Sam's death.

She wondered how Gwen had dealt with it over the years. Did she feel as guilty as Audrina did? She had obviously kept to her promise about never mentioning it to Charles, which Audrina was thankful for. There was absolutely no reason why the truth needed to come out now. After all these years, it wouldn't do anyone any good. Apart from the press having a field day with the story, the police would most definitely get involved. She couldn't bear the thought of having to spend a single minute in police custody, never mind the days, months or even years that might follow. What good would it do anyone for the story to come out now? Nothing at all. The past needed to be left where it was, untouched.

As she rested her head on the headrest in the back of the taxi, she allowed her mind to remember Gwen, something which she often repressed. She missed her so much, that thinking about their brief time together was still painful.

She hoped that Gwen felt better about herself these days. She had always been beautiful and kind and emanated a warmth that made people love her, but she had never managed to fully love herself and the episode with Sam hadn't helped one iota. For weeks afterwards, her self esteem had taken a nose dive. She had told Audrina that she hated herself and she couldn't understand how Charles could love her. She didn't deserve him. Audrina told her that she was being stupid and she needed to stop crying so often, as Charles would start to ask questions about what was really bothering her.

When they had first gone to lectures, Gwen was convinced that all the boys were looking at just Audrina, when in fact they were looking at both of them. Gwen had plenty of admirers. She was feminine, curvy, vivacious and sexy. It was such a shame that she didn't appreciate how lovely she was. Audrina had noticed Charles looking at her as soon as they walked in to the lecture theatre in their first week. Then, from the moment the two of them started dating, it was clear that he was smitten and as far as she knew, had never looked at another woman. Audrina had been shocked to read that it had been Gwen who had been unfaithful, but it seemed that Charles had forgiven her and they were still together.

Gwen had been so excited when Charles had asked her out on a second date, the day after their first. They had gone to Morecambe for a walk on the promenade. He had bought them hot chocolate with marshmallows from a kiosk and they had sat on a bench, holding hands and looking out to the sea. When their drinks were finished, Charles had taken the cups and put them in the bin and then gone back to the bench, where he took Gwen's face in his hands and kissed her gently on her mouth. Afterwards, he had taken her for dinner at The Midland Hotel, the magnificent art deco hotel overlooking the promenade. They had a roast beef dinner, which she said was the best she had ever had, followed by sticky toffee pudding.

When Gwen came rushing back to their shared room, her face was glowing and her eyes were shining with the excitement of the day. She said that the meal at the hotel was wonderful. There were fresh flowers in a tiny crystal vase on the table, the glasses were polished to within an inch of their lives, the table cloth was the finest cotton and the staff were attentive without being over bearing and the view from the table was amazing. But sitting on the bench with their hot chocolates and sharing a kiss had been the most romantic thing she had ever done.

"More romantic than when he pushed you up against the wall and kissed you yesterday?" Audrina had asked, laughing.

"Yes," said Gwen, "I can't explain it, but I think it's because last night's kiss was passionate and I know that the initial passion will fade, but today's kiss, and the whole outing in fact, is something that I can see us doing well into our old age. Do you know what I mean?"

"I think so," said Audrina. "But bloody hell, girl, you've known him for a day and you're talking about your old age together."

"My mum said that when you know, you know. And I think I know."

Audrina had asked her whether she wanted to cast her net a little wider and date other people before she decided that Charles was her future husband. Gwen had looked at her quizzically and asked her why she would do that when she had everything she wanted in him. She was serious too. She didn't see the point in going out with other people, only to find that they didn't measure up to Charles, by which time, he would have been snapped up by somebody else.

"No," she said, "As long as he wants me, I'm not looking elsewhere."

Audrina had told her that she was pleased that she had met him, but maybe she shouldn't go looking for the engagement ring yet. It might be good to slow down a little and maybe go on a few dates with other people, just for fun.

But neither of them did that. From what Audrina had read in the news, they had married less than five years after their graduation and had honeymooned in Jamaica. They didn't have any children yet and Audrina wondered whether it was their choice not to have them or whether they planned to have them in the future. She couldn't believe that Gwen had decided not to have children. She had desperately wanted them and had even talked about what she would call them. If she had a girl, she said she wanted her to be called Charlotte, so she could shorten it to Charlie, after her dad. Audrina laughed and said why didn't she just wait until she had a boy and then she could call him Charles. Gwen said that was boring, because Charles had been named after his father, who was named after his grandfather and she wanted to break the tradition. But she couldn't bring herself to break it entirely, so Charlotte was a nice compromise.

Audrina hoped that they did have children in the future. Gwen was such a lovely gentle person that if anyone should pro-create, it should be her. Her genes deserved to be passed on.

It was the weekend after Sam's funeral when Gwen had told her about her plans for children in the future. She said that she and Charles had talked about it and he had said that he would be happy with a couple of children, but if she wanted more, then he would go along with it. She was the one who had to bear them for nine months, so he would leave the choice up to her.

At the time, they were sitting in deckchairs in the garden of Charles' parents' house in Cheltenham, where they had been invited to spend the weekend. His mother had been concerned about them all having to go through a funeral of someone they knew and persuaded them that a weekend in the country wouldn't be a bad thing. She said it was no trouble, she had a freezer full of homemade food and all she needed was some young people to share it with. She and Charles' dad couldn't possibly eat it all on their own. They had arrived on the Friday night and planned to stay until Sunday afternoon. Charles' older sister, her husband and their four year old daughter, Katie, had arrived for tea on Saturday afternoon. Both she and Gwen had managed to relax a little and when Charles' mum began to fuss over them, giving them tartan blankets for their knees and persistently asking if they were alright and constantly plying them with food and drinks, neither of them argued. It was her way of showing love to her guests and they were happy to receive it.

"I still haven't done last week's assignment yet and it's due to be handed in on Tuesday," Gwen had said, as they watched Charles playing football with Katie.

"It isn't like you to be late with homework," said Audrina. "Are you struggling with it? Can I help?"

"Thanks, but it's not that. I'm struggling to concentrate and other things just seem to get in the way. I can't seem to focus. I've been spending a lot of time with Charles and then the funeral and stuff. It's all knocked me sideways a bit, you know what I mean?"

"Of course," Audrina had said. "I understand, it's been an awful couple of weeks."

As she said the words, she tried to work out how she really felt. Since the funeral, she hadn't cried and had barely thought about Sam. When he had popped into her mind, she forced herself to think of something else. She refused to allow him to enter her thoughts. Only the previous day, as she was pottering about, cleaning and hoovering while she waited for Gwen and Charles to get ready for their weekend at his parents', the afternoon drama on the radio wasn't gripping her like they normally did, so she switched over to Capital FM and found herself singing along to the music. When the cleaning was finished, she had made herself a cup of tea and as she sat down to catch up with her social media in the garden, she continued to hum the songs in her head. It occurred to her that she should feel sad, but she didn't.

Charles' mother, anxious that neither of them had eaten a mouthful of food for at least five minutes, came outside carrying a tray with two cups of tea and a plate of biscuits and place it on the table between the two of them. Gwen glanced at the biscuits, but didn't take one. Charles' old ginger cat, Nutmeg, was lying on a warm patch of grass in the autumn sun, trying to sleep, but she was distracted by the dozens of bees and butterflies on the lavender.

"I'm going to have to take her inside. She's going to get stung if she dives on a bee," Charles' mother said. She picked up her cat and took her inside.

As she closed the kitchen door behind her, Gwen whispered, "I wish she wouldn't keep bringing us food. I'm going to be the size of a house by tomorrow night."

"Rubbish," Audrina told her. "You can work it off at the gym when we get back to uni. Or you can take your bike up to the park, up that massive hill."

Gwen laughed. "I love your enthusiasm. If I had just a

fraction of yours, I would be out there every day, burning calories and fitting into a size ten pair of jeans. I think I'm just too lazy. I should face up to it and accept my flaws and stop trying to be someone I'm not."

"There's nothing wrong with being lazy. And there's nothing wrong you with, you're perfect." Audrina picked up her tea cup and clinked it against Gwen's.

"Thank you," said Gwen. "Cheers. I love lazy days. That's why I'm glad that Charles likes cats, rather than dogs. I'd hate to have to do all that walking, although it would burn a few calories I suppose. Then I wouldn't need to go to a gym or ride up a ridiculously steep hill."

"For goodness sake, stop worrying about calories," said Audrina. "You're the perfect size."

"Go on, say it, for an ordinary person. Someone who isn't a model."

"I wouldn't dare," laughed Audrina. "And that isn't at all what I meant, anyway. Do you know that my agent told me last week that I could do more lingerie shoots if I lost ten pounds."

"No way? Cheeky bugger. I wondered why you were avoiding the biscuits," said Gwen, reaching across to the plate and taking a digestive, which she dipped in her tea. "I can't believe he said that." She shook her head. "Honestly? He thinks you're over weight?"

"Not over weight, no, but there are some designers who want to see their models with abs, you know." She patted her stomach. "They want to show a lean and healthy body, not necessarily thin, but a low body fat."

"Thin by any other name," said Gwen. "But you would be too thin if you lost ten pounds."

"I'd be lean," said Audrina. "That's what my agent said anyway."

"What an absolute.. . sorry, I can't say it, I don't want to swear in case Katie hears me, but that's made me really angry."

"I'm used to it," said Audrina, shrugging her shoulders.

"Even so, I don't know how you could keep your mouth shut when someone said that to you."

"It's not my agent's fault, it's what he gets told by the designers. It's the industry I'm in."

"I don't care who makes the rules," said Gwen. "It's outrageous."

Audrina sighed heavily. "I find it hard to muster up any outrage these days," she said. "Thank you for doing it for me."

Gwen reached over and grabbed her hand. She knew what she meant. Gwen was dealing with their shared trauma by crying every day, releasing the tension that had built up and talking about Sam with Charles and Sebastian and Faisal. They were dealing with their grief together. But Audrina was numb. She didn't want to feel grief. She didn't want to feel anything and she certainly didn't want to talk about Sam with the boys. She wanted to forget him and the sooner the others forgot about too, the better.

"Mummy, can you tell him?" A little voice travelled down the garden.

"Tell him what Katie?" asked Charles' sister, coming out of the kitchen with a cup of tea in her hand.

"It's Uncle Charlie," shouted Katie. "He keeps tickling me."

"Right," shouted Charles, "Race you to the top of the

garden and back."

Screams and laughter floated in the air as they watched Charles racing with Katie towards the house. His sister joined Gwen and Audrina at the table and they relaxed again, knowing that the subject of Sam had been squashed once again.

Now, when Audrina's taxi pulled up at Piccadilly Train Station and the driver hauled her suitcase out of the boot, Audrina thanked him, tipped him a ten pound note and set off to find what platform she needed for her train to London. Now that she was away from home and she had the beginnings of a plan of how to deal with her stress, she began to feel better. The cloud of despair was slowly lifting. After the initial few weeks when she had felt numb and cold after Sam's death, her true feelings gradually rose to the surface and grief descended onto her. Grief for him and grief for herself, for the person that she was before he violated her.

But after nineteen years, maybe it was time to talk about him with Gwen. It might be what both of them need. Audrina certainly felt like she needed it. She had tried running away, from her feelings and from the people she once loved, but that didn't help. Emotions had a way of catching up with you. The tension had been building in her for some time and if she didn't release it, she would burst. She had been thinking about Gwen and Charles and Sam a lot lately and she knew that that was why she had been unhappy and snapping at the children.

She was looking forward to relaxing in the hotel swimming pool this afternoon, eating some good food and getting an early night, after she had spoken to Devon and the children. After the meeting with Jacob tomorrow, she would have brunch with her parents, who had promised to meet her at her hotel, then she would get the train back to Manchester so that she could be home before the children went to bed. Then they could spend the whole weekend together.

After being anxious about the weekend ever since the invitation had arrived, she was finally looking forward to going to Zara's wedding. She knew that Gwen would be there. She knew that they were close friends and work colleagues. After nineteen years of not seeing her, it was time for them to see each other again. They could talk about Sam if they got chance. Otherwise, she could make arrangements to see Gwen one day next week. She would love that.

Finally, she was looking forward to seeing Gwen and Charles. It was going to be a great wedding.

She took a photograph of herself about to board to train and posted it onto Instagram with the hashtags

#gratitude
#london
#lovemylife
#familyvibes.

Chapter Sixteen

Wedding Invitation

June 2022 - Thursday

Gwen didn't know how much longer she could keep up the facade of normality. She didn't even want to be here. She hadn't told anyone at work that Charles had left her. If she did, that would be an admission that it was real. If she carried on as normal and pretended that everything was okay, he might return and nobody needed to be any the wiser. So far, she had managed to control her emotions in front of the camera. She had read the news and interviewed guests as though it was just a normal day. As though her life wasn't falling apart and her heart wasn't broken into a thousand pieces. She plastered on her professional mask, focused on her work and only allowed her thoughts to drift when the programme was over and she was finally off air. The three hours that she was on air had been complete torture.

Thankfully, Charles hadn't booked himself into The Hilton after all, so nobody in the hotel knew about their troubles. As yet, the gossip mongers and the newspapers were still in the dark. She was thankful for that at least, but she wished she knew where he was. He hadn't said anything last night when he left and she hadn't heard from him today. If he had been in The Hilton, at least she would know where he was. When she was missing him, like she had done every minute of the day so far, she could picture his room and imagine him lying on the bed, missing her too. Hopefully he was missing her. Surely he was.

But she didn't know where he was. She didn't know what he was doing. He hadn't contacted her since he last night, when he had walked out and left her broken on the floor.

She had spoken to her sister and they had both cried buckets down the phone; Julia crying partly because of Gwen's pain and partly because of her own break-up that she was still coming to terms with. But she had assured Gwen that she didn't think that this was the end. She said they couldn't possibly break up and that he would be home soon. She said they went together; their names were always coupled together in people's consciousness - Gwen and Charles, Charles and Gwen. She told her to 'hang in there' and that he would be back soon. Gwen had clung to that thought as she climbed into bed, hoping and praying that Julia was right.

Now, as she sat in her dressing room, wiping away the day's make-up and tears at the same, she consoled herself with the fact that she was going to be kept busy this weekend at Zara's wedding and that, by the time she arrived back home on Sunday night, he would probably be back in their apartment (well, strictly speaking it was her apartment, which she had bought a few years before they were married) waiting for her. In all honesty, she didn't expect him to go to the wedding with her, but that was fine, she would know plenty of people from work and she would just make up a last minute excuse for him and say that he was ill. A stomach bug would be her life saver this weekend.

" 'Get fresh for the weekend, showing out, showing out.' I hope you're ready for...Hey, are you crying? What's wrong?" Zara burst into her dressing room, without knocking. The only person at the production company that was allowed to do that.

"No, no, I'm fine," said Gwen, with her best professional smile.

"Well you don't look fine."

"Honestly, I'm fine. I was crying at your singing, that's all. Was that Mel and Kim you were singing? I haven't heard that song in years."

"It popped into my head. I'm getting fresh for the weekend. I'm so excited!" She put the two coffee cups she was carrying onto the table and clapped her hands together like a child. Gwen couldn't take away her excitement, that would just be cruel, like taking candy from a baby. Zara had planned her wedding for over twelve months and Gwen wouldn't spoil a single minute of it for her. Yet when tears want to fall, they fall.

"Is it hormonal?" said Zara. "If so, I've got just the remedy." She rummaged in her handbag and produced a brown paper bag from the deli on the ground floor. "I've been on a chocolate ban all week and I treated myself to a humongous brownie, but I will donate it to you. You're a good cause."

"I'm a lost cause more like." Gwen wiped the tears with

the back of her hand, hoping that Zara wouldn't notice them, but the torrent was too strong. Zara knelt on the floor in front of her chair and waited for her to find the words to tell her what was wrong. "Charles left me last night," she said eventually.

"He didn't?"

"He did."

Zara didn't know what to say. She knew about the incident with James at the Christmas party and she didn't have to ask whether this was the reason. She hugged her friend close and offered her one tissue after another, until she finally stopped crying.

"I'm still coming to the wedding, but I can't speak for him. I haven't heard from him since last night."

"Don't worry about that now. Look, I know this weekend's going to be difficult for you and you probably won't feel like partying, so I understand if you don't want to come."

"I wouldn't dream of missing it," said Gwen. "I've been looking forward to it."

"And it will do you good to drown your sorrows in a tonne of Italian wine. Don't you think?"

Gwen smiled and nodded, wiping what was left of her mascara from under her red rimmed eyes.

"I'd love you to come," said Zara, "But only if you feel up to it. Hey, why don't you bring your sister? Oh my God, yes. Please do. The best man's single. We can do some matchmaking."

"Thank you," said Gwen, smiling at Zara's enthusiasm. "That's a good idea, I'd rather not have an empty seat beside me."

"Of course. And then when you get back home, you can give Charles a call and go and talk it through with him. You'll sort it out, I'm sure."

"Yes, I hope so." The thought of talking to Charles cheered her. All he needs is some space. He will be ready to talk after a few days apart. "I think a good wedding is just what I need, and having Julia with me will be lovely, I'll give her a ring. I was planning to spend the majority of the weekend in an intoxicated state, to stop myself from obsessing about where Charles is and what he's doing, so now I will have a drinking buddy. Thank you."

"Perfect," said Zara.

Gwen felt slightly better but she knew that the weekend wouldn't be easy and that, despite her best intentions, she would be spending most of the time thinking about Charles and wondering how he was. She had never seen him cry as much as he did last night. Her heart broke, not only for herself, but for him too. She had caused him immeasurable pain. She was tempted to text him and ask him if he was okay, but she didn't know the rules. What was the break-up etiquette in this situation? She hadn't broken up with anyone in the past. Charles had been her one and only boyfriend. Friends had dumped people and as far as she knew, they hadn't contacted any of them to see how they were. The ties had been cut, nice and clean and irrevocably. But this was different. Charles was her husband. Her life. Her other half. She knew that he was as devastated as she was. Maybe she should leave it until after the weekend and then contact him. But how was she going to get through the next couple of days without speaking to him? Whenever she spent a day without him, if she was out with her sister or a group of friends, she would have text conversations with him and at least one phone call. She would send him a plethora of messages throughout the day, with silly photographs of her and the girls, holding up wine glasses and laughing into the camera. But she wouldn't be doing that this weekend.

How would she cope?

How did a broken heart manage to keep beating?

"Aww love, please don't cry. You know you'll make me cry and I haven't got waterproof mascara on. Have some brownie." Zara picked off the corner of the brownie and placed it in Gwen's upturned hand.

"I don't think I can…"

"Eat!"

Gwen did as she was told and placed the piece of brownie on her tongue, struggling to swallow it passed the lump in her throat. Zara handed her a coffee to wash it down. She said that coffee was the answer to everything and if you had a fresh coffee in your hand, then all would be well. Gwen said that was a load of old bollocks and it was sweet tea, not coffee, that you were meant to hand out in a crisis. Zara hugged her and said that if she still had the capacity for humour, then she would be fine.

"He won't have me back, you know," she said.

"He might do." Zara didn't think that he would, but she wanted to say the right thing.

"I can't stay in this job now. And I'm going to have to put the apartment on the market. I don't want to live there without him."

"What are you talking about? You can't make any decisions right now," said Zara, "Especially life changing ones. You and Charles have argued before, who knows what's going to happen this time."

"I might kid myself into thinking that we'll get back together, but I know deep down that we won't. I've well and truly messed it up and I've got to accept that. I know that I'll get over him, eventually, but if I see him with someone else, I just couldn't cope. So I need to move out of Manchester."

"But you don't need to leave your job. You love your job. You can live in Cheshire somewhere."

"Yes maybe," said Gwen, taking another sip of coffee. "But the papers will hear about it. I don't want to become something that people gossip about, but it's inevitable, I suppose."

"It will be tomorrow's chip wrappings before you know it," said Zara. "People might gossip, for a day or two, then something else will happen and they'll forget all about you."

Gwen didn't reply. She stared out of the window, trying to organise her racing thoughts.

Zara didn't know what else to say. More platitudes wouldn't help. They both knew that the tabloids and even some of the TV news programmes would have a field day with this story. She was a famous face and the public loved a scandal. The story about James would be dragged up again and it would run for more than a day or two. Gwen would have to be prepared to navigate the paparazzi for quite a while. Maybe it would be better for her if she moved house, moved out of Manchester, maybe went to London for a while, until she figured things out. She still had some close friends there from when she was a junior journalist and they could keep her busy. She kept quiet for now. This was a conversation that they could have at a later date. Although Zara hoped that she wouldn't go. She had worked with Gwen for a long time and enjoyed seeing her friend every day at work.

"I thought he was The One, you know," said Gwen. "The one that was going to last forever. But when I look back, there were little signs. Funny how you don't see them when you're immersed in the relationship."

"What do you mean? What kind of signs?"

"He seemed like he was pulling away from me. Not just because of James, but before that. I think the thing with James was just the catalyst. I just made excuses because I didn't want to see what was really happening."

"But what did he do?"

"It was more about what he didn't do. He just wasn't as caring and considerate as he used to be. Like the other week, we'd been out, had a good time and I thought he might want to get a bit romantic when we got home, you know what I mean. So I'm going upstairs and he said 'I'll just check the cricket scores.' I mean, come on…"

Zara knew exactly what she meant. This situation was not alien to her. Her ex-boyfriend had always preferred watching sport to being 'romantic' with her. Thankfully, she now had a different relationship. A more normal relationship, one in which precious time together was more important than watching sport.

"That's not good," she said. "Not good at all." She popped a piece of brownie into her mouth, as though the luxurious chocolate would make everything better.

"I was literally half way up the stairs," said Gwen.

Zara shook her head. She knew that if your man chose cricket over a passionate night between the sheets, then the writing was on the wall.

"Did you say anything to him?" asked Zara.

"No, because I wanted to play the role of being the perfect wife. So I waited for him for over an hour. A fucking hour! I lit a scented candle and everything. I put nice underwear on, I sprayed myself with the perfume that he bought me for Christmas and I just waited and waited, like a fucking idiot." She sighed and wiped her eyes with the tissue which was already sodden with tears. "I kept changing position in bed, one minute I was on top of the covers, then under the covers, then I stood at the end of the bed, trying to decide which one would look the sexiest when he walked in, you know?"

Zara could imagine the scene. "The bastard. So what happened when he came to bed?"

"I was asleep by that time. I got my book out after a bit and then fell asleep. I didn't even hear him come to bed. For fucks sake, how could I have been so stupid?"

"You weren't being stupid at all. You were doing it because you love him."

"No, not that. I mean how could I have been so stupid with James?"

"Oh yes that. Well that was bloody stupid, let's be honest," said Zara.

Gwen laughed. A short laugh full of sadness, regret and resignation.

"Well, there's nothing I can do about it now. Live and learn, I suppose."

"I know you don't mean that. There must be something

you can do," said Zara. "Do you think you could work it out?"

"I would love to, but I don't think he does. If he could just get the image of me and James out of his head, then maybe he could move on, but he said he can't. He said that he sees me differently now." Another tear rolled down her face.

Zara passed her a clean tissue from the box. "I know you don't think this now, but maybe he isn't The One. I know you married him, but forgiveness and trust are so important and you need someone who will trust you, even if you make mistakes. You can't pay for that mistake with James for the rest of your life."

"I know, you're right. I need to get my big girl pants on and get over him. I told Julia that when she broke up with her boyfriend a couple of months ago. I told her that life's too short for crying over a man. Now I need to give myself the same advice." She signed. "He loved me so much, I can't believe that all of that has gone."

She smiled at a sudden memory.

"What is it?" asked Zara.

"We just used to laugh so much. He told me once that I was a cross between Tigger and Audrey Hepburn. He said that Tigger was really fun and bouncy and Audrey Hepburn was beautiful and elegant."

"Aww, that's really cute. I love that," said Zara. "I think it's true, too. Everyone loves Tigger and Audrey Hepburn."

"He doesn't see me like that now though. Who am I now, in his head, I wonder? The Joker? Or a nasty villain in a James Bond film? Why can't I just be Gwen Wilson, the person he fell in love with?"

"Stop torturing yourself. Sometimes you need to change your paradigm, or change your circumstances. But sometimes you should sit and wonder whether you need to do both."

"I thought it was only the polititians who spoke in riddles," said Gwen.

"No, it's simple. Like I said, he's not The One. He was just one that you were practising on. You haven't met your husband yet, but you will do."

"Can we change the subject?" asked Gwen. "Let's talk about the weekend. I want the whole itinerary. Would you and your bridesmaids have time to join us for cocktails on Friday? I'll ring the hotel and book us a VIP area."

"Hundred percent. Although we need to be careful, I don't want any hangovers on Saturday."

Gwen's phone pinged and she jumped up to get it from her handbag.

"It's just my mum saying hi," she said. "I'll ring her later. She'll be upset about Charles, so will my dad. They both love him." She sighed and wiped away another stray tear. She was surprised that she had any left, after last night. How long would this pain last? How long would she jump when her phone pinged and then cry when it wasn't Charles' name on her screen? She sat back down, taking her phone with her and placing it on the table.

"I'm going to leave my phone at home this weekend," she said, "It'll stop me checking it every two minutes. I'm going to be in-communicado. I'll do some thinking while we're away. Thanks Zara."

"What for?"

"Just for being so supportive. I know you should support

your friends when they're going through trauma and crying, but I know it's also a massive pain in the arse. A happy jolly friend is much better to have. Especially when you're about to get married."

"Yes, you're right," said Zara, laughing, "So get over yourself and stop moaning!"

"I will," said Gwen, "I promise I'll try."

Chapter Seventeen

New Day

June 2022 - Friday

Audrina had one of the best night's sleep she had had in years, certainly since the arrival of Harry three years ago. She reached across the bed to turn off the alarm on her phone at seven o'clock and was greeted by a video that Devon had sent half an hour earlier of him and the children dancing in the kitchen while they were eating their cereal. This is what she was looking forward to when she got back. She wanted to dance with the children and her husband. She wanted to greet each new day with a smile and be grateful for what she had and what the day was yet to bring. Her thoughts of Sam and the guilt that she had carried for years had been dragging her down for too long. Today was a new day.

She sent a Whatsapp message to Devon,

Love the video. Wish I was there with you, dancing the kitchen. Xx

He sent an immediate reply,

Kids are cleaning their teeth. All under control. Can't wait for tonight. Don't use up all your energy, you will need some for later xx

She smiled to herself. After a long and hectic day, usually the last thing she wanted was Devon's amorous advances. But she would treat herself to a bubble bath when she got home and then she would show him how much she loved him.

By eight forty-five, after a room service breakfast of yoghurt, strawberries, blueberries and a croissant, a hot shower and a short taxi ride, she was waiting in the reception of Choice Modelling and Talent Agency for her meeting with Jacob. She took a selfie underneath the huge banner behind the reception desk and posted it onto Instagram with the hashtag #thebitchisback.

After a couple of minutes, the main door was thrown open and Jacob burst into the reception area, carrying a large canvas bag across the crook of his elbow and a coffee in each hand. She stood up to meet him and took the coffees from his hands.

"Darling, it's so lovely to see you. You look amazing, as always," he said. So it seems that I have passed the first test, she thought. The wonders of a good night's sleep. They air kissed each other's cheeks on both sides. "I bought us some coffee on the way in," he put his right hand to the side of his mouth and whispered loudly, "I'm sorry to say that Georgia hasn't yet got the hang of making a decent cup."

"I heard that," laughed Georgia, from behind the glass reception desk. "My talents lie elsewhere, I'm afraid."

"Yes, well, when you find them, let me know," said Jacob, giving her a wink. "Follow me, darling."

Audrina followed his cloud of expensive aftershave into one of the meeting rooms. He dumped the canvas bag onto the large oak table in the middle of the room and Audrina put the coffee cups onto the small round glass table in the corner of the room, next to the jug of fresh water and glasses. Everyone knew that drinks of any kind were not permitted on the conference table, ever, as usually there were client samples hanging around and nobody wanted to be the one to admit that an original piece of clothing had been ruined by someone being clumsy and knocking a drink over.

Audrina walked over to the window while Jacob emptied the contents of his bag onto the table.

"I've missed this view," she said, looking across to The Shard and Tower Bridge. "It's no wonder that tourists love this city. I mean, where else can you get something so old next to something so beautiful and new?"

"I don't know, the Choice Modelling Agency maybe?" laughed Jacob.

"Oi, you cheeky sod," laughed Audrina. "I'm not that old!"

"No, not you darling," he said, "But you've got to admit that Victoria has been here for a thousand years."

"It seems like we all have, to be honest. Anyway, what have you got for me? I'm excited about going to Paris. I hope the designer likes me. I'll be gutted if she doesn't."

"Oh, it's practically a done deal," he said. "Just look at this." He waved his arm across the multi-coloured fabric pile in the middle of the table, "This is from a young design house called Summer Falls, headed by a young lady called Summer Harrison who graduated from Heriot Watt

University last year. She's the next big thing, let me tell you, and I wanted you to meet her. She will love you."

"Swim wear?" asked Audrina, picking up one of the swimsuits and holding it up to the light from the window. "Aren't I too old for that? Or is she going for the older market?"

"Not just swim wear, darling. There are some amazing beach cover-ups, floor length and short, together with a couple of sarongs," said Jacob. He grabbed a white cotton shirt with wide sleeves and held it against his chest.

"That's beautiful," said Audrina, "The cotton is so soft."

"Egyptian obviously," said Jacob, "But everything is hand finished and the attention to detail is just spot on. Anyway, to answer your questions, it's no and no. You're not too old and she's isn't going for the older market."

"Who is her target?" asked Audrina.

"Women like you," said Jacob. "You're perfect for this client. She is aiming for the over thirties, probably, but her target lady could be younger, as long as she has a little more class than the average. Someone with a little panache, shall we say."

"So no more arse cheeks on the beach then?" said Audrina.

"Oh my goodness, no. The thought of all those bare cheeks while you're sipping your Champagne cocktail is just too much," he said, fanning himself with one of the bikini tops and pretending to faint.

Just then Georgia knocked on the door and introduced the designer, Summer.

"Come in, come in," said Jacob. "Let me introduce you two. This is Audrina, the model I've been telling you about.

Audrina, this is Summer, the very talented designer of these amazing items."

It had been a long time since Audrina had met a young designer and she was shocked at how young she looked. Her baggy boyfriend style jeans, flat Converse pumps and plain white t-shirt made her look like a teenager. Or was this a sign that Audrina was getting old, when people of working age, doctors, police officers and designers look like they have been out of school for less than five minutes? But Audrina was careful to show her the respect that she deserved and the meeting went well. Summer confirmed that she wanted Audrina to be her main model and the final arrangements were made for her trip to Paris.

As soon as she left the agency, Audrina hailed a black cab back to the hotel to meet her parents, who were waiting for her in the Grille Bar at her hotel. She had promised to treat them to brunch, so her mum didn't have to cook. By the time she arrived at the restaurant, her parents were already there and were waiting for her at the bar. She rushed over to them and her dad wrapped his huge arms around her, making her feel like a small girl again. Her mum hugged her from behind and for the second time in twenty-four hours, Audrina was grateful for her family.

"I think you can let me go now, dad," she said, laughing and kissing him on the cheek.

"Do I have to?" he said.

"Well, only if you want something to eat," she said. "It's pretty hard using a knife and fork in this position."

He let her go, but kept his arm around her shoulder as they were shown to their table. Many pairs of eyes furtively followed them. The beautiful famous model who was married to the Premiership footballer often drew attention. Audrina, if not oblivious to it, was used to it, but her parents not so.

"I don't know how you deal with all these people watching you all the time," said her mother, when they were seated at a round table next to the picture window.

Audrina shrugged. "There's nothing I can do," she said. "If you smile at them, they usually look a little embarrassed to be caught staring and then they look away." To prove her point, she turned to the right and smiled at the people on the next table, two men and two women in their fifties. Immediately, they all looked down at their food and began busily eating. She knew that they would look again at some point within the next few minutes, but she had long ago accepted that, with the amount of work she did and the amount of exposure she had, it was inevitable that her face would be recognised.

"So what's new in Audrina World?" asked her dad, after the waiter had brought over their bottle of white Rioja that her dad had ordered and poured each of them a glass. "I want to hear everything."

She loved that about him. No matter how mundane she thought her life was, her dad was always there, on tenterhooks waiting to hear all about it, usually with a glass of expensive wine in his hand.

"Yes, tell us about your meeting with Jacob," said her mum.

"It was amazing," she said. "I met the designer, who looked about twelve. I'm not kidding, I've never met anyone so young in that position."

Her mum laughed. "You probably have, but you would

have been the same age, so you didn't notice."

"I think you're right," she said. "Anyway, she confirmed that she wants me to go to Paris for the shoot. She said that she chose me in particular because I remind her of her mum."

Her mum and dad laughed so much that the four middle aged people on the next table couldn't help but stare again. This time, Audrina didn't mind.

"I've got more news," she said. "Remember Gwen from university?"

"Yes, of course we remember Gwen," said her mum. "Lovely girl."

"Excellent news reader," said her dad. "She gave the Chancellor a right royal telling off this morning, did you see the interview?"

"No," said Audrina, "I didn't really have time to watch it this morning, but I think I'm going to get back in touch with her."

"Oh, you should," said her mum. "You were such good friends. It's such a shame that you lost touch."

"Yes it is," said Audrina, as lightly as she could. She didn't want her parents thinking that her and Gwen losing touch was anything other than because they both had busy careers. By the time Gwen graduated, Audrina's work schedule was taking her all over Europe and America and she very rarely had free time in England, so the fact that she didn't keep in touch with her best friend was understandable, from her parents' point of view. "But I've found out that she will be going to the wedding we've been invited to tomorrow. Do you remember me telling you about Zara, the lady that I met on the maternity ward when I had Harry?"

"Yes, I do, she had a little girl didn't she?" said her mum.

"Yes, she did. Well, it's her wedding, and she now works with Gwen at the BBC, so that's how Gwen will be there too."

"Wow, what a wonderful coincidence. That will be lovely for you both to catch up. And what a lovely surprise for Gwen."

Yes, it would be, she thought, and she couldn't wait to see her.

***

On the train back home to Manchester, Audrina mulled over her mum's words about it being a lovely surprise for Gwen to see her at the wedding. More than likely, it would also be a huge shock to her and Audrina decided that she should probably ring her, or at least send her text or a Whatsapp message, before the wedding, to let her know that she would be there. In Audrina's heart, their reunion would be something special, full of heartfelt regrets and tears and plenty of hugs and talk about the lost years. But in her head, she knew that the reality could be entirely different. The last time she had seen Gwen, they had argued and then Audrina had left. She was under no illusion that Gwen would be angry with her for leaving so suddenly. The question was, was her anger a thing of the past, or was it still fresh and raw?

It was towards the end of November, around three weeks after Sam's funeral that Gwen's anger had made its first appearance. Charles had been spending more and more time with Sebastian and Faisal next door, often coming home after Audrina and Gwen had gone to bed. After a week or so of him doing that, Gwen had become irritated and asked him why he was there so often. Charles, immediately defensive, told her that it was obvious that he wanted to be with his friends. He had just lost one and he enjoyed spending time with them. They were processing it together, talking about Sam and dealing with their own grief in unity. In normal circumstances, this wouldn't be unusual behaviour. Friends getting together to mourn the loss of another friend is understandable, encouraged even. But this wasn't a typical bereavement and Gwen was struggling with the fact that she was the cause of Charles' grief. There was no escaping the fact that Sam had been run over and left for dead in the road. Doing that to a stranger was bad enough, knocking them down and then driving over their vulnerable body and driving away without a second glance is enough to drive a person crazy with guilt, even more so if it was an accident, which this obviously was. But to do that to your boyfriend's friend and to have to watch the victim's friends grieving was just too much for Gwen to bear.

The anger that she felt towards herself, which had been building since the accident, came out in a torrent of hostility towards Charles. She told him that she could understand Sebastian and Faisal being upset, after all they were his room mates, but wasn't he being a little bit self indulgent? He should give them some space. He had only known him for five minutes, he couldn't be that upset. Charles said that he had never heard anything so heartless. He reminded Gwen how much she had cried at the funeral and then asked her if those were crocodile tears. She said, no, of course not, the funeral was very upsetting, but she didn't want to spend the next few months grieving over a boy that they hardly knew. Charles reminded her that they had known him for months, had spent virtually every day with him and that he had bonded with him immediately and he thought that Gwen had too. Gwen said that he was being overly dramatic and yes, she had liked him, but she wanted to enjoy her life at university, not spend it wearing sackcloth and sitting in ashes. Christmas was coming up and she was determined to enjoy the festivities, like all the other students.

They were in the kitchen when she said this. Audrina heard her words through the living room wall and sat with her head in her hands, wishing that Gwen would hold her tongue. She had never heard her say such horrible things and she knew that Charles would be hurt and it was absolutely obvious that Gwen would know that too, as she knew him better than most. She waited for Charles' response, but there wasn't one, except for the sound of a cup or a plate breaking on to the floor, followed by the sound of Charles' heavy footfall down the hall and the sound of the front door being slammed shut.

The ensuing storm lasted over a week. Angry words and vile reproaches were thrown around in a whirlwind between them. Sometimes they shouted at each other and sometimes the silence between them was defeaning. As much as Audrina tried to keep out of it and let the couple work through their issues, the atmosphere in the house was inescapable.

One Friday afternoon, after Charles had again stormed out, shouting that he was driving to his parents' house for the weekend and he expected to see a little more compassion in the house on his return, Audrina knocked on Gwen's bedroom door and told her that they needed to talk.

"Oh not you as well," she had said. "I'm tired of talking."

Audrina sighed. She had never seen her friend like this. The lovely kind Gwen that she was used to, the one who cried at the RSPCA adverts on the television, the one who gave ten pounds a month out of her meagre student's income to Shelter, a charity for the homeless, the one with bucket loads of empathy was nowhere to be found. Anger had replaced kindness and stolen all the words of comfort that she should be using on her boyfriend.

"I can't let you carry on like this," said Audrina.

"Like what?" Gwen snarled at her.

"Gwen, for fuck's sake. You're destroying your relationship with Charles. You're shouting at him all the time…"

"He shouts at me too."

"Oh stop being so petulant. This is serious. I don't know what self destruct mission you're on, but someone has to stop you. You're being so mean to him. Can't you see how upset he is?"

For a moment, Gwen stared at Audrina, her brow furrowed into a look of genuine perplexion, as though this was the first time that she had contemplated Charles' feelings. Then she burst into tears, throwing herself onto bed and hiding her face in her pillow. Audrina sat on the edge of the bed and rubbed her back, waiting for her to finish.

"What have I done?" said Gwen eventually. "I can't stop myself from doing it."

"You're grieving too," said Audrina. "You've been

through a lot."

"Not really," said Gwen. "Not like you. Like you said that night, I'm not the victim. It's not about me, it's about you and Charles."

Audrina shook her head.

"No, it is," Gwen persisted. "I'm not the one who got attacked and I'm not the one who has lost a friend."

"But you were driving the car," said Audrina. Gwen looked visibly shocked, as though someone had just imparted the most terrible news. "You need to cut yourself a little bit of slack. Be kind to yourself and be kind to Charles."

Fresh tears fell and Audrina rushed to the bathroom to get Gwen some toilet roll to wipe her eyes and her nose.

"I'm going to have to tell him," said Gwen. "I can't cope with this guilt."

"Yes you can," said Audrina firmly, like she was talking to a recalcitrant school girl. "You have to. We promised not to tell anyone. What we did was illegal."

"You said it wasn't," said Gwen, on the edge of hysteria.

"Well it fucking is," said Audrina. "And keep your voice down. You know how thin these walls are."

"But it was an accident," said Gwen. "They'll understand, won't they?"

"Who will understand? His parents? Do you think they'll understand that you knocked over their son and didn't stop the car. Or Charles? Do you think he will understand when you tell him that he has been unreasonably grieving for a friend that you killed? Or the police? Do you think they will understand that you left the scene of an accident and then had the audacity to go to the dead man's funeral?"

"Audrina!! That's a wicked thing to say. You were the one who told me not to stop."

"You had the steering wheel in your hand. Do you always do what people tell you, without question?"

Both of them were raising their voices now, neither of them able to control their rising levels of anger. Gwen felt as though she had been riding the same wave for weeks. She was beginning to forget how it felt not to feel so much anger. Adrenalin was a regular visitor for her these days.

"You absolute bitch!" said Gwen.

Now it was Audrina's turn to slam the door.

Those were Gwen's last words to Audrina. Absolute bitch. As Audrina re-lived those horrible few weeks and that last conversation between them, she wondered whether that was Gwen's lasting memory of her, that she was an absolute bitch? Time was a great healer, everyone knew that, but not everyone could forgive and forget.

Neither of them had taken Sam's life on purpose; they weren't murderers. It was doubtful whether you would even call it manslaughter. She was afraid to google the definition in case she had to admit that their actions fit the criteria of the crime. But what she did know for sure was that both of them had gone through a terrible trauma and that if she hadn't asked Gwen to help her find her phone, Gwen wouldn't be in the position she was in. Gwen had been forever burdened by the guilt of what she had done, at Audrina's behest. Of course she could have stopped the car, but the poor girl was in shock. She was doing as she was told and keeping her foot down on the accelerator was the easy thing to do. Both of them wanted to get out of that horrible situation as quickly as possible.

For a couple of weeks, Audrina felt as though they had got away with it. Nobody suspected anything, not even Charles when he found out that his car was damaged. He readily accepted that Gwen had caused the damage when she borrowed his car to go and buy some wine and he was so upset about his friend's sudden death, that he didn't question it. Not only that, but he had paid for the repairs himself.

But she should have known that it wouldn't be that easy. Every action has a consequence, an equal and opposite reaction. The consequence was visible to see in the way that Gwen was taking herself down the path of self destruction.

Chapter Eighteen

Harsh Words

June 2022 - Friday

Charles was waiting for Gwen in the staff car park, standing in the rain, typing something into his phone. As soon as Gwen saw him, her first thought was that he was texting her, probably asking her where she was and what time she was due to finish work so that they could talk. It was a little later than usual and he must have been waiting for her for at least fifteen minutes. Although she hadn't heard her phone ping and a quick glance at it confirmed that there were no messages from him.

"Hi," he said, as soon as she appeared next to her car, quickly putting his phone into his jeans pocket.

She was completely lost for words. After a morning of interviews and discussions, where she never faltered and her words had flowed freely and easily, now she was struck dumb. She didn't know what to say and she didn't know how to feel. Her husband was here, waiting for her as though this was their 'thing'. As though he had come to take her to for a late lunch at the end of her long working week. As though this was something that they had arranged and she had been expecting him. Except that it wasn't. She hadn't spoken to him or heard from him in nearly two days. She wasn't sure whether she was pleased to see him or angry that he had left her suddenly and hadn't been in touch to see how she had been coping. Surely he would have known how devastated she was and the fact that he hadn't called just made her pain worse. As though he were deliberately ignoring her. It was bad enough that he had broken her heart, but did he have to pour salt into the open wound? But now wasn't the time to get angry or upset. He was here, that's all that mattered.

She looked down at his jeans pocket, which was hiding his hand and his phone.

"What?" asked Charles.

"What?" echoed Gwen, shaking her head as though she didn't know what he meant.

"Why are you looking at me like that?"

"Nothing, I just…" She couldn't prevent her eyes from wandering again over to his jeans pocket.

"No, no, no," he said. "Don't you dare even think that."

"Think what?" she asked, confused.

He seemed suddenly and irrationally angry and she could feel unwanted tears coming. She didn't want to make him angry again. She wanted this meeting between them, the first meeting since he had told her that he was leaving her, to be a nice pleasant experience for them both. Calm and full of love and apologies. She wanted to hug him close and tell him how miserable she had been these past few days and how much she loved him and missed him. The bed was cold without him. The apartment was empty without him. She was lonely without him. And so unbearably sad. Then he would repeat the words and tell her that he loved her too, he was sorry for over-reacting and he wanted to come home. He wanted to enjoy the weekend with her at Zara's wedding and put all this nonsense behind them.

But none of that happened.

"You want to question me about my phone, don't you?" he said.

"No, I don't," she said, hoping that he would believe her, whilst at the same time knowing that he wouldn't. They had been together for so long that he knew what she was thinking before she did.

"Look! Here!" he said, fumbling in his pocket and taking out his phone. "You can see if you want. I'm not the one with anything to hide. I don't have any secrets."

"Charles, please," she was crying properly now and she wiped away the tears with the back of her hand. The fact that he remained angry and insistent on showing her that he hadn't been texting anyone, but had in fact been commenting on one of his sister's Instagram posts, rather than being contrite about making her cry and being completely unconcerned that she was crying, made her cry more. Before she knew it, she was sobbing and taking deep breaths and covering her face with her hands. There was nobody else in the car park, but she no longer cared whether there was or not. Her single concern at that moment was her marriage and what could she do to fix this awful mess.

What could she do to persuade him that the thing with James had been a one night stand, which neither of them wanted to continue? It hadn't meant anything. Why couldn't he see that?

She had told him everything that he had wanted to know. She has answered all his questions in an open and honest manner. She didn't have any secrets. She had told him that it was a one-time thing and it was over before it had even began. It wasn't ever an option for them to have an affair. Neither of them wanted to go down that route. Both of them knew instantly that they had made a drunken mistake and they agreed never to speak about it again. She didn't have James' number in her phone and he didn't have hers, so she had never had any need to hide her phone from Charles. She didn't have anything to hide from him. If only she could convince him.

Obviously, if the low-life paparazzi photographer hadn't taken the picture of her and James kissing in the hotel lobby while they waited for the lift, she wouldn't have gone home and confessed to Charles about what she had done. She would never have hurt him, just so she could offload her guilt. He was never meant to find out. But the fact was, she had told him, because she hadn't any choice. She was famous and she had been seen. But she thought that they had moved on from that. Their marriage had been strong, hadn't it? They had talked about it, both on their own as a couple and with the counsellor, and he had agreed to forgive her and to try and forget. She didn't know why he had now decided that he had to end their relationship. She couldn't believe that it was over.

After a few minutes, Charles softened and his anger dissipated a little. He handed Gwen a tissue from his pocket.

"Look, let's start again shall we?" he said.

"Yes, can we?" said Gwen, immediately brightening and

stepping towards him, her arms held open for a hug.

"No, not that. I mean let's start the conversation again," he said, stepping away from her.

It was as though he had slapped her across the face, sharply and suddenly. The shock was enough to stop her in her tracks. Not just the shock of his words, as though he were telling her for the first time that he was leaving her, as though she hadn't actually believed him before. But the fact that he stepped away from her. When had he ever done that before? Whether it was an subconscious act or he had done it deliberately, both scenarios were equally painful.

She wiped her eyes with his tissue and waited for him to continue speaking.

"I need to get some of my things from the apartment," he said. "Clothes and stuff."

"You've got a key," said Gwen. "You can go in there whenever you want. Are you asking my permission?"

"Well, yes," he said. "I suppose so." Another metaphoric slap. "I didn't want to just go in and empty my wardrobe and then it be a shock to you when you got home. I was trying to do the right thing."

"You're making me look like an idiot," said Gwen. "You're making this much more difficult than it needs to be." She didn't mean to say that. She didn't want to make him angry or accuse him of anything. She didn't want any harsh words to travel between them. He was hurting just as much as she was, if not more, and she should be doing everything in her power to take the hurt away. To heal him. But she wasn't thinking straight and the words kept coming before she could stop them. "I mean, why are you waiting here to tell me that you want to go to the apartment? Why didn't you ring me? People from the studio could be looking out of the window. They could see us."

He looked up at the tall building, as it trying to figure out which windows had spectators.

"I thought it would be better than phoning you," he said. "I didn't know whether you'd pick up."

"Well, it's not better," she said, pushing him out of her way and opening her car door. "I was alright until I saw you. I was calm and composed, getting on with my life, and now look at the state of me. Do you want people to be gossiping about us?" Why had she said that? The counsellor had told them that if they could see the other person's point of view, they were half way there to solving any argument or issue they might have. So why wasn't she focusing on Charles' hurt? Why was she throwing unnecessary accusations his way? She needed to tell him that she was sorry and she would do anything she could for him. But instead, she was throwing accusations around like stones, waiting to bruise him, as though this whole situation was his fault.

She was no more getting on with her life than she was preparing to fly to the moon. She didn't want him to think that she had moved on and that she didn't want him back. It was such a mess. They couldn't even have a conversation without shouting at each other.

"I'm sorry," she said. "You just caught me off guard." She took a deep breath and tried to stem the tears with the already soaked tissue. "If you want to follow me back to the apartment, that's fine." She got in the car and closed the door. She didn't want to say any more words right now, as none of them seemed to be right. And her work car park

211

was definitely not the right place to be discussing private matters. She had learned the hard way that paparazzi photographs were crafty little bastards who hid in quiet corners of the lives of well known people, waiting for them to trip themselves up by being human.

Charles still had his car park pass to the Beecham Tower residents' car park and as he pulled into his space beside hers, it was easy for Gwen to believe that they were still a couple. Here he was, home from a day's work, ready to spend time with his loving wife. But his tight lipped smile and icy demeanour rather than his warm, open arms and welcoming hug told her that the old Charles wasn't home yet. This was New Charles. The one who she didn't recognise. The one who didn't live here.

The shared lift ride was awkward and silent. She had been hoping to get there before him, but he had been right behind her all the way home. She stared at the numbers on the wall as they lit up, one after the other, until the lift opened on the forty-fifth floor and they could escape the confines of each other.

She stepped out first and he followed her to the door, making no effort to get his own door key out. She opened the door and went straight to the kitchen, where she flicked on the kettle. She didn't ask him whether he wanted a drink, she simply got on with the preparations, frightened of turning her back to see whether he was behind her or not. If he was stood at the breakfast bar, or looking out of the window, or ever hovering at the door, then at least that would mean that he wasn't packing. Within a minute, the fast boil kettle had done its job. She poured boiling water over the teabags and then stirred them, taking her time before she was forced to take them out and turn around to put the teabags in the bin and get the milk from the fridge. She took a deep breath and turned around. He wasn't there.

She could hear the drawers in their bedroom opening and closing. She left his tea on the counter top and took hers into the living room area, where she sank into the sofa. She turned the television on to drown the noise of his impending departure. Inspector Morse was giving instructions to Sergeant Lewis and she tried hard to focus her concentration on what he was saying, as though he wasn't a fictional character, but someone that she had to interview tomorrow about a terrible murder of a university professor.

"I think I'm done," said Charles ten minutes later, appearing in the doorway, seemingly unsure of whether to cross the threshold into their living area.

"That was quick," said Gwen. He didn't answer, but then again, it wasn't really a question. "I've made you some tea, but don't feel obliged to drink it, if you want to get going." She didn't want to give him permission to leave, but she didn't feel like New Charles wanted to stay.

"Thanks," he said.

Inspector Morse was driving his Jaguar Mark Two along the leafy streets of Oxford on his way to interview a potential witness. Sergeant Lewis had been sent back to the police station to undertake some mundane task that nobody else was available for. Opera music filled the living room. Mozart? Wagner? Gwen had no idea and no intention of finding out. If Charles hadn't been here, she would have turned the volume down to drown out the annoying screeching of the opera singer but Charles was a fan of classical music. He had grown up with it playing around his childhood home. He once told her that it was the background to his life and when he heard it, it always reminded him of his parents' home and the endless piano lessons that he and his sister had endured for years. He wasn't bitter about the hours he had spent learning about quavers and crotchets and where they sat on the piano keyboard. He respected and loved his parents and he was lucky enough to have had a very privileged childhood. Gwen loved his parents too, but doubted whether she would ever see them again. Isn't that what happened when people separated? The two families separate too. All those strangers that met at the wedding and then became friends, will they be torn apart and be forced to take sides? Gwen pictured the guests at their wedding, sitting on uncomfortable wooden pews in their best formal clothes in the church, the two families separated by the aisle, only to come together over a shared meal and a small dance floor. Friendships were made that day, not just a husband and wife.

As Charles walked over and perched on the end of the sofa, his cup of tea in his hand, Gwen snatched up the remote control and changed channels.

"I fucking hate classical music," she said angrily. She knew that he didn't like her to swear, but he didn't react. He ignored her outburst.

"I don't want this to be difficult," he said. "Can we try to be one of those couples who separate without paying thousands of pounds to lawyers? It's such a waste of money." He smiled at her as though he was suggesting something pleasant which he was waiting for her to agree to. A day out in the Peak District or a night out at the cinema, rather than the under use of legal advice.

"So you really want to do this?" she asked, trying not to cry again.

"I don't want to do it, Gwen," he said, with an air of resignation. "I think we have to. It's the end of the road for us."

"I haven't got there yet," she said quietly, more to herself than to him. "I don't want to go there."

He stood up. "Maybe now isn't the time to talk about dividing the assets," he said. "But we will need to talk eventually. Probably sooner rather than later."

"Dividing the assets?" she said, looking up at him. "What are you even talking about? I'm not selling this apartment, if that's what you mean."

Yesterday's conversation with Zara about her selling the apartment and giving up her job was now forgotten, as she became defensive about her living space, wanting to preserve it, as though somehow by holding onto it, she would be holding onto a part of Charles.

For a moment Charles was nonplussed. He carried his cup over to the breakfast bar, without speaking. Gwen hated that about him, the fact that he took time to think before he spoke. Why did he have to be so bloody English, uptight and staid? Why can't he have a bit more fire in him and say what was on his mind without choosing his words so carefully? He was breaking up with her, not writing his dissertation. But this was Old Charles, the one who she chose to marry. She used to like that aspect of his character, the fact that he wouldn't throw words around like weapons to hurt people needlessly. He wouldn't hurt her needlessly, at least not in the past. So he must really mean it, to be doing it now. She allowed that thought to settle for a moment until it dawned on her that this was real. She was losing him. She had to let him go.

"Gwen, we can discuss it another time," he said.

"I don't want to discuss it another time," she said, finally feeling some strength and authority returning, replacing her tears. "I want to make it clear that I'm not selling this apartment. If you want to manage this without lawyers, then you need to know where I stand."

"But you can't say that. You'll have to sell it to give me half. Or you can mortgage half, if you still insist on living here," he said.

"Insist on living here? You say it as though it's something completely unreasonable. I bought this flat before we began living together. I'm not selling."

"You didn't buy it," he said, beginning to raise his voice. "You moved into it, yes, but you didn't own it. The bank did."

"Oh get lost, Charles," she said. "You know what I mean. My income is the one that managed to pay off the mortgage ten years earlier than planned." She followed him into the kitchen area, put the cups onto the top shelf of the dishwasher and slammed the door closed.

"Oh here we go. I didn't think it would take long for you to throw the fact that you're the higher earner into my face."

"That's not what I'm doing. I'm just making the point that the mortgage only lasted fifteen years and for five of those, I was living here on my own."

Charles gripped the side of the breakfast bar. For a moment, Gwen thought she had over stepped the mark. But then told herself that no, she hadn't. She was right. Women in general needed to stand up for themselves more often and that's what she was doing. He might be entitled to some fraction the apartment, but not half and she certainly wasn't going to sell it. She loved living here. She loved the view, she loved the neighbours and she loved the apartment.

"Am I expected to walk away from this marriage with nothing?" he asked.

"No," she said. "We will need to divide whatever we have in the bank accounts and cash in the Premium Bonds. I don't know, I mean we have a car each, so I'm happy to keep our own cars, are you?"

"And the shares portfolio?" He seemed to be smirking at her. She couldn't quite read his expression.

"You said that as though I was ignoring the shares, trying to dwindle you or something." She could read him well after all these years.

He looked at her with raised eyebrows. "Well if the cap fits," he said.

"Are you serious? You can't be?" she asked.
"It crossed my mind whether you were hoping I might forget that we have nearly twenty thousand pounds tied up in shares."

"No!" Gwen screamed at him suddenly. "How dare you accuse me of that. Here," she opened one of the wall cupboards and pulled out a manila file and slid it across the breakfast bar towards him. "Everything's in there. You can see it."

He took his phone out of his pocket, opened the file and began taking photographs of each of the share certificates and letters from their broker.

"What are you doing?" asked Gwen.

"I just want copies, that's all," he said. "I don't know what's in here."

"Well that's not my fucking fault," she screamed at him again, hoping the next door neighbours didn't hear her, but unable to stop the fury from building. "You weren't ever interested in it and one of us had to make the money work. You can't just leave it in the bank, you know. One percent interest doesn't go very far these days."

"Don't patronise me," said Charles. "There's no need for that, I just want what I'm entitled to, that's all, after everything you've done."

"Right, that's it." She snatched the file back from him and threw it to the ground. "Get out! Go on, fuck off! I don't want to talk to you right now. I'm done with apologising for one drunken mistake that lasted less than ten minutes." She pushed him away, her hands on his chest as he backed to the door.

"I don't know you anymore," he said, shaking his head at her. "I don't think I've ever really known you, to be honest."

How dare he say that? He was the one who was acting like a stranger, not her. She hadn't changed at all. She stopped pushing him and dropped her hands by her side, momentarily ashamed that she was acting like a deranged woman and using force against the man she loved. He was right, she wasn't acting like herself right now. She shouldn't be forcing her husband out of the apartment like that.

"What do you mean, you don't know me?" she said. "I'm still Gwen, your wife. Alright, alright, I shouldn't let myself get so heated, but it's only because I want to fight for us." She stepped towards him, but he stepped back again, almost tripping over one of the suitcases which he had lined up in the corridor, filled with his half of their shared life.

"No, Gwen," he said. "I don't know who you are. I've always kind of thought that, but that behaviour just then has confirmed it." He wagged his finger disparagingly towards the kitchen. "You're a liar and a cheat. I'm sorry to say it."

Only Charles would apologise whilst at the same time saying something so hurtful. He had always had such impeccable manners. She almost laughed.

"I haven't lied to you, Charles," she said softly. "I told you about James as soon as I could."

"Because you had no choice," he said.

Fair point, she thought.

"But you're still a liar and you always have been." The words were loud and clear and venomous, enunciated like a declaration.

"Charles, I never lied to you." She tried to defend herself, but she could tell it was hopeless. The case was already lost, the jury's decision was final. He was no longer listening to the evidence that was put before him. All she could do was await her punishment.

He picked up his holdall and threw it over his shoulder and grabbed the handles of his two suitcases, one in each hand.

"The night that Sam died," he said. "I know what you did."

The blood rushed from Gwen's head into her feet and she held onto the door handle to stop herself from keeling over. Charles looked at her in a way that she had never seen before. It may have been bordering on hate, if she had to describe it to anyone. It was certainly intense dislike. Her heart raced with the shock of what he was saying and how he was looking at her.

"I know you killed him. You might be able to live with that, but I can't, not anymore. This has never been about James, it's just that your infidelity tipped us over the edge."

He opened the door and dragged his suitcases to the lift. Gwen closed the door behind him, held her head in her hands and sobbed.

Chapter Nineteen

Welcome Call

June 2022 – Friday

Gwen wasn't sure how long she had been sitting in the hallway, sobbing like an abandoned baby. She was unable to process what had just happened and what Charles had said. She wasn't even sure that she had heard him correctly. "I know what you did. I know you killed him."

His words reverberated around her head, but had he really said that? Or had she imagined it?

These past few days were beginning to feel like a nightmare, so maybe she would wake up in a minute. Maybe it had all been a dream, after all. She could get out of bed and carry on her life, with her great job and her loving husband, living in harmony in this perfect penthouse apartment. Sam was in the past and unless she forced herself to, she didn't need to think about him from one day to the next. She could ignore her bad dream and Sam and keep him buried, metaphorically speaking.

Except that it wasn't a dream and now that Charles had dropped his explosive bombshell, she was beginning to understand that her past had finally caught up with her.

The young Gwen who had attended Lancaster University seemed like a different person, who lived in a different lifetime. She was so unlike the Gwen of today, that she was hardly recognisable at all. Of course, today's Gwen still had some of the same hang-ups that her younger self had, for example, she still worried about her yo-yoing weight, she berated herself for not taking enough exercise, she felt guilty when she had too much sugar in a particular week and some days, she worried that she wasn't good enough at her job and that she would soon be replaced by a younger, more dynamic, more stylish version of herself. But overall, she was much happier with herself than she used to be. She had come to realise, whether it was because of Sam's premature death or whether it was simply because she was growing older and wiser, than life really was too short to sweat the small stuff and as long as she continued to work hard, everything would be fine.

Her life was good and her impressive salary gave her and Charles the lifestyle that they deserved.

Except that there was no longer a 'Gwen and Charles'. The two names that had so easily fitted together for nineteen years would no longer be said in the same sentence, except when people were gossiping about them, discussing their separation and whose fault it was. She knew that eventually, the newspapers would get tired of their story and would move on to someone else, but for the time being, as well as dealing with her heartbreaking split from the love of her life, she knew that she would also have to negotiate their story with the tabloids, so that she came out the other end in one piece. How that was going to happen, she had no idea. For the moment, she didn't want to think about it.

Each time she replayed Charles' words to her in her mind, her heart began racing and she had to take deep breaths just to calm her racing thoughts. She couldn't believe what he had said.

"I know you killed him. You might be able to live with that, but I can't, not anymore."

How did he know? Had Audrina told him? Surely she wouldn't have done. They weren't in touch with each other. Well not as far as she knew. Maybe they were. But after all these years, why would she do that? They had vowed to each other than they wouldn't say a word to anyone. At first, fear of being arrested had made Gwen keep to her side of the bargain and as the years went on, fear of losing her job and her reputation were added to the omnipresent fear of a prison sentence. Surely it would be the same for Audrina? And what did he mean when he said that he couldn't live with it anymore? How long had he known?

She needed to ring him and find out. She couldn't manage a moment longer with all these unanswered questions going round in her head. She had no idea where her phone was, but then she heard a faint ringing coming from the kitchen. She jumped up from the floor and ran into the kitchen, where the ringing was coming from the inside of her handbag.

"Hello," she said, grabbing her phone and pressing the green button quickly before it stopped ringing. "Charles, is that you?" The screen had said Unidentified Caller, but he could be ringing from someone else's phone.

"Hello, Gwen?"

She knew the voice immediately, but she didn't want to say her name, in case she was wrong. So much was going on in her head that she couldn't seem to process anything right now.

"Hello," repeated the voice. "Gwen, are you there?"

"Yes, I'm here," she said eventually, through her tears, which were now freely coursing down her cheeks.

"It's Audrina. How are you?"

"Awful," said Gwen, through her sobs. "Charles has left me."

"Oh my God, when?" asked Audrina.

"A couple of days ago," said Gwen. "But he's been over this afternoon and packed his stuff and gone."

"I'm so sorry. I thought you two were forever."

"Yes so did I."

"Is it something you can fix?" asked Audrina.

"No. He said that he knows I killed Sam."

"What?" The way that Audrina screamed the word confirmed to Gwen that this was news to her and that she couldn't have been the one who was responsible for telling him.

"Did you tell him what happened?" she asked, nevertheless needing the clarification.

"No, of course not. I haven't told a living soul, I swear. I haven't even told my husband that we were friends. He has no idea that I know you."

"Why not?" asked Gwen, feeling that revelation like a punch to the stomach, as much as the earlier revelation from Charles. Wasn't their special bond and the things they had shared special enough to Audrina for her to tell her husband about them? That hurt. "You never said anything when you saw me reading the news? I gather you know that I'm on a breakfast news programme?"

"Yes, of course I do, and every time I see you, I want to tell him, but I was trying to protect you," said Audrina softly, as though she had picked up the hurt in Gwen's question. "To protect us both. I didn't want anyone to make the connection, especially when you got the job on the news."

Gwen didn't know what to say.

"Gwen, are you still there?"

"Yes, I'm thinking, there's a lot to process today. Of all the people to ring me just now, I never would have thought it would be you."

"Sorry to ring you out of the blue and at such a bad time."

"No, no, it's fine, it's good to hear you. But how did you get my number?"

"We have a mutual friend, Zara," said Audrina. "I asked her for your number."

"Zara?" asked Gwen, trying to figure out how Audrina would know her.

"Yes, we met on the maternity ward a few years ago and we've stayed friends."

"So you have children then?" Gwen asked with a smile in her voice. She wasn't jealous of anyone else's motherhood, especially not Audrina's. She was pleased for her.

"Yes, I'd like to tell you about them but, listen, I'm on the train on my way back to Manchester, and I was thinking about you because tomorrow…"

"Do you want to come over?" The words were out before Gwen had properly thought about it, but what the hell. Charles wasn't here and she could do with some company. She couldn't bother Zara with her matrimonial issues right now. Learning of someone else's impending divorce the night before your wedding wasn't something that a bride would want to deal with. She could talk it over with her sister, Julia, later tonight at the hotel, but right now she needed someone and Audrina was exactly who she wanted to see.

Audrina said she would love to see her. She said that her husband was picking her up from Piccadilly Train Station but she could ring him and tell him that she was going to see an old friend and to give her another hour or so. She could be with her in less than an hour. Gwen gave her the address and Audrina said that she would get a train to Deansgate Station from Piccadilly, and would walk over.

Gwen had no idea that Audrina lived in the north west. She assumed that she lived in London. She couldn't help but know that she was married to Devon and that he played football in Manchester; they were photographed so many times together, that everyone knew that. But she purposefully didn't follow her social media accounts, so she was unaware of other details of her life. She always thought, for some reason, that Audrina would be in London with her family, so that she could work. Knowing that she was living so close was another blow. How many more could she take this week?

When she put the phone down, Gwen began to think that maybe seeing Audrina wasn't such a good idea and she contemplated calling her back. She didn't need added complications in her life right now, although she did need a friend.

It was so long since she had heard Audrina's voice and there was so much to talk about, but where would she start? How could you begin to discuss your life when the chasm over the years was so wide? Do you talk about the big stuff, or chat about small inconsequential events that had happened recently? Small talk.

The huge celebration that she had had when she first got the job with the BBC was a special day. Should she tell her about that? Before then, when she had collected the keys from the estate agent and moved into her penthouse, she had wanted to ring Audrina and tell her about it. She would have loved the apartment and she would have loved to help choose the furniture, the blinds at the floor to ceiling window in the living room, the colour of the sofa and the cushions and even the dinner plates, cups and wine glasses. Audrina had always loved that kind of thing.

They had often talked about where they would live when they left university and what kind of place it would be. They decided that they would probably have to live in London because Gwen wanted to be a journalist and Audrina would carry on modelling, and they could share a flat, probably in Fulham or Chelsea, somewhere trendy and middle class. Clapham at a push. Audrina wanted a basement flat, so they could have a garden. She said that there was little enough sunshine in England, so they had to make the most of it when it appeared and it would be a shame not to have any outdoor space. Gwen had wanted to be on the top floor, so she could have a view, but Audrina said that the places they could afford wouldn't have a view worth looking at. So when she had moved into the penthouse, with its wonderful views of the Bridgewater Canal, Castlefield and the beautiful Pennine Hills in the distance, she knew that Audrina would have loved it. But she didn't have her number and had no way of contacting her.

Gwen left her phone on the kitchen worktop and wandered into the bedroom, where she checked her reflection in the full length mirror. She had no energy for choosing another outfit and Audrina would have to accept her in her work clothes, creased as they were from the time spent on the hall floor.

She wondered what Charles would say if he knew that Audrina was coming round. Her first instinct was to call him and tell him. "Guess what," she would say excitedly, "The prodigal student returns to the fold."

Old Charles would be thrilled and would be dialling down to the Hilton Hotel, ordering bottles of Champagne and canapes for their guest while Gwen ran around plumping cushions and emptying the bin in the kitchen and lighting smelly candles. But the New Charles wouldn't do that. She didn't know him very well, so she didn't know how he would react for sure, but she had a feeling that she should keep Audrina's ad-hoc visit to herself for the time being.

Gwen wondered what had prompted Audrina's phone call and made a mental note to ask her when she arrived. When she left university, she had said that it was best that they never saw each other again and, although this was never what Gwen wanted, she had no choice but to capitulate.

She sat on the edge of the bed and reached into the back of the bottom drawer of her bedside cabinet, a place normally used for headache tablets, tissues, old pens, paperback books long ago read and anything else that needed its own private place. She pulled out a sheet of A4 paper, which had been folder into four. She unfolded it and smoothed out the creases. It had been a long time since she had read this hand written note from Audrina, left for her in the bathroom the night that her and Charles had had a huge argument and he had stormed out and stayed at his parents' for the weekend.

Dear Gwen,

You know how much you mean to me, so I am doing this for you. Please don't be angry with me. You probably will be, but in years to come, I hope you will accept that I have made the right decision, with your best interest in mind.

I am leaving university and I am going back home to London. I have sent an email to Professor Lumley. He will know that my heart was never in it, so he won't ask questions. My agent has been asking me to commit to them full-time for a while and now seems to be the right time. He has assured me that I won't be short of work.

My presence in this house is too much for you to bear, I know it is. Every time you see my face, you must be reminded of that night and what we did. Yes, I have said 'we' because that unfortunate incident was every much my fault as yours. Probably all my fault, if I'm being completely honest. If I hadn't asked you to go back and search for my phone, then the accident wouldn't have happened. If I hadn't told you to drive on, then maybe we could have saved him.

Everything that happened is because of me. You are not to blame at all.

Don't think that I don't dwell on every single minute of that night and how things could have been different, because I do. The only difference between me and you is that I can control my emotions more and keep them hidden. I have given myself a strong outer shell, for protection. But you, my darling Gwen, are a much nicer person than me. Your emotions are part of you and I don't want you to change for the world. You are the most beautiful person I have ever met. I know I am surrounded by models when I go to work, but they aren't as beautiful as you, because you are so kind and caring. Your beauty shines out of you.

Keep shining, Gwen. Keep being the kind person that you are. I am sorry that I have changed you. I hope I haven't damaged you too much and I hope that you can return to your true self very soon.

It hurts me to see the way you have been shouting at Charles this week and I know that it is my fault. The hurt, guilt and pain that you are feeling is coming out in anger and if you don't stop and think about what you are doing, you could lose him.

Maybe if you didn't have to see me every day and you weren't reminded of that tragic night, you would get over it quicker. So that is why I am leaving.

By the time you read this, I will hopefully be on a train so don't come after me. I won't answer my phone. I'm going to get a new number as soon as I can. I really think that a permanent break is for the best and we shouldn't see each other again.

I will keep our secret, if you will. If we don't see each other, we won't be tempted to talk about it ever again and nobody will ever find out.

Please destroy this letter as soon as you have read it.

With love,

Your dearest friend,

Audrina xx

As she re-read the words that had brought an end to her friendship, Gwen sat and cried. The emotions of that evening all those years ago came flooding back. She had sat on the edge of her bed in Lancaster, as she was doing right now, and she had sobbed for her best friend and the loss that she knew she would have to get used to. An hour or so before she found the letter, she had heard Audrina moving about in her bedroom, but she had no idea what she was doing and she had no idea that she would never see her again. If she had known, she wouldn't have stayed in her room pretending to read, she would have begged her to stay. They could have talked about it over large mugs of steaming hot chocolate and buttered toast, or better still, a bottle of chilled wine and all would have been sorted. But Gwen was being petulant, like Audrina had said, and she was being stubborn. She had no intention of seeing Audrina until the morning, so she had stayed in her room, with the door firmly closed until the noise of Audrina moving about had subsided and the house had fallen into the quiet peacefulness of a late autumn evening. By nine pm it was dark outside and the only reason that Gwen ventured from her room was because she needed the toilet and a cup of tea. She intended to check that the front and back doors were locked and creep back to bed before she bumped into Audrina. She wasn't in the mood for another argument.

But as she opened the door to the bathroom, she couldn't miss the letter that had been left on the closed toilet seat for her. The word GWEN was written in large block capital letters on one side and Audrina's neat joined up handwriting imparted the awful news that their friendship was over on the other side.

She dialled Audrina's phone immediately, but it went to voicemail. She didn't leave a message. She then rang Charles but he too was avoiding her calls. She imagined that he would be sitting in his parents' comfortable living room in front of the fire, watching a movie on their giant television screen and he wouldn't be giving her a single thought. He would be relishing their time apart. A refuge from their arguments. She left him a voicemail asking him to call her, but he didn't.

When he arrived home late on Sunday evening, she ran to him, throwing her arms around him and sobbing, while at the same time hurriedly telling him that Audrina had left. She said that she had been offered a tonne of work by the modelling agency and she couldn't refuse their offer. Charles had said that it was a shame that she had given up her studies, but it was wonderful news for her and Gwen had been forced to agree with him and say that she was happy for her, but she would miss her. She couldn't tell him that she had no idea where Audrina was and that she was refusing to take her calls. She couldn't tell him that she would never see Audrina again and the best friend she had ever had had left her life for good.

At the time, she didn't know how she would explain to Charles the fact that she would never see her again. She would have to make him think that they had just drifted apart. Maybe she would need to lie to him for a while and tell him that they had had some phone conversations and that Audrina sent her love to Charles, all the way across the Atlantic from where she was taking part in New York fashion week. Then their pretend phone calls would become less and less frequent, until they eventually lost contact.

Gwen knew she would think of something, but her first priority was to fix her relationship with Charles. She couldn't lose him as well. In between kisses, she had told him how sorry she was and how this weekend had made her think how special he was to her and how horrible she had been. She said that Sam's accident should be a wake-up call to both of them and they shouldn't let silly arguments get out of hand.

She remembered that Charles had looked at her in a way that she couldn't decipher. Was he about to tell her that it was her fault and that she shouldn't be telling him not to let arguments get out of hand when she was the one who had caused them? She waited for him to say what he was thinking, as there was clearly something on his mind. But he didn't say anything. He took her face in both hands and told her that they had a bright future ahead and they should focus on that and on each other and this terrible, dark episode of their lives would pass. He kissed her and then she led him upstairs to bed.

The following morning, as she switched off the alarm clock, she wondered whether Audrina would yet be awake. She presumed that she had gone back to her parents' house. She quietly climbed out of bed and dialled her number, hoping that she would answer, tell Gwen that she had made a mistake and would get the next train back to Lancaster. But the phone was still switched off. She left a voicemail for her telling her that she was sorry for shouting and that she needn't worry about her and Charles, because they had made up and everything was fine. She then sent a text message giving Audrina her parents' address and told her to keep it safe, as she was likely to move around, but her parents would always be able to tell her where she lived.

Something in the back of her mind told her that Audrina would never listen to the voicemail and would never read the text message, so as soon as nine o'clock finally arrived, she rang the university and asked Student Services for Audrina's home address. If she wasn't answering her phone, then she would go and see her. But they refused to give it to her, quoting some data protection issues. At that point, it hit her that Audrina was serious about them never seeing each other again and the tears flowed again, although this time she had to stem them. She couldn't let Charles see that she had been crying. She wouldn't be able to explain to him what she was crying about. She had to pretend that she was happy for Audrina, as she ventured to London to chase her dream.

Now, as she held the letter in her hand, Gwen wondered whether this was how Charles had found out the truth about Sam's accident. Maybe one day he had gone into her bedside cabinet for something, a pen or some paracetamol and had found the letter and read it. Sam's name wasn't mentioned but that didn't mean that the letter was obscure. It wouldn't have been difficult for Charles to put two and two together and work out what had happened, especially if he remembered about the damage to his car. She should have destroyed the letter as soon as she had read it, like Audrina had told her to. She had no idea why she had kept it but that stupid decision not to destroy the letter had now destroyed her marriage too.

Chapter Twenty

Reunited Friends

June 2022 – Friday

Audrina wasn't sure what to tell Devon about her last minute change of plan. She knew that he would be excited to see her and she would have been able to see the children before bedtime too, if she hadn't arranged to go and see Gwen. But Gwen sounded like she needed her and she couldn't let her down. She wasn't going to see her out of a sense of atonement, but because she wanted to offer her a friendly shoulder to cry on.

She ignored Devon's pleas and his guilt inducing disappointment, telling herself that his eagerness to have her home was probably more to do with the fact that he wanted help with putting the kids to bed, rather than the fact that he couldn't wait to see her. He had put his friends before her on many occasions in the past, not to mention on their moving in day on Monday, when he hadn't come home until midnight, so she refused to allow him to make her feel guilty.

"So who is this old friend that you're so desperate to see?" he asked.

"She's called Gwen," said Audrina, her mind racing at a hundred miles an hour, wondering how she was going to tell Devon that she was close friends with the famous news reader from the BBC and that she just hadn't mentioned it in all the years they had known each other, despite watching her on the television most mornings. She didn't want to lie to him, but she absolutely could not tell him the truth of why she left university. As far as he was concerned, she had left her course because she was a successful model with plenty of work to keep her busy and there was no point in wasting time on a degree that she would never use. That was partly true. Even if Sam's accident had never occurred, she probably would have left before the end of the academic year anyway, so technically she hadn't lied to him. She just hadn't told him the whole truth.

"And you said that she's going to the wedding tomorrow?" asked Devon.

"Yes, I found out from Zara that she's a close friend of hers too."

"So if you're going to see her tomorrow, then why do you need to see her tonight as well?"

"Devon, I told you, I just rang her to say hello and she told me that her husband has just walked out after an argument, so I said I'd go and see her. She was upset. We won't get chance to talk properly tomorrow. You know what it's like at a wedding."

She didn't want to tell him that Gwen had told her that Charles had left with all his belongings and it seemed that their marriage was over. After all, it might not be permanent. All married couples argue and they could work it out. Devon didn't know either of them and, even though he was her husband, her loyalty to Gwen prevented her from gossiping about them.

"So what time will you be home?" he asked.

The added tone of irascibility in his voice irritated her. Unless she was working, she was at home with the children every day. If she had lunch with her friends, the children went with her more often than not. If she was going somewhere special, Devon's parents looked after them, so Devon had no basis of an argument that he was left home alone with them on a regular basis.

"I don't know," she said curtly. "I'll get a taxi, so if it gets late, just go to bed and I'll see you later."

She told him that the phone signal wasn't great and he kept cutting out and she had ended the call before he asked any further questions about Gwen. He knew that Zara was a make-up artist for the BBC and he knew that the morning news reader was called Gwen Morris, so it wouldn't take a genius to work out that the Gwen she was going to see was the newsreader. He would inevitably ask her why she hadn't mentioned that she not only knew her, but knew her well from university. If he didn't think to ask her when she got home, he would definitely want answers to his questions tomorrow at the wedding, when he would see that Gwen Morris the news reader was a wedding guest.

Audrina had between now and then to think of something.

It was just after seven by the time she arrived at Beetham Towers. As she took the lift up to Audrina's apartment, her heart began to race. She was looking forward to seeing her old friend, but she wasn't looking forward to facing her past. That whole horrible episode of her life had been parked safely away in the back of her consciousness. The night that Sam raped her, the awful morning when the policeman had knocked on their door, the funeral, the subsequent arguments between Gwen and Charles and the day when she had finally decided to leave and packed her bags, leaving university and her friends behind, was a part of her life that she didn't like to dwell upon. It was almost as though it had happened to someone else. Not even her husband knew many of the details of her university days. She had told him that her mum had persuaded her to take the course in case her modelling work didn't keep her busy enough, but she had no interest in it and had left as soon as she was able. Of course, she had told him that she shared a house with someone, but that they had drifted apart when she left. She had never mentioned a particular name and Devon had never asked. He probably assumed that they couldn't have been that close, if they didn't keep in touch.

When the wedding invitation from Zara had arrived, Audrina's first instinct was to tell her that she couldn't go. She knew Gwen and Charles would be there and after nineteen years of avoiding them, it seemed foolish to put herself in the position of having to face them, especially in the social setting of a wedding, when people always want to know how people know each other. Are you the bride's side, or the groom's? She quickly checked the football fixtures and was disappointed to find that Manchester United weren't playing that weekend, so she couldn't use that as an excuse. Even if they were, she knew that Zara would tell her that just because Devon couldn't make it, didn't mean that she had to miss the wedding too. She would have told her she was welcome to bring a friend and that Devon could join her later.

It took her over two weeks to send back the RSVP. Eventually Devon had picked it up from behind the clock on the fireplace.

"You need to reply to this," he had instructed, holding it out to her with one hand while he clicked his Playstation on with the other. "Callum's been asking me. They need to tell the caterers what we want to eat."

Callum and Devon had been introduced to each other by Zara and Audrina over dinner. The two women thought that a double date was a good idea and although they had had a good time, it wasn't something that they repeated often. Zara and Audrina preferred to spend time together without their other halves, so that they weren't subjected to an evening of football talk. Callum and Devon hadn't questioned the arrangement and seemed quite happy to get together for an occasional bout of squash followed by a couple of beers without the women.

Audrina knew that the caterers wouldn't be pushing for the final menu numbers six months before the wedding, but rather Zara would be getting stressed about the arrangements and would want to get the seating plan organised, so she could then organise the favours and table decorations etc. What food people wanted to eat was one of the final things that needed to be sorted. But she had clearly asked Callum to give his friends a nudge and ask for the RSVPs to be returned.

Audrina had been there, she understood. She wouldn't have called herself a bridezilla exactly; she had just wanted to be precise and meticulous. Weddings didn't arrange themselves and there was a lot to do, if the day was to run smoothly and without a hitch. Her mum had told her that she was bordering on being finicky when she had insisted on visiting virtually all the luxury candle shops in London, searching for the right scent for the church. She told her mum that was rubbish and even if it were true, as a bride, she had a right to be finicky when details such as the church's welcoming fragrance were so important. It had to compliment the flowers and the whole ambience relied on it. There was a world of difference between sandalwood and musk or lavender and bergamot. One of them said summer wedding and one of them said male changing room. Her mum had looked at her in bemusement and said that she had no idea which one said what and she refused to go into one more shop until they had stopped for lunch and rested her weary legs. In the end, she had settled on a peony and rose fragrance, to match her flowers and as her mum entered the church, taking deep breaths to stem the flow of tears that threatened to ruin her carefully applied make-up, she had to admit that the candles added to what was a perfect scene.

So Audrina had taken the wedding invitation from Devon's outstretched hand and had sent her reply to Zara, telling her that she, Devon and the children would be delighted to accept the invitation and that they would all prefer the vegetable soup, roast beef and the chocolate fondant. As soon as she saw the blue tick on Whatsapp, she knew there was no going back. She knew that in six months, she would be coming face to face with Gwen and Charles and that she had six months to tell Devon that they were old friends and to think of a reason why she hadn't mentioned it so far. Until now, she hadn't yet done it and now she had only eighteen hours before the wedding. Maybe she should mention it to Gwen and they could come up with a story together.

She knocked lightly on Gwen's door, which was opened almost immediately.

"Hi," she said shyly. She wanted to grab hold of Gwen, who was clearly in the need of a hug, looking at the state of her red rimmed and swollen eyes, but she wasn't sure whether that would be welcome. As though the last nineteen years had been erased, she stood on the threshold of Gwen's apartment waiting to be berated for leaving her so suddenly, without talking about it. She knew that Gwen would have been angry and upset and she deserved whatever wrath she wanted to throw at her. Having watched her on Morning News Live for the past six or seven years, Audrina knew that Gwen wouldn't be short of words and she would have no hesitation in telling her how she felt.

But any anger and dismay that Gwen had held for Audrina had disappeared many years ago. She held out her arms and welcomed her old friend into a hug, into her apartment and into her life without a second thought.

"I'm so glad to see you," said Gwen, when they finally pulled apart. Both of them were crying and Gwen wiped away Audrina's tears with her thumb, gently holding her hand to the side of her head for a second. Such a maternal gesture. "Wine?"

"Of course," said Audrina. "I'm sorry, I didn't bring any. I didn't think, I could have called into Marks and Spencer at the station, but…"

"Don't be silly, I've got plenty," said Gwen, leading Audrina into the kitchen.

She opened the door of a large glass fronted wine cooler and took out a cold bottle of Chablis and took two glasses from a shelf. She handed one of the glasses to Audrina and invited her to sit at the breakfast bar. She poured the wine into their glasses, which they clinked together, as said 'cheers'. Gwen didn't ask Audrina which wine she liked. She knew that Chablis was one of her favourites, if she wasn't drinking Champagne. Audrina wouldn't have asked for red wine, knowing that Gwen avoided it, so that it wouldn't stain her teeth.

As they took their first sip of the cold and very welcome alcohol, any fears that either of them had that this first meeting would be awkward had evaporated. There were no signs of recriminations or accusations, just love and friendship.

"I'm sorry to hear about you and Charles," said Audrina. She didn't ask whether they could work it out. It probably wasn't a question that Gwen would be able to answer right now.

"I can't believe it, to be honest," said Gwen. "I've been trying to process it all week, but I can't believe that he's actually gone. He's packed all this clothes and everything."

"Tell me what he said about Sam."

Gwen took another large gulp of her wine. "It was when he was leaving. He was so angry. He said that he knew what I did, the night that Sam died. He knew that I'd killed him." Gwen wiped away fresh tears with the back of her hand.

"But how?" asked Audrina. "Is he bluffing, do you think? How could he actually know?"

"I don't know," said Gwen, staring into her wine rather than into Audrina's face. She didn't want to admit that she hadn't destroyed the letter.

"You didn't tell him, did you?" asked Audrina.

"No, of course not, did you?"

"No!" said Audrina fiercely. "How could I have done?"

"I don't know," said Gwen.

There was a moment's silence while each of them tried to process what had happened and what they would do next. Both of them knew that Charles was basically a decent human being and that they could talk to him and he would be rational and, if he knew the truth, if he had all the facts about what had happened that night, he would understand that they had both been caught up in terrible events beyond their control. Allowing the truth to be told to anyone else, apart from the three of them, would not have advantageous consequences for any of them.

"It'll be alright though, won't it?" said Audrina. "We can talk to him."

"I hope so." Gwen took a deep breath. "I think he found your letter. I never destroyed it. I kept it in a drawer in my bedside cabinet." She couldn't keep the admission from escaping any longer.

"Oh for fuck's sake, Gwen! Why would you do that?"

"I don't know," said Gwen, swiping at another tear.

"Well, alright, let's not panic. It doesn't matter how he find out, it just matters what we do next. Like I said, we can talk to him, right?"

Gwen shook her head. "He was so angry. I've never seen him like that before. I think what's bothering him the most is that I've lied to him. He called me a liar and said that he has never known who I really am."

"That's rubbish, of course he knows who you are," said Audrina. "People always throw horrible words around when they argue. You're not a liar, you just didn't tell him the truth, which isn't the same at all."

"But don't you see," said Gwen. "I didn't just lie to him about that night. I lied to him many times over the next year or so, when I pretended that I'd spoken to you. I fabricated a whole friendship."

"Why would you do that?"

"Look, it was easy for you, you just walked away and you didn't need to talk about me to anyone, but Charles knew you almost as well as I did. He knew that we were like sisters and that we wouldn't just let each other go like that. He would have asked questions. So I made it out as though we were in touch for a while, just by phone, and then we both got busy with our careers and we drifted apart."

Audrina doubted that Gwen would have had to use such subterfuge, but she couldn't judge her. She was right in a way, it was easier for her, travelling the world and meeting new people, none of whom had met Gwen and Charles and none of whom needed an explanation. And she hadn't yet told Devon about Gwen, so who was she to judge?

"So what are we going to do?" asked Audrina.

Gwen smiled briefly. She was so glad that Audrina had said 'we'. She felt the tension in her shoulders relax a little. Knowing that she had an ally was half the battle. "I'll talk to him on Monday. I'm sure he would have calmed down a little by then. I'll have to tell him everything. He needs to know what Sam did to you and why we took the car. Everything. Is that okay?"

"Yes, of course," said Audrina. "Don't worry about it. I know we can trust him."

"Yes, I hope so. Anyway, let's change the subject. I've got so much to ask you," said Gwen. "It's hard to know where to start. I want to know everything."

"Well, I'm still modelling," said Audrina. "I was just on my way back from London, after seeing my agent and a new designer. I've got a job in Paris coming up."

"I had no doubt that you'd make it big," said Gwen. "I've seen you in lots of magazines and I saw that TV advert that you did. I'm so pleased for you."

"You didn't do so badly yourself," said Audrina, waving her arm around to indicate the lavish penthouse apartment.

"I knew you'd like this place," said Gwen. "I wanted you to see it when I first moved in. I've been here fifteen years now. It was such a blank canvas, you would have loved to put your stamp on it and I needed someone to help me out with furniture and decorating." Tears welled again before she could stop them. "Sorry, I didn't mean it to sound like an accusation. I know you had your reason for leaving."

"I'm so sorry," whispered Audrina. She thought that when she was finally able to say those words, the words that she had wanted to say to Gwen for so many years, that she would feel lighter. Happier, or at least a little less burdened. But she didn't. Regret still lived in her veins and had become such an integral part of her, that she was doubtful that it would ever leave her.

Gwen reached over the breakfast bar and held tightly to Audrina's hand. "I'd like to say that there's nothing to be sorry about, but that it's not true is it?"

Audrina shook her head.

"I'm sorry too," said Gwen. "About everything that happened. I'm sorry Sam was such a bastard, I'm sorry he violated you, I'm sorry he died, I'm sorry you felt you had to leave. But having said all that, I don't think that it was our fault. Any of it."

"You don't?"

"No, not really. What choice did we have? We were young and we made decisions at the time that we thought were right. You can't base those choices on what we would do now. We're different people now, older and wiser."

"We could have stopped the car," said Audrina.

Gwen shook her head. "The policeman said he died instantly, there was nothing we could have done to help him, even if we had stopped."

"But we should have reported it as an accident," said Audrina. "That's all it was, an accident. Didn't the policeman call it an RTC?"

"Yes, but I'd been drinking, don't you remember? They would have breathalysed me. I could have been charged with causing death by reckless driving or something like that. I could have gone to prison."

Audrina shrugged. "I'd like to say je ne regrette rien, but it's not true. Whatever you say, I have so many regrets."

"Are you sorry for leaving university?" asked Gwen.

"Actually no, I can't say I am. Work was so hectic at that time. It was definitely the right thing for me to do, but I should never have left you. I've missed you so much."

"We need to stop crying like this, both of us. Here, wipe your eyes." She passed Audrina a cotton tea towel, which she used to dab underneath her eyes. "I'm going to look a state in the morning and I've got a wedding to go to."

"I'm going to Zara's wedding too," said Audrina. "That's why I phoned. I didn't want it to be a massive shock for you when you saw me there."

"Ahh," said Gwen. "So that's why you phoned? Because of the wedding?"

"Yes," said Audrina, not following Gwen's train of thought.

Gwen got up from the breakfast bar and wandered over to the window. She gazed out onto the familiar view of Castlefield and the tiny cars and tiny people going about their business on Deansgate forty-five storeys below the apartment.

Audrina joined her. "I bet you never get tired of this view, do you?" she said. "Gwen? Are you okay?" She could feel a sudden frostiness in the air.

"I thought that you'd got in touch with me because you wanted to, not because you wanted to avoid a scene at the wedding?" said Gwen.

Audrina didn't know what to say. There was no point in telling lies. Gwen knew her too well.

"Initially, I suppose that's true, but I had time to do a lot of thinking on the train yesterday and this afternoon, and I really wanted to see you, despite the wedding. Please believe that."

Gwen sighed. "Okay, fine," she said. "I don't want to argue with you. Are you hungry? Do you want me to order some food?"

"Not really," said Audrina. "I had something on the train."

Gwen could have eaten something, but she didn't want to eat alone. She would love to get her pyjamas on and sit in front of the television, watching a crappy romantic film and munching her way through a pepperoni pizza, but Julia would be waiting for her at the hotel, anxious to get their weekend celebrations underway. She had told her and Zara that she had some work to finish off and would be at the hotel later. Julia said that Zara had asked her to join her and her bridesmaids for cocktails in the bar and told her not to worry.

She looked at the giant clock on the wall. "I'm going to have to leave soon," she said. "Julia's already at the hotel. We're staying there tonight and tomorrow."

"Charles too?" asked Audrina.

"I don't think so," said Gwen. "He hasn't said one way or the other, but the way things were left earlier, I don't think I'll be seeing him this weekend."

"Maybe that's for the best," said Audrina. "Let's deal with one husband at a time. I haven't yet told Devon that I know you and he knows that I watch you on the news every morning. He's going to think it's very odd that I've not mentioned it. I don't know what to tell him."

"Oh that's easy," said Gwen. "Just tell him I was really fat at university and I had bright red hair and you didn't recognise me. After all, it's been nearly twenty years and I didn't have the same surname then."

"Yes, that might work. This might be one of those occasions when I'm actually glad that my husband never

249

listens to a word I say. I'll just distract him with a whiskey and coke and whisper rude promises in his ear."

They both laughed.

By the time Audrina had left and Gwen had packed her small suitcase with her new dress and shoes for the wedding, she was beginning to look forward to the weekend. It would be good to spend some time with Audrina and meet her husband and children. She sent a message to Julia telling her that she was on her way and would see her soon. Then she turned off her phone and put it in the glove compartment of the car.

Chapter Twenty One

Summer Wedding

June 2022 – Saturday

The English summer hadn't let Zara down and was putting on its best show for the bride and groom and all the wedding guests. The sky was a beautiful cobalt blue with a smattering of fluffy clouds and the temperature was an agreeable twenty-five degrees. There was no wind to blow away a carelessly fastened veil and untidy a bride's hair and the rain promised not to fall until the wedding was well and truly over.

As they drove up the long winding drive to the Grand Hotel in Chester, past the ancient oak trees and the smattering of wild summer flowers in the grass, Audrina could see that Zara had kept her promise and had made provisions for all the children that had been invited. A huge inflatable bouncy castle, a couple of swings and a slide were in full use on the front lawn. Dozens of children screamed and screeched their way from one to the other. Two older boys chased a football around and used two trees as goal posts. Shiny shoes were quickly becoming scuffed and miniature suits and party dresses were quickly becoming creased. But the children, their shiny faces sparkling with excitement, were loving it and the parents were taking a welcome break to mingle amongst the other adults in peace.

Devon parked the car in the car park around the back of the hotel and released the children from their seat belts in the back seat. As soon as their door was opened, they careered across the car park and onto the front lawn and dived onto the bouncy castle. A young waiter in a black suit and crisp white shirt handed Devon and Audrina their first glass of cold Prosecco, with a small strawberry bobbing up and down on top of the feisty bubbles.

Devon took their suitcases into the hotel reception, where he checked them in to their room. The receptionist assured him that their cases would later be taken upstairs into the family suite. As she waited for him, Audrina sipped her Prosecco and tried to locate Gwen in the throng of guests on the patio. Audrina was looking forward to seeing her, now that she had broken to Devon who she actually was.

Devon had been in the living room when Audrina had arrived home last night but thankfully he wasn't in the mood for a detailed conversation about whatever old friend she had just been to see. Gran Turismo on his Playstation Five was stealing his attention and for once, Audrina was thankful that he had a one track mind and wasn't fully concentrating on her. She handed him a cold beer from the fridge and poured herself a glass of wine and then sank into the sofa, tucking her feet underneath her. He sat cross legged on the floor, staring at their giant TV screen, but she didn't ask him to turn it off and join her on the sofa, despite the fact that they hadn't seen each other since she had left for her to trip to London the day before. She was happy that he was keeping himself occupied on something else while she imparted her lies.

"Did you have a good time?" he asked. She knew that he wanted her to say a quick yes thanks, and then leave him to his game. But it was now or never. She had to tell him.

"You'll never guess who my old friend was?" she said, trying to keep her voice light.

"What?" asked Devon, skidding his on-screen car around a sharp bend on the track and overtaking another careless driver. "Yes! Got ya!"

Ordinarily, this would have sparked an argument, with Audrina claiming that she never got any of his attention unless he wanted a shag, and it just wasn't good enough, she was worth more, wasn't she? She would tell him that she was sick of his selfish behaviour and she was sick of being ignored and the next time he wanted to tell her about how his training went and what the boss had said to them all, she would ignore him, pretending that online shopping was more important than saving their marriage. Devon would huff and puff and say that in a million years, he would never understand women and tell her that he was just having a bit of down time, like when she went to get her nails done or lay face down on a bench having her neck rubbed by a total stranger for an extortionate amount of money. Audrina would tell him that she needed time in a spa to get away from him. There would be door slamming and stamping of feet, followed by frosty silences.

But not today.

"Gwen, who I went to see tonight, you'll never guess who she is?"

"Gwen who?"

"Gwen Morris the newsreader." Audrina rushed out the rest of her words while Devon was negotiating a particularly tricky part of the race course, another car hot on his heels. "She was called Gwen Wilson when I knew her. I didn't recognise her at all. I mean, I did recognise her, because she's Gwen Morris from the telly, but I didn't know it was her. I didn't know it was the same person. She's so different nowadays. She used to have short red hair and she's thinner these days. I couldn't believe it. And she never used to wear glasses."

She was aware that she was waffling and hoped that it all made sense. She waited a moment for the information to settle into Devon's consciousness. She used to share a house with the news reader, but she didn't recognise her, despite watching her every morning on the telly. Really? She waited a few more seconds, then Devon crashed his car.

"For fuck's sake!" he shouted at the screen. He put the controller down on the floor and span around to face her.

Why did he have to crash? thought Audrina. I want to talk to the back of his head, not his eyes.

"So the girl you knew at uni is Gwen Morris?"

"Yes, amazing isn't it? It took me a few minutes to work it out. I was expecting someone else to answer the door, the person who I remembered and then Gwen Morris was standing in front of me."

"And you didn't know that it was her on the morning news?"

"No," said Audrina, hoping that she sounded convincing. The whole story sounded like a pile of tosh to her and she couldn't believe that Devon would fall for it for one moment. "To be fair, she never used to wear glasses (she knew she had already said that) and I'm usually busy in the mornings, it's not like I sit and actually watch it. It's on in the background while I'm getting the kids ready."

Devon shrugged and nodded at the same time, as if he was acknowledging the possibility of this bizarre situation. He crawled over to her, stroked her thighs and rested his head on her lap. She stroked his hair.

"I've missed you," he said.

She told him that she had missed him too, as she drank the last bit of her wine and then led him upstairs to bed. Distraction was better than confrontation any day.

This morning, he hadn't mentioned it.

"Audrina, hi," the voice behind her said. She turned around to see Gwen and her sister, Julia.

"Hi," she said, hugging them both and giving air kisses to each cheek.

"You look amazing," said Julia. "I haven't seen you for years. How have you been?"

"Great, thanks," said Audrina. "It's lovely to see you. We haven't seen each other in what feels like forever."

"I know, eighteen, nineteen years?" said Julia.

"Yes, something like that."

Julia had travelled over to Lancaster and stayed with her and Gwen for a weekend once, in the spring of their first year. The time just before the end of year exams glued everyone to their seats as they ploughed through text books and hastily hand written notes in an attempt to stick to an impossibly strict revision timetable. They had had a great time. Julia was still at college doing her A'Levels and was in the process of visiting various universities before making her final choice. They had got through dozens of bottles of wine, stayed up too late, eaten junk food and laughed and laughed the whole weekend. Audrina had loved every minute of it. But she hadn't seen her since. When her friendship with Gwen had ended, her fledging friendship with Julia had died too.

"It's a shame that Charles isn't here, but it means that we get to have a catch up. Every cloud has a silver lining, they say," said Audrina, smiling at Gwen. Gwen knew that she didn't mean it and that she wished that Charles was there as much as she did, holding hands with his wife in a show of married bliss. Gwen gave her a conspiratorial wink to let her know that she understood.

"This handsome man is your husband, I presume," she said, as Devon arrived back from the reception desk. He took Gwen's outstretched hand, kissed her and told her that it was lovely to meet her.

"This is him," said Audrina, putting her arm around Devon's back and pulling him towards her. "Devon, this is Julia, Gwen's sister."

"Good to meet you both," said Devon, kissing Julia. "I've spotted Callum, I'm going to go and wish him luck before we all go in." Audrina was happy to let him go. He was happier when surrounded by men, and today she was happy to stay with Gwen and Julia.

"You'll be able to see the children over there somewhere, in the tangle of other kids on the bouncy castle," she said. "You can meet them later."

"Is someone giving them plenty of sweets to keep them quiet?" asked Gwen.

"They are topped up with Haribo, don't worry," laughed Audrina. She squashed the thought that Gwen should be the one offering her children sweets in her role as Godmother. The fact that she had never met them was too sad to contemplate.

"Is that the best man?" asked Julia, looking over to where Devon was standing with Callum and another man of a similar age, wearing the same suit with a matching rose bud in his lapel.

"Looks like it might be him," said Gwen. "Or a groomsman or something. Zara told me that the best man's single, so we might be doing some matchmaking later on," she told Audrina. "Julia needs some recreation."

"Oh well, that's one of the jobs of the best man, isn't it, to provide 'recreation' on the wedding night?" said Audrina. "Although doesn't he usually have to do that with one of the bridesmaids?"

"May the best girl win," said Julia.

They laughed and clinked their glasses together and Audrina was transported back to 2003, back to a nightclub in Lancaster where Gwen was trying in vain to keep her younger sister from wandering off with one of the local boys. She had promised her mum that she wouldn't let her out of her sight and watching her sister snogging a stranger was not something that she wanted to do. She had dragged her back by her arm, back onto the dance floor and back into the safety of female company.

"Having a good time, are you?"

Despite the years that had separated and aged them, Audrina recognised Charles immediately. But his expression didn't invite a welcoming smile from her, the delighted greeting of an old friend. His scowl told all of them that he wasn't here to hand out best wishes. Not to them, anyway.

"Charles? I didn't think you'd be coming," said Gwen. The shock of seeing him was clearly visible on her face.

"Why not?" asked Charles, as though it was the most natural thing in the world to leave your wife one day and then accompany her to a wedding as her plus one the day after.

"I don't know, I… why didn't you tell me?"

"I tried to, but it seems you don't want to answer your phone," he said.

"It's in the car," said Gwen. She didn't add that she had deliberately left it there to avoid his calls.

The disconsolate Gwen that Audrina had seen last night was back again. For a few moments, she thought that she could be brighter and happier, albeit temporarily, and enjoy the day. But not now that Charles had arrived.

"Audrina," said Charles, with a nod in her direction, by way of a greeting.

Nobody had said her name with such accusation and hostility before. She was used to warmth when she heard her name, love and kindness from her friends and family. How dare he say her name like that, with such cold. She fought against the resentment that was beginning to build inside her. He was angry at the news about Sam, she understood. If he had only just read the letter, this would all be new to him. He would be having to deal with all kinds of emotions, some new and some regurgitated from the past. He would be shocked and aggrieved, but he needed to get over it. At this moment, he only had one side of the story and that was the story that he was concocting in his own head. He needed to know the truth and he shouldn't be waving his judgement around until he had heard all the evidence.

"So how long have you two been seeing each other again?" he asked. "I didn't know that you were in touch."

"We weren't," said Gwen hastily, hoping that he would believe her. The last thing she wanted was for him to think that she had been lying to him about something else. "Audrina got in touch with me last night and told me she'd be coming to the wedding."

"I'm a friend of Zara," said Audrina. "We had our babies in the same hospital."

Charles glanced over to the bouncy castle and the cacophony of children. He didn't ask her any questions about which child was hers, whether she had more than one, a boy or a girl?

"Ladies and gentleman," shouted a loud voice from the entrance to the hotel. The Master of Ceremonies clattered a silver knife against a glass to get the attention of the gathered guests. "Please take your seats inside the hotel to await the arrival of the bride."

He disappeared inside, followed by some of the guests. Others collected their reluctant children from the play area and followed, whispering to their excited offspring that it was now time to sit down and be quiet, while crossing their fingers and wondering what were the chances.

"Are you staying?" asked Gwen.

"At the wedding? Of course, I am," said Charles. "Unless it's easier for you if I leave. You've got your friend back now and Julia's here, so I don't suppose you need me. I didn't want you to be on your own, that's all…"

"No, no, that's very thoughtful of you," said Gwen.

"It's okay," said Julia, giving Gwen a quick hug, "I'll spend the day in the spa and I'll see you later."

"No, please don't," said Gwen. "I'm sure they can set you another place at the table."

"No, of course they can't. I'll be happy in the spa, I promise you."

Gwen glared at Charles. She didn't need to tell him that he had cocked up her plans by his unexpected arrival.

He glared back at her and walked off towards the hotel.

Chapter Twenty Two

Honest Discussion

June 2022 – Saturday

The wedding ceremony was beautiful and moving. Chairs had been placed in rows on either side of a red carpet in the conservatory at the back of the hotel, which looked out onto manicured gardens and well stocked flower beds. The altar was an arch of white and pale pink roses, in front of a long table with two chairs, where the happy couple would sign their wedding certificate after sharing their vows. The music was provided by an elegant all female string quartet playing Kissing You Des'Ree from Romeo and Juliet as Zara walked down the aisle on the arms of her father. Their young daughter scattered rose petals under her feet. The order of service held a pink tissue, for the sentimental guests, of which there were many.

Audrina, Devon and the children sat behind Gwen and Charles on the left hand side of the red carpet, the bride's side. By the time Audrina had gathered the children and Devon had joined them, the bride had glided down the hotel's curved staircase into the impressive reception hall, her bridesmaids carrying out last minute scrutinies of her veil and gown. They quickly took their seats. There was no time for introductions, so Audrina just whispered to Devon that the man he was sitting behind was Gwen's husband, Charles. He didn't question why he was there, after he had walked out on her, presumably forgetting that piece of information that she had told him yesterday.

After the ceremony, canapes and more Prosecco were served in the bar while Zara and Callum had some photographs taken outside in the garden with their close family.

Gwen watched them through the window as she sipped her drink, remembering her own wedding day. Hers had been a small wedding in Charles' family church in Cheltenham, following by afternoon tea, drinks and dancing in a marquee in his parents' enormous garden. The sun had shone for them, like today, and she had spent the whole day smiling, unable to believe how lucky she was to have met such a wonderful man. She had a few moments of tears early in the day, when her two bridesmaids, Julia and her friend from work, Joanna, were helping her into her dress, as she wished that Audrina was with her. She had always wanted three bridesmaids and she wanted to tell her that she had been right. He was The One and she was glad that she hadn't dated anyone else in university, like Audrina had advised. Other than that one moment of sadness, she loved every other minute of the day. They had danced until their feet hurt and after all the guests had left, she lay on her back, next to her new husband, in the garden looking up to the bright stars and Charles had told her that he had meant every single word of his vows.

"Well, of course," she had said. "So did I."

"No, I mean, I really really meant it. I'm going to love and honour you all my life. Always."

He had kissed her then and she knew that in that moment, she was the luckiest person on earth, because she had found her love so young.

The following day, they flew to Jamaica for their honeymoon and two weeks later, tanned and jet lagged, Charles had moved into her apartment in Beetham Towers. The apartment that she had decorated and furnished and loved, and which he now wanted her to sell.

She looked over towards where Charles was waiting at the bar. He didn't like Prosecco so he was ordering himself something else. She thought that was rude. The bride and groom had gone to the trouble and expense of paying for Prosecco for everyone, the least he could do was to bloody well drink it. It wouldn't poison him. She watched the bar man put two shots of whiskey into a small glass and place it on the bar. There was no ice to dilute it. Charles wouldn't dream of adding ice to his whiskey. Proper Scotsmen drink it neat, he would say. Gwen hadn't wanted to tell him that, actually, she had heard that the reason they don't add ice is that it's too cold in Scotland and whiskey is traditionally used to warm people. It's nothing to do with machismo, like he had intimated.

Charles waved his bank card at the machine and then took a large sip from the glass. He turned around, leaning on the bar and caught Gwen's eye. Gwen looked away quickly.

Within moments, he was by her side.

"Do you want to talk?" he asked.

"What about?" she said, not facing him. "How lovely the ceremony was, how cute Zara's daughter looked in that little white dress or how that lady over there is going to struggle with those high heels on the dance floor?"

"There's no need for that," said Charles, although he couldn't help peering over his shoulder to look at the high heels in question.

"If you think I want to talk about us, then the answer's no. It's hardly the time and the place, is it?" She knew that they needed to talk about Sam. She couldn't avoid it and it was clear that Charles had something to say, but she couldn't face it right now. She hadn't expected him to be there and his very presence had left her discombobulated.

"We can go to my room," he said. He took another sip of his whiskey. The fumes wafted over to Gwen. She used to like the smell. It reminded her of their long and cosy winter evenings, when the two of them would stay inside, battened down against the harsh winter rain and wind, their love keeping them warm.

"Your room?" She knew what he meant. She hadn't expected him to share her room. He couldn't anyway now, as Julia was with her. But the fact that he had booked another room, not knowing that Julia had been invited to the wedding, was another dagger to her heart.

"I didn't think you'd want me to share with you, so I booked my own," said Charles. For a moment, she thought she saw a flash of contrition. Was he sorry for leaving her? Was he sorry for breaking her heart? Right now, she couldn't tell. She still had to get used to New Charles, the man that she didn't know. She wasn't sure that she liked him very much.

They each sipped on their drinks for a few minutes, their silence drifting over the chattering voices of the other guests.

"I can't keep it in, I'm sorry," said Charles, suddenly. "We need to talk about the huge elephant in the room. At least I do."

"The elephant in the room?"

"Sam!" He almost shouted it and Gwen told him to keep his voice down.

"I told you, now isn't the time and place. We can meet on Monday, if you want."

"No, I don't want. I want to talk now. It's been eating me up inside for ages. I can't hold it in any longer, now that I've told you that I know. We need to talk about it."

What did that mean, he can't hold it in? Gwen thought. Surely that doesn't mean that he wants to talk about it to anyone other than her? She couldn't take a chance, so she suggested they talked on the front lawn. Some of the parents were supervising more bouncy children, but they could stand to the side, out of hearing.

Audrina watched them, as they walked out of the bar, through the reception area and towards the front door. Neither of them were smiling and she didn't for one moment think that they were going outside to kiss and make up. Harry, Mary and Martha had been asking for another go on the bouncy castle, so she took the opportunity to suggest to Devon that she took them outside for half an hour, let them burn off some excess energy before the meal. He was more than happy to stand at the bar and keep the groomsmen company.

She took the children over to the play area and made sure that they were playing nicely, without any fighting, before she walked over to where Gwen and Charles were standing at the side of the hotel, close to the car park. She could see by their gesticulations and expressions that they were arguing already.

"What the fuck do you want?" asked Charles, glaring at her, as she got closer to them.

"Charles!" said Gwen. "Stop it! This is between you and me, there's no need to speak to Audrina like that, she hasn't done anything wrong." She didn't to hear him swear. He used to be an old fashioned gentleman who would only swear when in the company of other men. Lately, that hadn't been the case and he had sworn at her a few times, during arguments. Just another of those red flags that she had chosen to ignore.

"She was with you, wasn't she, the night that Sam died?"

Gwen burst into tears and Audrina stroked her arm and told her to calm down, everything would be fine.

"Charles, I know you're having a very private conversation with Gwen and I know you're upset about Sam but I thought that we should all talk about it together," she said, as gently as possible. She tried to hit the right mark so as not to add further fuel his anger, but she was aware she was getting it wrong. She sounded somewhere between a gentle school teacher talking to a young child and a patronising psychologist talking to a troubled patient.

Charles walked away, rubbing his hands through his hair. He looked like a lost soul, which made Gwen cry even more.

"You should never have written me that letter," she hissed at Audrina, pulling her arm away from her. "You should have knocked on my bedroom door and we could have talked about it. You didn't need to put it in writing."

Charles stopped, turned around and looked at them, confused.

"You should have thrown it away!" Audrina shouted back. "Why would you keep something like that? It's your fault."

"What are you two arguing about?" said Charles.

"She's right," said Gwen. "If I hadn't kept the letter, you would never have found out. And if you hadn't found out, then you wouldn't have left me."

"I'm sorry, can someone explain to me what you're talking about?"

"She means the letter that I wrote to her, saying I was leaving university and we shouldn't be in contact with each other anymore."

"I don't know what you're talking about," said Charles. "Can you two sort out your argument another time, I really need to speak to Gwen on her own."

"Then how did you know about Sam if you don't know anything about the letter?" asked Gwen.

"Because I saw you," said Charles. "I was there. I wish that I hadn't seen it, but I did."

Nobody spoke for a moment. Charles drained the last of his whiskey and gripped tightly to the glass with white knuckles. He put the glass onto the floor, as though frightened that it might break.

"You saw the accident?" said Gwen. Charles nodded. "So you've known about it the whole time? All these years?"

"Yes. I was walking home from the university, we had somehow all become separated and I saw you run over Sam. I saw him fall to the ground." He put his hands over his eyes, as though to block the memory of that horrible event.

Gwen felt light headed. She stepped back and held onto the wall of the hotel with one hand and pressed her back against it, to steady herself.

"I feel sick," she said. Then she vomited all over the grass, narrowly missing her new shoes.

Audrina ran inside to get her a glass of water, while Charles led her to one of the benches at the front of the hotel. Gwen sat down and put her head between her knees, as instructed by Charles. When Audrina re-appeared with a glass of water, she was thankful to sit up, as having her head down was making her feel worse.

"You know you can't take drink on an empty stomach," said Charles.

"Oh shut up, I've only had half a glass. We didn't get chance to have one before the ceremony."

"It's the shock of all this," said Audrina. "I don't feel too good myself, it's bringing back unwanted memories." Tears sprang to her eyes, which she wiped away hastily. She didn't want to cry. She wanted to be strong. Gwen needed her support. It was the least she could do, after all, if it wasn't for the events of that night, Gwen and Charles wouldn't be in this position, arguing and bickering. They should be inside with all the other wedding guests, getting drunk, eating too much and enjoying themselves.

Suddenly Gwen was furious. She stood up and faced Charles.

"So let's get something straight. You witnessed the accident?"

Charles nodded.

"So when the policeman came round and told us about it, you already knew?"

He nodded again.

"Did you know he was dead? Wait, did you even try and help him? Don't answer that, I don't want to know. You complete and utter bastard!"

She threw what was left of the water into his face while she waited for him to respond. She was ready for his anger now. She felt strong enough to deal with it. Adrenalin worked wonders for confidence building.

"Hang on a minute," he said, wiping his face with his hand. "I'm not the one who ran him over. Why are you getting mad at me? I didn't kill him, you did! And now here you are, back with your old friend, showing no remorse whatsoever."

Audrina looked over to where the children were still bouncing. A couple of mothers were watching them, laughing together and sipping Prosecco. They didn't show any indication that they had heard anything.

Gwen took a step towards Charles with both fists raised, but he stepped back and avoided her blows. Audrina grabbed hold of her arm and led her back inside, telling Charles over her shoulder that it would be better for all of them if he went home.

Chapter Twenty Three

Very Impressive

June 2022 – Saturday

Audrina walked with her arm around Gwen through the hotel reception and straight to the lifts, where she pressed the button for the third floor. When the lift door opened, they saw that thankfully the lift was empty, so they managed to get to Audrina and Devon's room without anyone interrupting them and asking why Gwen was crying. As soon as the bedroom door was closed behind them, Audrina phoned Devon and asked him to keep a watch over the children on the bouncy castle, while she re-did Gwen's makeup for her. She told him that she had had an argument with Charles, but he was going home now, so they would be down soon.

Gwen held tightly onto the sink in the bathroom and stared at her reflection in the mirror. Audrina waved a makeup brush behind her and smiled.

"Don't bother with that," said Gwen. "I feel like shit, I can't go back to the wedding now. Everyone will know that

I've been crying and now Charles' seat will be vacant and…"

"Shhhh, don't worry about that. I'll ask the wedding planner to put you on our table. Nobody will be asking any questions. You can sit with us. Or ring Julia, get her to come back down."

"She'll be in the jacuzzi by now," said Gwen. "No, that's not fair on her. Her hair will be wet…"

She turned quickly, pushed Audrina out of the way and just managed to get to the toilet in time before she vomited again. She fell to her knees and clung onto the side of the toilet bowl. Audrina moved her hair out of the way with one hand and passed her a bunch of toilet tissue with the other hand.

"You've done that a few times, haven't you?" Gwen said, when she had finally finished. She smiled weakly, as she got up off her knees, went into the bedroom and flopped down on the bed.

"How good was that?" said Audrina. "I managed to hold your hair and get you some tissue at the same time."

"Very impressive," said Gwen. "I owe you one."

"I'll make us some tea," said Audrina. She picked up the tiny kettle, filled it with water in the bathroom and then switched it on. She put the teabags into the cups and fiddled with one of the tiny plastic milk cartons, struggling to open it. "Why do they still make these fucking awful things? They're not environmentally friendly and a fucking pain in the arse to open."

Gwen got up and went to give her a hug. "Come here, you're shaking. I think it should be me making the tea for you. Why don't you sit down?"

"I'm alright, honest. I'm trying not to cry. Look, I've done it now." She poured the milk into one of the cups. Gwen picked up the other milk carton, opened it easily and passed it to her. "I can't believe what Charles has just said. He saw the whole thing? And yet he never said anything?"

"I know," said Gwen. "What was that all about? And then he has the audacity to say that I'm the one who's a liar. He told the policeman that he was in Lancaster in one of the pubs, but he wasn't."

The kettle flicked itself off and Audrina poured the boiling water into the cups, squeezed the tea bags against the side of the cup and left them on the tray, next to the kettle. Gwen didn't need to ask why she hadn't put them in the bin. She knew that cold teabags were the perfect remedy for tired and swollen eyes. They had used that beauty treatment many times at university after a late night.

"You know what's the worst thing about all this?" said Gwen, taking her cup of tea and wrapping her fingers around the comforting warmth. Audrina waited for her to speak. "We didn't need to spend the last nineteen years apart. If Charles knew all along, then why did we do that? We've lost all those years."

"Don't make me cry again," said Audrina. She took her tea and sat down on the bed close to Gwen. "I'm not sure that it could have been any different," she said. "I mean Charles knew, yes, but nobody else did. If we saw each other week after week, it was bound to come out. One of us would have slipped up in conversation."

"Would we? I don't think so."

"Well who knows. It's too late now. We're here and that's the main thing."

"And after all that, he wants me to sell the apartment and give him half. It's not happening, I can tell you right now."

"You'll need to get yourself a good lawyer," said Audrina. "But don't worry about that today." She looked at her watch. "Look, it's almost quarter to three, the meal starts in fifteen minutes. What do you want to do? Are you coming down, or do you want to stay here for a bit?"

"I don't want to eat anything," said Gwen. "I still feel a bit sick. But I'll go my own room and then I'll be there when Julia gets back from the spa."

Audrina told her that she would speak to Zara, when she got a minute, and tell her that she was having some time out in her room, but she would join the party this evening. Gwen assured her that she would be fine by then, when her nerves had settled.

***

Downstairs, Devon was coping with the children, which isn't to say that he wasn't pleased to see his wife again. The children climbed off the bouncy castle and ran to her when she told them that their dinner was about to be served. Copious amounts of sugar had heightened their appetites. She managed to get their hands washed just in time to be called into the dining room. As she walked back through the bar, Devon was waiting for her.

"I've just ordered them some lemonade from the bar," he said. "The waiter said we can sit down and he'll bring it over." He grabbed hold of her and kissed her neck. "Have I told you how beautiful you look right now?"

"Get off me, you'll crease my dress," she said.

They both laughed and he patted her arse as she walked past him. She whispered 'later' to him and in line with her new mindfulness app, she thanked the universe for her wonderful and sexy husband. It was awful to see Gwen so upset. Any breakup was painful, but especially when a couple had been together for almost twenty years, like they had and right now, after the blip she and Devon had at the beginning of the week, she was glad that they were now on a firm footing.

As they walked into the dining room, most of the guests were already seated at large round tables, each seating ten or twelve people. Their table was on the right hand side of the room. Zara had seated them with other friends of theirs who also had children. As they walked over to their table, she spotted Charles, sitting next to Gwen's empty space at another table. They had no option but to walk past his table to get to theirs. She had no intention of speaking to him, but as she got closer to him, he reached out to her, touched her arm and asked her where Gwen was. She was aware of being watched, so she bent down close to his ear.

"I thought you'd gone home," she said, pulling her arm away, as discreetly as possible.

He shook his head, picked up his napkin, shook it out and placed it on his knee. She walked on.

"What did he want?" asked Devon.

"He wants to know where Gwen is, but she's not coming down. He got her so upset before that she threw up outside, all over the grass, and then again upstairs."

Devon laughed, "Sounds like she's up the duff to me."

"What?"

"Sounds like she's pregnant." Devon laughed. "Since when does someone throw up just because of an argument?"

No more was said about it, as they joined the table and introduced themselves to the other guests. All four of the other adults were football fans and two of them were Manchester United fans, so most of the conversation throughout the meal centred around football. For once, Audrina didn't mind. She was glad that there was another focus, so that she didn't have to make small talk. Her mind was whirring with what Devon had said. She hadn't considered that Gwen might be pregnant and she wondered whether she was and hadn't told her. Not that she had had the time to tell her, since last night there had been a lot going on. She knew that Gwen had always wanted children, so it would be wonderful and it might also be the thing that got her and Charles back together. Devon was right, Gwen was made of stern stuff and even though this morning had been horrendously emotional, it was unlikely that emotions alone had caused Gwen to be sick.

As expected, the food was delicious, the wine was cold, the speeches were funny and the bride looked dazzling. Everyone at their table commented on what a good time they were all having and what an unforgettable wedding it was. That was one word for it, thought Audrina. She wouldn't forget today in a very long time.

"Harry's getting a bit grumpy," she said to Devon when the pudding had been served and they were waiting for coffee. "I'm going to take him upstairs and see if he'll have a nap. Will you be okay for half an hour or so?"

"Yes sure," said Devon. "You go up, I'll see you in a bit."

She gave him a quick kiss and then lifted Harry out of his seat. He clung to her neck and wrapped his legs around her waist. As she began walking out of the room, he rested his head on her shoulder, already almost half asleep. She didn't see Charles getting up from his seat as she went past him, but she couldn't avoid him as she stood waiting for the lift.

"Is Gwen alright?" he asked. "Look, I know you think I'm the bad guy here, but I still care about her, you know. Where is she?"

"It's not for me to get involved, Charles. You and Gwen need to talk next week. I just want to get my child to have a nap, so if you don't mind…"

The lift doors opened and she stepped inside. Charles followed her. The doors closed behind him.

For a moment neither of them knew what to say and they travelled in silence.

"Are you getting out here?" asked Audrina, when they arrived at the third floor.

"Erm, yes, I mean, my room's on this floor but I wanted to speak to Gwen really. Do you know where her room is?"

"No, I don't and even if I did, I wouldn't tell you. She needs some space, after what happened outside." Audrina put the key card into the slot in the door and it opened with a beep. Charles followed her inside and watched as she gently lay Harry onto the bed and stroked his hair as he closed his eyes and began sucking his thumb. Charles passed her the throw that was placed across the bottom of the bed and she took it from him and covered Harry with it.

She straightened up and when she was sure that Harry was asleep, she walked away and sat down on one of the chairs in the living room area at the far end of the room. Charles followed and sat down in the opposite chair. She hadn't invited him in and she didn't particularly want to talk to him right now, but he needed to know the truth of what had happened that night. He needed to know why she had left and why she and Gwen hadn't spoken for so long. Now was as good a time as any.

She started by telling him about the incident in the kitchen, before they had gone out to see the reggae band at the Pendle Bar, when Sam had knocked her Champagne flute onto the floor and as she bent down to pick up the broken glass, he had grabbed her head and forced her towards him, saying "While you're down there." Charles said that would have been a joke, something that boys do, just messing around, having a laugh. She said that it wasn't funny and he had to be there to witness everything before he could properly judge the situation. She told him that Sam was always around her, with a lecherous look and a smutty comment. She said it was like being in the nineteen seventies, her mum had told her about those days, when men had no respect for women and treated them like sex objects, something for them to look at and paw at. She said times had changed and he shouldn't have done it. Charles agreed that it wasn't gentlemanly, but he was young and she should have just told him to back off. She did, but it hadn't worked and when he broke the glass, she had lost her temper and shouted at him. Charles said he vaguely remembered some commotion in the kitchen, but he hadn't taken much notice.

"He must have got really angry then and," she paused and took a deep breath in. "He raped me."

There was no other way of saying it. No nice, gently way to convey those horrible words.

Charles said that he couldn't believe it. Not that he didn't believe her, of course he did, if that's what she was telling him, but Sam didn't seem the sort. Audrina said that she thought he was exactly the sort. He was so smarmy and lascivious and gave her the creeps. She knew there was something about him that she didn't like from the first moment they met. Charles shook his head and said that Sam was a good looking boy, he didn't need to get sex like that, with force. When Audrina explained to him that it was nothing to do with sex and was more to do with power and dominance and Charles admitted that yes, he had heard that before.

She told him how Sam had forced her to the ground and said disgusting things to her. When it was over, she walked home but realised that she had left her phone behind, so she asked Gwen to help her to find it.

"So that's when you took my car?" he asked.

"Yes, I asked Gwen to tell you and ask your permission, but she said you wouldn't mind if we borrowed it."

Charles said that he would have given Gwen anything she asked for at that time.

She told him that on the way back, Sam had stepped into the road and they didn't have time to stop. It was an accident, pure and simple and they couldn't avoid it. He must have been drunk. Charles nodded and said that they were all very drunk that night.

They sat in silence for a moment, Charles digesting the news of what his friend had done and Audrina trying hard to dismiss the flashbacks of that horrible night.

"I thought you were going to stop," said Charles. "I couldn't believe it when you drove off."

There was no compelling defence that Audrina could put forward.

"He was already dead when I got to him," he said.

Both of them sat with that information. Charles was glad that his friend hadn't suffered and at least he had died immediately. Audrina wondered how her life would be different if he hadn't died. If he had just suffered a broken leg and some concussion.

"Why didn't you tell us that you knew?" asked Audrina.

"You were both so upset, I don't know. I've asked myself the question a million times before, but I couldn't admit it when the policeman came round, otherwise we would have all been in trouble. I knew that my car had been damaged and they would have thought it was me driving, so I didn't say anything. After that, what was the point?"

"Did you ring for an ambulance?"

"No, I just left him. It was obvious he was dead." He paused while he remembered his friend's cold, grey face and his blank eyes. "I hated that I had to do that."

"But why have you brought it up now, after all these years?" asked Audrina.

"Don't you know what she did?" said Charles. The grief that visited him moments ago had quickly been replaced by anger.

"What do you mean?"

"That guy that she shagged, it was all over the papers, you must have seen it?"

Audrina admitted that she had seen it, but she assumed they had got over it, because they were still together.

"It was just another lie on top of another lie. It was one too many. I tried to forget it, but it tipped me over. It finished us. I just had to tell her that I knew what she'd done. I don't want to argue with her anymore, but it's definitely over. We just need to sell the apartment, sort out the bank account and the shares and go our separate ways."

"Oh she won't do that." The words were out before Audrina could stop them. It wasn't her place to tell him Gwen's plans, but he was going to find out sooner or later. "You need to talk to Gwen about it, I shouldn't have said that, sorry. But I know she doesn't want to sell the apartment."

"Well, we'll see about that. It's half mine, so she's got no bloody choice."

It was Charles' angry loud words that woke Harry. It was Charles storming out of their room and slamming the door that made him cry.

Chapter Twenty Four

Let's Party

June 2022 – Saturday

Zara and Callum cut the cake to loud applause and the flashing of cameras and phones. They declared the party started and the lights were lowered. The children were ushered off the dance floor to make room for the happy couple's first dance. After a few minutes, everyone else was asked to join to them. Devon danced with both Mary and Martha and Audrina danced with Harry. As she twirled him around to the music, she could see Gwen and Julia watching from the bar. She waved to them.

"Come with me," she said to Harry. "I want you to meet a very good friend of mine."

She took him over to the bar and gave Gwen and Julia a hug and introduced them to Harry. While Julia was crouching down to him, asking him if he was enjoying himself, who he had made friends with today and what he had been doing, Audrina told Gwen that Charles hadn't gone home and was still here, unfortunately. She told her about their conversation in her room earlier and that she had told him what Sam had done to her. She also admitted that she had blurted out that Gwen didn't want to sell the apartment.

"Don't worry about it," said Gwen. "I've already told him that anyway, so it wouldn't have been news to him."

"He got quite annoyed though," said Audrina. "He stormed out and slammed the door."

"I didn't slam the door," said Charles. "I just didn't hold it while it closed."

He appeared suddenly at the bar next to Gwen. How much of their conversation he had heard, he didn't say and neither Gwen nor Audrina wanted to ask him.

"Do you want a drink?" he asked.

"I've just got one, thanks," said Gwen.

Charles ordered a double whiskey, no ice. Gwen looked at Audrina, not sure whether to stay and talk to him, or to walk away and try to avoid him for the rest of the night.

"Shall we go and have a dance?" said Audrina, making the decision for her.

Gwen nodded. Harry had already disappeared and Julia was busy talking to the handsome best man. Zara had tipped him off that there was a beautiful single lady invited and he had made a bee-line for her as soon as he noticed her arrive.

"You know Faisal's a lawyer now, don't you?"

Charles' words stopped Gwen in her tracks on the way to the dance floor. She turned to face him. The sooner she let him say his piece, the sooner she could escape him.

"Faisal Patel, from university. He's a lawyer now."

"I know who he is, Charles," said Gwen impatiently.

"I rang him before. His letter is on its way to you."

"What letter? Are you drunk? How many of those have you had?"

"None of your fucking business," he shouted. His whiskey breath and slurred words told her that he had had his fair share and probably shouldn't be having any more. "You won't get away with it, you know."

For a terrifying moment, Gwen thought that he meant Sam's murder. Was it murder? She wasn't sure, but that word had popped up so many times in her mind that the word 'accident' just didn't seem to cover it. After the lengths that she and Audrina had gone to to keep the secret, he wouldn't tell anyone now, would he? What would be the point? Just to hurt her? Would he be that cruel?

"It's a matrimonial asset and I'm entitled to half. The letter will set it all out."

She let the air out of her lungs and was relieved that he only wanted to take her apartment, not her liberty.

"We'll talk about it next week," she said. She didn't want to tell him that only yesterday, he had wanted to deal with their breakup without expensive lawyers. She knew that he had had too much to drink and he wasn't in the right frame of mind to see sense. Right now, it seemed that they were on their way to acrimony.

"What will he say when I tell him about Sam, I wonder, and how you and her were involved?" He shouted to her as she walked away and the music almost drowned out his alarming words, but they managed to reach her. "Do you think he'll advise me to go to the police? I think so. I hope you like prison food!"

"Ignore him," said Audrina. "He's trying to goad you and frighten you into selling, that's all."

"What did you say?" Charles grabbed Audrina's shoulder and span her around to face him. "Tell me what you said to her. She doesn't need you whispering in her ear, she can fight her own battles."

"Battles?" said Gwen. "Is this what it's going to be?"

"You wanted it like this," he said. He took another gulp of his drink and staggered backwards, almost knocking a drink out of a man's hand behind him. "Sorry mate," he said. The man, who was equally drunk, told him not to worry about it and continued on his way to the dance floor, his arms waving about in the air in time to the music.

"Charles, please, we really can't talk now. The music's loud and there's too many people about. Just leave it." She tried to walk away again.

"I used to have a wife I could trust!" he shouted, making no attempt to keep their conversation private.

"You still have a wife you can trust," said Gwen, close to tears. "I'm still the same person that I've always been."

"Yes, and that's the trouble," said Charles, a little more quietly. "You've always been a liar and a cheater and I should have left you years ago."

"Right, that's enough." Julia, having excused herself from her chat with the best man, grabbed hold of Charles' arm and dragged him towards the door and out into the corridor. Audrina took hold of his drink, which he relinquished. Thankfully, most of the guests were dancing or talking or queuing at the bar and Gwen and Audrina were confident that nobody had actually witnessed the short argument. When Julia walked Charles towards the door, she smiled broadly and held onto his arm as though she were his girlfriend or his wife and those who didn't know them, wouldn't have been any the wiser.

Chapter Twenty Five

Evening's End

June 2022 – Saturday

The party was still in full swing when Audrina and Devon agreed that they should take the children upstairs and put them to bed. If Gwen and Julia had still been around, Devon would have offered to take them on his own and let Audrina continue to enjoy the dancing. But after the altercation with Charles, they had checked out of the hotel and gone home early. Gwen had made her apologies to Zara, who understood that she didn't want to spend another minute in the same room as Charles. Gwen went home with a huge slice of the chocolate fudge wedding cake and Julia went home with the best man's telephone number.

The children fell asleep before their heads hit the pillows, exhausted from a long day full of sweets and bouncing.

"Aren't they beautiful?" said Audrina, as she tucked them into the double bed next to theirs and kissed their cheeks, one after the other.

"Yes, they are," said Devon. "Just like their mother."

He began to kiss her neck and then her mouth. As his hand reached to her back and searched for the zip on her dress, she pulled away from him.

"I need to tell you something first," she said.

"Can it wait?" asked Devon, knowing from the sincere look in his wife's face that it couldn't.

She shook her head.

"Promise me that you won't get angry," she said.

"Have you cheated on me?" he asked.

"No, of course not."

"Then I won't get angry."

Tears welled in her eyes and this time she let them fall. It didn't matter now that her makeup got ruined or her eyes became swollen. She needed to let it out.

"What is it baby? I'm here for you, just tell me."

"Let's go and sit down." She led him by the hand and for the second time that day, she sat in the chair in the living room area opposite a man that she was about to tell about her rape. Devon reached across to her and held her hand, which he kept hold of the whole time that she unburdened herself.

"Do you remember that I told you that Gwen was my friend at university, but that I didn't realise that she was Gwen Morris, the news reader?"

Devon nodded.

"Well I lied to you about that. I'm sorry. It's a long and complicated story, but I don't want to lie to you anymore. I've known for years who she was. I knew the minute she got the job on the BBC that it was my Gwen. She used to be called Wilson, but she married Charles Morris, the man who you met today."

She waited for Devon to shout at her, for him to get angry that she had lied and demand explanations. But he didn't.

"Okay, carry on. I'm sure you've got reasons, just tell me," he said calmly. "I love you."

His kind words made her cry even more.

"Well, I haven't told you the real reason why I left university. It was partly because I had too many modelling jobs, like I told you, but it was also because of something that happened. I haven't seen Gwen since the day that I left. I didn't even tell her that I was leaving. Well, I told her in a letter, but I didn't tell her in person. I left her a note in the bathroom and just walked out and got the train home to London. I told her never to contact me again and I changed my phone number."

"Wow, what the fuck, babe? What did she do?"

"No, it wasn't her, she didn't do anything. But we swore to each other that we wouldn't tell a soul."

She paused then, while she gathered her thoughts and wondered how to phrase it. There was no nice way to tell your husband that you had kept a secret throughout the whole time you'd known each other. No sugar coating was going to make it any easier.

"We had been out one night to a concert at the university and, to cut a long story short, I got separated from Gwen and this guy called Sam, who lived in the house next to ours, well… he raped me on the lawn outside the bar."

"What? Baby, why haven't you told me this? You're not blaming yourself, are you? You know it wasn't your fault.

There's nothing to be ashamed about." He got up from his chair, knelt in front of her and hugged her tightly.

"I know. I'm not ashamed at all, but that's not it," she said, as she gently pushed him away. He sat back onto the chair. "That's not the reason I left. I probably could have got over that, in time, and carried on with the course. Gwen wanted me to report it to the police, but I didn't want to. I just wanted to have a shower and go to bed, I didn't want to be kept in the police station for hours and hours, being examined and questioned."

Devon nodded. "Understandable."

"But I'd dropped my phone on the grass at the university and I needed it back, it had all my contacts in, you know. So Gwen offered to take me back to help me find it. The problem was that we couldn't get a taxi, so we took Charles' car without him knowing."

Devon smiled, impressed that his law-abiding wife had done something criminal. It was so unlike her to break rules. She knew what he was thinking and she slapped his leg.

"No, Devon, we shouldn't have done that," she said.

"Admit it, he's a prize prick, that bloke."

"He wasn't then, he was nice. But anyway…" she paused again. "Please don't hate me!"

"Baby, I won't."

"We were young and…"

"Just tell me."

"We were involved in an accident, with Charles' car. Sam was drunk and he staggered into the road and stood in front of the car and we ran him over."

"Were you driving?"

"No, Gwen was driving, but I say 'we' because we were in it together. He hit the bonnet and fell into the road and banged his head and, well, he died."

"Shit," said Devon. He sat back in his chair. "And that's why you left university? I guess the police got involved?"

She shook her head. "Well, yes, they did, because they found him, but we didn't get involved in any investigation. They didn't know it was us. They put it down to a hit and run."

"What do you mean they didn't know it was you? Didn't you report it?"

"No. We drove off and left him." She broke down then and sobbed the tears that had been waiting to come out for the last nineteen years. The grief for her lost friendship with Gwen and the pressure and stress of having to deal with the fact that they had caused someone's death was too much for her to bear. The face of Sam's mother as she walked down the aisle in the church behind her son's coffin was something indelibly marked in her mind forever.

And now she was terrified that her husband would hate her, like Charles hated Gwen. She couldn't bear to lose him.

She looked over at their sleeping children, which made her cry even more. If they had to grow up with their parents separated, it would be awful for them. No more family Christmases and holidays. No more climbing into their parents' huge bed in the morning and cuddling until breakfast time. No more board games around the dining room table on rainy days.

Devon didn't say anything. What could he say? she thought. He was probably too busy planning where he would live and how often he would get to see the children, in between football matches. He wouldn't be on his own for long, she knew that. He would get snapped up by some young gold digger, who would want children of her own, to keep him by her side and to justify the fact that she would then be unable to work.

Losing her husband was the price she had to pay for killing someone. She had to accept that. If you take someone's life, whether by accident or whether on purpose, why would you then be entitled to go on and live a life of luxury, surrounded by a loving family? The universe didn't work like that. She had to be punished somehow and here it was. The time for her punishment had arrived. The universe had decided that she didn't have to spend time in prison, and let's face it, she wouldn't last a minute, but she was finally being punished by losing her husband and becoming a part-time mother. Soon, her children would be spending mornings in bed with their daddy and a new step-mother and would be returned to her at three thirty on Sunday afternoon, dropped off at the gate like some parcel from DHL.

Suddenly Devon stood up, took hold of both of her hands and pulled her to her feet. He wrapped his arms around her and buried his face in her neck. She could feel his soft breath on her neck and she wondered if this was their last hug. Was this his way of saying goodbye? She held onto him tightly.

He then pushed her away and held her at arms' length, staring into her eyes intently. This is it. This is the moment that he tells me he's leaving me, she thought.

"I love you so much," he said. "More than anything in the world, you know that don't you?"

"Yes," she said.

"And I'm here for you, I want you to know that."

"You're here for me?"

"Yes, of course I am." He frowned at her. "Why wouldn't I be?",

"Because I killed someone," she said.

"No, you didn't," he said. "You were involved in a tragic accident, that's all. You didn't *kill* someone. Not with malice aforethought."

She managed a short laugh. "Look at you with the legal jargon."

"Hey, up there for thinking and down there for scoring goals." He pointed at his head and then his feet. "I've heard that phrase on the telly."

"Obviously," she said. "I didn't think you'd turned into Rumpole of the Bailey."

"Who?"

"It doesn't matter." She pulled him towards the bed and lay down next to him, resting her head on his chest. "I'm sorry for not telling you about it sooner," she said.

"It's okay," he said. "I kind of understand. It must have been hard for you to re-live it. I wish you had told me sooner though."

She understood that he felt a little betrayed, like she hadn't trusted him enough to give him her secret, in case he left her and later used that knowledge against her in divorce proceedings. Used it as a threat to get what he wanted, just like Charles was doing. When she had first met him, how could she have told him something like that? Trust had to be built up over a period of years; she couldn't have told a man that she had just met her deepest darkest secret, not even when they became engaged. And then later, when they were married, should she have told him then? No, she couldn't. No matter how bruised his ego might be now, she had sworn to Gwen that she wouldn't ever tell anyone. Devon could tell her now that he loved her until he was blue in the face, and he could assure her that he would never leave her and that he wouldn't tell anyone what had happened. But couples break up. It happens.

"I suppose you're wondering why I'm telling you this now?" she said.

"I am, but I'm more thinking, if the police didn't suspect you, then why would that mean that you had to break off your friendship with Gwen?"

"I don't know. I thought at the time that it was the right thing to do. I thought that if we saw each other, we were bound to reminisce about our student days and it might come out, what we did. As time went by, it seemed even more vital to keep it hidden. You've got to understand that Gwen was working as a journalist, and then later on she got the job on the TV, so it would have caused a massive scandal."

"Yes, I get that. So you're telling me now because Gwen got invited to Zara and Callum's wedding?"

"Not really," she said. "It's Charles. He's threatening to tell the police unless Gwen agrees to sell her apartment and give him a good divorce settlement."

"He's blackmailing her?"

"Well, I didn't think about it like that, but I suppose he is, yes."

"And is she going to sell the apartment?" asked Devon.

"She doesn't want to. She bought it before Charles moved in, but I suppose she'll have to now. She's got plenty of money, so she can get another one."

"That's not the point though, is it? The bastard."

"So, if he goes to the police, or the papers or something, I need you to be prepared. I'm going to get dragged into this." She began crying again. "I'm going to go to prison."

"Stop that now, you're not going anywhere. You weren't even driving."

"But isn't it interfering with a police investigation, or perjury or something? Or harbouring a criminal?"

"I've no idea, but it's a good job they don't have the death penalty anymore, that's all I can say."

"Devon, I'm being serious."

"I know, but what are the chances of Charles going to the police, seriously?

"He seemed pretty serious earlier on. That's why Gwen went home. She was really upset. He's already got a lawyer, one of Sam's friend from uni and he said that he would tell him what happened."

"Shall we watch a film?" Devon said, suddenly changing the subject.

"If you like," said Audrina.

"Why don't you choose one from Netflix while I go and get us a drink from downstairs?"

"There's stuff in the mini-bar, you don't need…"

"There's nothing I fancy in there. Let's have cocktails!" He jumped off the bed and began putting his trainers on. "Espresso martini?"

"Yes please," said Audrina. She was finding it hard to believe that Devon was taking what she had told him so well. Maybe when he had had time to process it, things would be different. For now, she would try and relax. She would help Gwen to deal with Charles next week. Hanging onto her apartment, however much she loved it, wasn't worth getting Charles angry, so she would tell her to give him what he wants.

Blackmail or not.

As Devon was leaving the room, she said, "I'm sorry for not telling you sooner. I know I've been hard to live with for a while, especially this past week. It's because I knew that I had to come face to face with Gwen and Charles and I didn't know what to do about it."

He blew her a kiss and told her to stop worrying and that he would be back soon with their cocktails.

***

Devon hadn't lied to Audrina. He did want to go downstairs for cocktails. He needed a couple of shots of alcohol and Audrina would too, no doubt. But the main reason he wanted to go downstairs, was that he needed to speak to Charles.

Just a quiet word in his ear.

He wasn't going to allow him to blackmail his wife and Gwen, and a gentle reminder was in order.

The wedding was still in full swing, nineties dance music thudded through the walls of the wedding suite, getting louder as he sprinted down the stairs. He didn't have the patience to wait for a lift at the best of times and especially not right now. He needed to get hold of Charles as soon as possible.

He opened the double doors and waited for a few seconds for his eyes to adjust to the relative darkness. The chairs around the dining tables were now empty. Used party poppers, empty wine glasses and disposable cameras, provided to each table by the bride and groom to record their special day, were discarded amongst the fresh flower arrangements in the centre of the table. A few people were congregated around the bar, at one end of the room, but most of the guests had squashed themselves onto the dancefloor. If Devon was going to find Charles, he would have no option but to push his way into the crowd.

As he walked towards the dancefloor, he could see Zara and Callum in the middle, surrounded by the bridesmaids and groomsmen, who were looking decidedly more dishevelled than this morning. Waistcoats had long since been abandoned and the cravats were now non-existent. Callum looked as though he had taken his shirt off at one point as the buttons had been fastened back up wrongly. The left side of his shirt was much longer than the right side. As soon as he saw him, Callum grabbed hold of his hand and pulled him into the dancing crowd. Devon didn't mind; it gave him a chance to have a good look around.

But Charles was nowhere to be seen.

At the end of the song, when Neil Diamond's voice began to belt out Sweet Caroline, Devon knew that that was his cue to exit. He pushed his way off the dancefloor and made his way to the bar.

Still there was no sight of Charles.

He ordered two espresso martinis from the weary bar man and took them back upstairs. When he reached the third floor and turned the corner at the top of the stairs into the corridor that led to their suite, he spotted Charles at the end of the corridor, struggling to put his key card into the door which was presumably his room. Devon put the cocktails on the floor outside their door and walked towards him.

"Having a bit of trouble, mate?" he asked.

Charles looked at him through blurry eyes and then tried again to open his door. Devon took the card off him, slotted it into the door and pushed the door open for him. Charles stumbled inside and steadied himself by holding onto the wall. Devon followed him inside and closed the door.

Chapter Twenty Six

Mrs Morris

June 2022 – Sunday

The storm arrived the morning after the wedding. As the weather forecasters had predicted, the tropical storm had made its way over from Florida and had hit the north west of the UK in the early hours of the morning. Gwen sat up in bed, a large mug of coffee waiting to cool on the bedside table next to her new book. Today, she planned to stay in bed for as long as possible, only leaving the comfort of her feather quilt to top up her coffee cup and pop some bread in the toaster. She opened the bedroom blinds with the remote control and sat watching the rain rivulets falling down the window. She had no plans for today, other than staying inside with Julia, who was still fast asleep in the spare bedroom.

She was glad that they had made the decision to leave the hotel early yesterday, as coming across Charles in the breakfast room was the last thing she wanted to do.

She had just picked up her mug of coffee when she heard the ringing of the doorbell. Assuming that Julia must have gone to the local shop for something, milk, bread or chocolate, and forgotten to take a key, she climbed out of bed, put on her dressing gown and went to open the door.

A police woman introduced herself as PC Harrison and asked if she was Gwen Morris. She thought to herself that this young police woman obviously didn't watch the breakfast news, as most people knew her face. She nodded to her and when PC Harrison asked if she could come inside, holding her hat in her right hand, she imagined that Julia must have been run over on her way to the shops. Those Manchester trams went too fast and didn't give people time to cross the road safely. Someone should look at that and do something about it, before someone got killed. But when Julia came out of the spare room, still wearing her pyjamas and with nothing on her feet, Gwen was confused and thought that she really shouldn't go outside in this weather in just her night clothes.

"I have some upsetting news about your husband, I'm afraid" said PC Harrison. "Can I come in, please."

Gwen apologised for keeping her standing outside in the corridor and ushered her inside the apartment.

"What's wrong?" asked Julia. "Some news about Charles, did you say?"

Gwen's thoughts whirred. She didn't know what to do or what to say. It occurred to her that they were still in the hall and that she should be leading the police woman into the kitchen and making her some tea, like she did the last time a police officer was in her home, when he called to tell them that Sam had had an accident. But she didn't want to make tea this time. She wanted the police woman to say what she had to say and leave as quickly as possible. She didn't want her lovely home to be sullied by bad news.

Julia took the lead and showed PC Harrison into the living room area, where she sat on one of the sofas. Julia and Gwen sat down on the other sofa. Julia took hold of Gwen's hand, knowing that the only reason that the police visit your house first thing in the morning and hold their hats in their hand, is to tell you that someone has died.

"I'm afraid your husband… I'm really sorry to tell you that Mr Morris was found dead in his hotel room this morning. His body was discovered by a member of the hotel's cleaning staff."

"Dead?" asked Julia, as though they needed clarification.

"I'm afraid so," said the police woman.

Julia burst into tears and PC Harrison handed her a tissue from her pocket. How kind of her, thought Gwen. She must have been anticipating tears and she had the foresight to put a handful of tissues in her pocket. She really must email her sergeant and tell him or her that that was a lovely thing for her to do. Very thoughtful indeed.

"How did he die?" asked Julia.

Gwen seemed to have lost all her powers of speech and she was glad that Julia asked the question that she had wanted to ask, but was unable to form the words for.

"There will need to do a post mortem to be absolutely sure, but from what we can gather, it seems to have been a tragic accident. He was found in the bathroom and it looks like he fell onto his back, cracking his head on the floor."

As the police woman's words took their time to sink in, Gwen wondered whether he had suffered. Sam had hit his head on the floor too and apparently had died instantly. Had Charles died instantly too? Or did he lie there on the floor, with blood pouring from his head, unable to reach his phone? She silently prayed that it was the former.

"Mrs Morris, are you okay?" asked PC Harrison. "Is there someone you'd like me to call?"

"I'll make all the necessary calls for her," said Julia. "Thank you."

Gwen was still searching for her words. And why wasn't she crying? Right at this moment, she didn't feel anything at all, which she found odd. If someone had told her on her wedding day, as she stood side by side with her new husband, smiling at the many cameras that were being pointed at them to capture such a precious moment, that she wouldn't cry when she heard the news that the love of her life was dead, she wouldn't have believed it for a minute. All those years ago, she couldn't have contemplated a life without him and she would have been shocked and appalled at such a thought. Yet here she was right now, feeling nothing.

She looked out of the window and watched the activity on the bird table on their wrap around balcony. There was plenty of seed and two giant fat balls and yet the sparrows pecked and shrieked at each other and wanted the same seed that another bird had. They were brutal. She marched over to the window and banged on the glass, sending the sparrows shooting skywards.

"Nasty little bastards, stop fighting!" she shouted.

But now the bird table was empty and none of them could hear her.

Suddenly she felt sick again and rushed to the bathroom, where she vomited in the toilet. Before she had chance to finish, she felt Julia's hands rubbing her back and asking her if she was okay. She managed to nod that she was.

"I must have eaten something dodgy at the wedding," said Gwen, finally finding words.

Julia shook her head. "We didn't eat at the wedding, remember? We had an omelette from room service and then a sandwich when we got home last night and I'm fine, so it couldn't have been that. And you don't get food poisoning from cheese or eggs."

Gwen splashed cold water on her face and wiped it on the towel that Julia handed to her.

"Do you think you might be pregnant?"

Gwen flushed the toilet, closed the seat and fell down hard on it. This was just too much for her to work out. She didn't know whether she was coming or going. She couldn't remember when her last period was.

First Charles and now this. She buried her face in the towel and cried like a baby.

Epilogue

Charles' post mortem concluded that he had died of a bleed to the brain following a head trauma. The verdict of the coroner was accidental death.

Gwen's solicitor advised her that she might have a case against the hotel for negligence, as their bathroom tiles were particularly slippery. He said that she could sue for the future loss of earnings of her husband, which could be a tidy sum. He said that she would be thankful for it, when the settlement finally came through, with a baby to support.

She didn't take his advice.

On the night of the wedding, Audrina and Devon enjoyed their espresso martinis in bed, while their children slept soundly beside them.

Audrina was beginning to become concerned when Devon had been gone for more than half an hour, but just as she was about to telephone him, he appeared. He told her that he had been caught up in a dance with the bride and groom. She had smiled at him and had pictured the happy scene in her head.

The morning after the wedding, when they were about to check-out of the hotel, they saw the police arrive, closely followed by an ambulance. They continued on their journey home, but she later heard the terrible news that Charles had been found dead in the bathroom.

When Gwen phoned, she could hardly speak to her, she was crying that much, but she managed to tell her that she had done a pregnancy test that morning and it was positive. So when Audrina visited her later that afternoon, she took her flowers, to commiserate for the loss of her husband, together with a tiny white baby sleepsuit, to celebrate the future birth of her baby.

Seven and a half months later, baby Charlotte entered the world weighing seven pounds and eight ounces.

Julia, Audrina and Devon were Godparents.

All of the guests in the hotel were questioned by the police, who concluded that there were no suspicious circumstances.

There was no CCTV in the corridors at the hotel.

THE END

Author's Note

This is a story about friendship, but unlike in my first novel, Just Breathe, Gwen and Audrina haven't just met. Their friendship was made many years ago at university and they bonded like sisters, sharing a room and confiding in each other and relying on each other. I think that friendships made at that age are so special, as you may know, as this is the time when you have left home and are starting out on your own. So it's good to have someone close. A new family.

The tragedy here is that the friendship didn't continue after university and the two women had to navigate their adult lives without each other. Of course, they had other friends, but when you meet that special someone, nothing else compares somehow. I hope that I managed to portray how much they missed each other over the years.

I hope that I didn't offend anyone with my descriptions of Audrina's beauty and how she found it harder and harder to get work as a model when she reached her late thirties. I don't know any models but I know from adverts in magazines and on the television, that models come in all shapes and sizes these days. Age and size is no longer a barrier. But I had to make her thin and beautiful, so that Gwen felt ordinary and dumpy beside her. The irony is that

Gwen was just as beautiful, but she failed to see that in herself.

I don't know whether models ever get to meet designers in their agent's office, but I wanted Audrina to meet the young designer who chose her to wear her swimwear, because at that point in the story, Audrina needed a boost. She was so happy to get the new job and she was looking forward to travelling to Paris for the shoot, so it made the events at the wedding more tragic.

If you have enjoyed reading this book, you might enjoy Just Breathe, which is my debut novel for adults.

If you have enjoyed either of my books, please leave me a review on Amazon. It really helps.

Caroline x

If you would like to read more from this author, have a look at the five star reviews for Just Breathe on Amazon. Here are just a few.

*****

"Absolutely loved this book. Bought it on a whim and was pleasantly surprised."

"A beautiful story with a few twists and turns."

"Fantastic book, loved it!"

"I was saving this for holiday, but once I'd read a few pages, I had to finish it! Really enjoyed it."

"A beautiful story of true friendship, love and perseverance and how women can be incredible drivers in supporting each other, especially in times of adversity."

"A really good read. I was hooked from chapter one. I couldn't put it down and didn't want it to end."

"A beautiful novel with two strong female characters, one horrible husband, one incorrigible ex, and one adorably decent man. Oh, and a slightly unhelpful and infuriating neighbour. This book is a delicious mash up of mystery, drama and romance, with a side of violence and a sprinkle of gorgeous scenery."

Printed in Great Britain
by Amazon